PRAISE FOR THE DANCIN' MAN

"Mary Ann Claud moves easily between past and present and her descriptions are often poetic. But secrets drive this story. The death of a strong matriarch and CEO of a family company unleashes a range of problems. Claud's characters experience family dynamics with heartbreak and humor, and consider the impossible compromises required to keep life moving. As secrets are revealed, understanding and healing begin to occur. The emotional struggles in this story will be familiar to readers with complicated families, but no one who reads this book will fail to be moved by the dramatic resolutions."

– **Elizabeth Cox**, author of *The Slow Moon, The Ragged Way People Fall Out of Love*

The Dancin' Man

Mary Ann Claud

LYSTRA BOOKS
& Literary Services

The Dancin' Man

Published by Lystra Books and Literary Services
391 Lystra Estates Dr., Chapel Hill, NC 27517

This book is a work of fiction, produced from the writer's imagination. Any similarity to real people or events is coincidental and not intended by the writer.

ISBN printed book: 978-0-9884164-9-9
ISBN ebook: 978-0-988416-6-8
Library of Congress Cataloguing-in-Publication Number: 2014934960

Book design and cover design by Kelly Prelipp Lojk

WWW.LYSTRABOOKS.COM
Publication managed by Lystra Books & Literary Services, LLC

Printed in the United States

For Olin

DANCIN' MAN: An eighteenth-century Appalachian toy made from laurel or apple wood, sometimes referred to as a jig dancer or a limberjack.

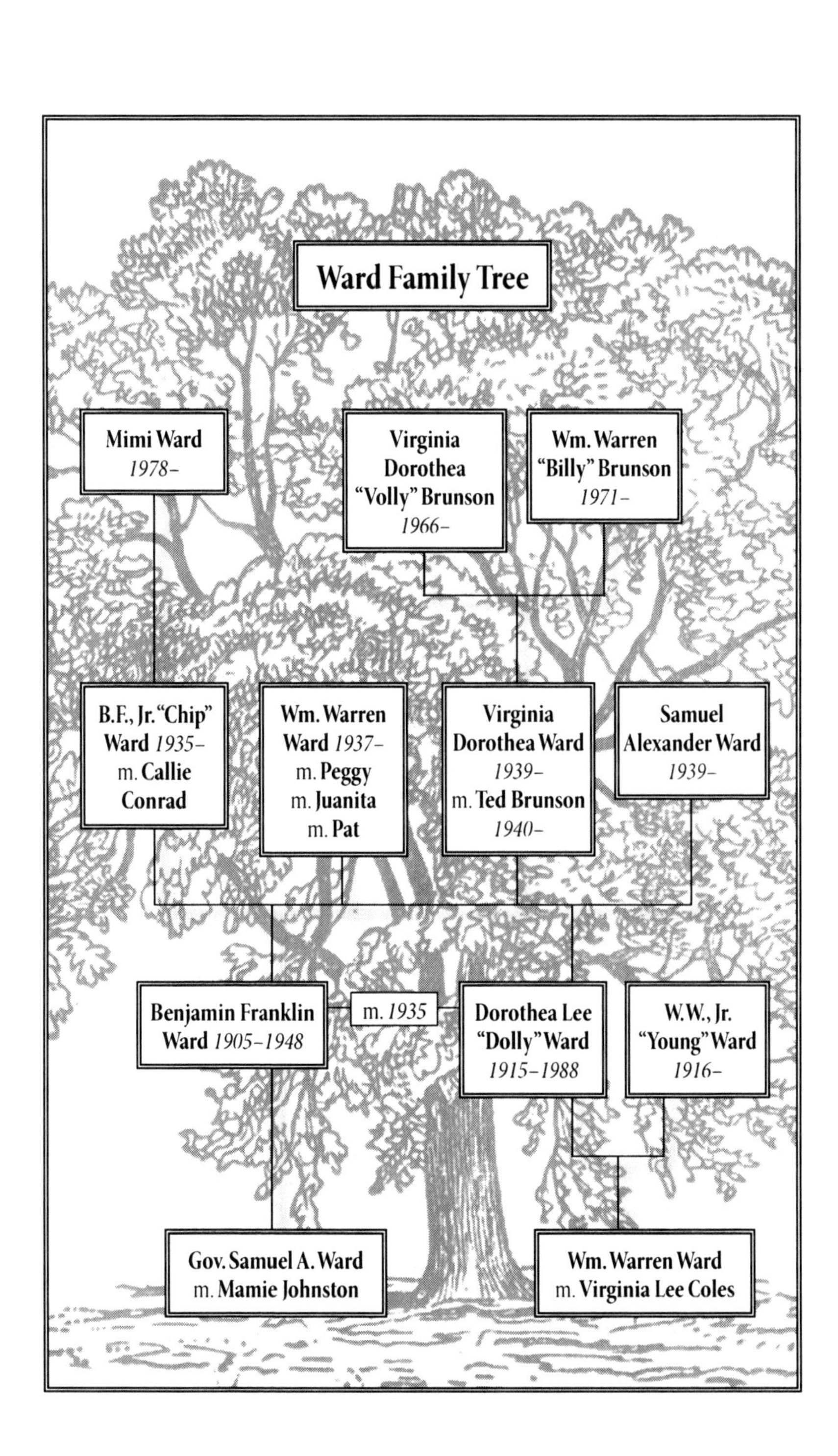
Ward Family Tree
Mimi Ward 1978–
Virginia Dorothea "Volly" Brunson 1966–
Wm. Warren "Billy" Brunson 1971–
B.F., Jr. "Chip" Ward 1935– m. Callie Conrad
Wm. Warren Ward 1937– m. Peggy m. Juanita m. Pat
Virginia Dorothea Ward 1939– m. Ted Brunson 1940–
Samuel Alexander Ward 1939–
Benjamin Franklin Ward 1905–1948
m. 1935
Dorothea Lee "Dolly" Ward 1915–1988
W.W., Jr. "Young" Ward 1916–
Gov. Samuel A. Ward m. Mamie Johnston
Wm. Warren Ward m. Virginia Lee Coles

PROLOGUE

Parkersburg Daily News
January 2, 1966
Widow Succeeds Brother, Husband, and Father as President of Ward Mills, Inc.

Ward Mills, Inc., today announced that Mrs. Dorothea Lee Ward, widow of former company President Ben Ward and daughter of the company's founder William Warren Ward, will assume the presidency of the company effective immediately. Mrs. Ward succeeds her brother, William Warren Ward, Jr., who is taking early retirement.

In a prepared statement, Mrs. Ward explained that there will be no radical changes in operations at the company, one of the oldest textile manufactures in Parker County and a member of the informal textile manufacturing group known as the Big Five.

"We are committed to our location, to our employees and to maintaining the high production standards which have been our trademark for the last sixty-five years," she said.

Mrs. Ward has been active in the management of the company since her father's death in 1948. In assuming the presidency, she becomes the first woman to lead a textile manufacturing company and one of the few female CEOs in the United States.

1

Near Leesville, N.C.
Friday, October 19, 1988

Driving his new BMW through the downpour, Ted Brunson hydroplanes just before he crosses the state line. When it happens a second time, he forces himself to slow down, to concentrate on the shiny blackness before him and ignore the endless hypnotic flow of headlights in the opposite lane. He exits the interstate as the digital clock rolls over. Seven, three, zero. Ten more minutes. He's been on his feet for the last five hours and he's aching with fatigue. He wants this day behind him, wants to be home.

Sheets of rain wash across the narrow two lane road to the farm. Halfway up the drive he rounds the barn, looking ahead for the sharp brightness of the garage flood lights, the yellow glow from the kitchen windows, but the house looms dark at the top of the ridge. Ginny's SUV is not in the garage. He finds her note on the refrigerator.

Gone to hospital.

Anguish shoots through his body.

No, no, Dolly. No. Please God. It's too soon. The doctor said it could be another month.

He knows he should have stopped by the hospital or at least called before he left Parkersburg, but he didn't. He breaths in, exhales, starts back toward the garage, catches sight of the red light flashing on the answering machine and hits the play switch. Sam's voice sounds hoarse, barely recognizable.

— Ted, Dolly's gone and Ginny said she had to talk to you. She's on her way home.

Dammit Ginny. Out there in this storm. He dials the number. Four rings, five.

— *You have reached 864*. Ted hangs up, dials again.
— Ted? Sam says.
— What happened?
— Her heart just stopped.
— When?
— Around five. Where have you been?
— There wasn't anyone to drive Ginny?
— Only me. What? You expected me to call a cab for a fifty-mile round trip? I told her to wait, I'd bring her, but she ripped out of there like a hound on a scent.
— How was she?
— Wound up pretty tight.
— About the arrangements. Do you need help?
— Under control.
— Volly will want to stay with you.
— No problem.
— And Billy?
— Talked to him as soon as I got in from the hospital.
— You called Chip and Warren?
— I will.
— You were both there? In the room with her ... at the end?
— Can we do this tomorrow?
— Of course. I'm so sorry.
— Yes, well. Aren't we all? Sam hangs up.
Ted blinks, tears stinging his eyes.
Dolly is dead. His mentor, his mother-in-law, his friend.

He looks at his watch then out into the blackness, willing his wife to drive safely, imagining where she might be on the familiar road. Past the mammoth north side church with its flashing Come to Jesus billboard and acres of asphalt, past the roadside stand where they buy the first peaches of the season every summer, maybe as far as the exit off the interstate. He looks at his watch again, blinking back the other reality.

He steps into the small room he uses as a home office, listening for sound of Virginia's car, glancing out repeatedly to catch the glint of her headlights when she passes the barn and heads up the hill. The windows are streaked, but the rain is slaking off. The dancin' man, a gift from Dolly, sits propped on one of the sills slumped forward, forlorn like a drunk in a doorway.

He picks up the framed picture from his desk, the photograph made at Dolly's seventieth birthday party three years ago. Posed in the garden at Montvue, Dolly's perfected vision of southern gentility. The azaleas, the house in the background, her children and grandchildren captured in vibrant color. The Wards, like the film cast of a Pat Conroy novel. Blond, healthy, handsome. Even Sam in his wheelchair. Chip and Warren, their wives. Chip's daughter, Mimi. In the middle, a triangular composition of the three women Ted loves most in the world. The three Dorotheas — Dolly in the middle, Virginia perched on the arm of her mother's chair, and Volly standing behind them to the right.

That one. His Volly, all grown up. Looking straight at the camera, as if it were all about her. Strong-willed like her mother, independent, beautiful. Hair streaked with sunlight, like that song from *Camelot*. Ted remembers the photographer told him to put his hand on Virginia's shoulder, his arm around Volly's waist.

Trying to make me look like I belonged.

Billy standing next to me, looking off to the side somewhere. Always. Poor kid. Tall, gangling. Just like I was at his age, all feet and elbows and thick dark hair. My genes. We don't look like Wards, do we? But Dolly didn't care.

"New blood," she said. "This line needs it." The day Billy was born she had congratulated him. "A son," she said, her eyes shining, as if he had sired royalty, accomplishing some magnificent feat single-handedly. He blinks again, puts the picture down, looks away. His eyes come to rest on the gun cabinet between the windows.

"Not local, but very good," Dolly had said. She spotted the cupboard in the shadows of a Jefferson County antique shop. "Probably Pennsylvania. There is nothing like old wood," she said. "Not even the best of them can fake it. This is perfect for your office at the farm."

"But I don't hunt," he said.

"Something fine, then," she said. "To pass on to my grandson." She had seen to the cupboard's refitting and placement herself. They had stood where he stands now admiring it together, one piece in a collection, built over years, the way he had helped her build the company. What he knows about antiques and about textile manufacturing, Dolly taught him.

Once he married into the Ward family, he was miraculously reborn. Their social clubs made room for him, their church confirmed him, their business group, the Big Five, welcomed him. All because Dolly made it so. They absorbed him the way a spinning machine absorbs raw cotton and turns it into thread.

The phone rings, startling him. A reporter from the *Parkersburg Daily News* wants a statement. How did they find out so soon?

— The public relations people will issue a prepared release in the morning.

— We've got plenty of information in the files, Mr. Brunson. How about a brief statement?

— Dolly Ward's death marks the end of an era.

His voice breaks on the last words. He coughs to cover the emotion, hangs up, pulls the monogrammed handkerchief from his back pocket and wipes his eyes. The handkerchief, another gift from Dolly. A dozen under the tree every Christmas. No more. He can't bear the thought of Christmas without Dolly.

The dog, Beau, rises from his cushion in the mud room and goes to the door wagging his tail. Ted sees the headlights as her car makes the turn above the barn, hears Virginia's Blazer pulling into the garage. He meets her at the door, reaches to embrace her, but she sidesteps.

— Get me a drink?

She pulls off her trench coat and throws it over the back of a kitchen stool. Ted catches the smell. She's smoking again. She is dry-eyed but her color is off. Her usually bright complexion has a yellow tint, the result of too little exercise and too much stress. He hurts for her.

— Funeral's Monday, she says.

— That soon?

— Why not? Will you call Volly?

— I thought you might want to talk to her yourself.

— No, I don't think so, she says. She is standing tight, pulled into herself the way she sits on a horse, aloof. She takes the glass without so much as a nod of thanks.

— I don't want to make this any worse for you, but I've decided, when the funeral's over, as soon as we can get everything settled, I'm leaving. Her voice is as hard as the ice cubes in the glass of Johnny Walker Black.

— Good, he says. — This has been a hell of a year. The diagnosis. Now this, so soon. Do you have some place in mind? Where are you thinking? Maybe I can …

— No Ted. I'm leaving here to get a divorce. Or you're leaving, I don't know which. She tosses the words out carelessly like a handful of gravel.

His mind won't process. He almost asks her to repeat what she has just said.

— I know the last few months have been hard on you, but …

— It's not the last few months, it's the last twenty years.

He cannot believe she's doing this, throwing his brief affair in his face again.

— I told you, he says, — that was over long ago.

— Not even close, she says. — I've gotten over your obsessions.

Dolly. Mary Helen. I just don't care anymore.

— You're upset tonight. We'll talk about it later.

— There's nothing to talk about. She takes a deep swallow of Scotch, draining the glass, and heads toward the bar. His instinct is to follow, to put his arms around her. He takes a step after her, but hesitates. She has wrapped herself in some sort of psychic barbed wire.

— Virginia, listen to me. Dolly's gone. We've got what amounts to a state funeral to get through. The family will be all over us, all of your cousins from Atlanta.

She wheels around to face him, her voice ringing across the large empty room.

— She's been dying for six months. Six months! You're supposed to be the one that loved her so much. At least that's what you're always telling me. How much you love Dolly. How wonderful Dolly is.

She stretches out the vowel sounds, mocking him, unaware that she has used the present tense. Her breathing is shallow, her pupils are dilated. Shock, he thinks. Or maybe the doctor gave her something.

— Well your precious Dolly has checked out, but she paid you off in advance, didn't she? You're president of Ward Mills. The first person in three generations who doesn't bear the name. That's what you've been waiting around for, isn't it? You finally got what you wanted. You've eaten this family alive. Now you can do what you want to and you won't have to put up with me or my brothers or my horses or my children anymore.

— Ginny, he says, — you're angry and upset. You've been through a terrible ordeal. You need to give yourself some time.

Turning back to the bar, she refills her glass. She takes a shuddering breath, which from any other woman would signal tears, and walks to within a foot of him, daring him, her voice intense.

— So you think I'm … what? Irked? Crazed with grief?

— Just … naturally you're … upset. He's repeating himself but he doesn't know how else to explain. He struggles to make her hear what he is saying, trying to connect with her and to control himself at the same time.

— Hysterical? Is that the word you're looking for? Although God knows I have reason to be, I am not, thank you, out of control. I'm relieved and I'm exhausted. And I'm sick of living with a man who married me for my money and my mother in that order. Well she's gone. She won't be around to take your side any more.

— I … I don't know what it is you expect me to say.

— How about I'm sorry? I've been sitting in that hospital room holding Dolly's hand, watching her die, and who did she ask for over and over? You. You and my brothers. Where the hell were you? Sam's the only one I could count on.

— You said …

— What did I say? Don't come? I can handle it? I'm okay? Didn't you know she needed you? That I needed you? Did I have to ask?

Anger pours out of her like rainwater gushing through a downspout. She makes a familiar hopeless gesture, flexing her fingers and balling them into tight fists as she turns away from him. She takes another gulp of Scotch.

— I don't know why I'm even trying to explain. You never pay one damn bit of attention to my feelings any more than she did. I know why you didn't come. You were scared you'd be there when she died.

He winces at the word. He's defensive, lacks experience dealing with death.

— I did come. I came almost every day.

— And checked by the desk and chatted up the nurses and peered into the room like we were under quarantine. I almost felt sorry for you. God, Teddy! You are so afraid of showing any honest emotion for Dolly, for me.

She's pacing back and forth taking short urgent steps. He wants to shout, that's not true. You're the one who bottles things up, not me, but her brittleness alarms him so he says nothing. She walks past him to the terrace doors, stares out into the darkness, crosses her arms as if she's holding herself together.

— She loved you like a son.

The sibilants hiss with barely contained disgust, but her words come slower, more controlled. He hears the condemnation, or was it irony? He cannot understand how he has failed her or Dolly or any of them. Her shoulders sag in a way that begs him to walk up behind her and embrace her but she has put miles between them.

They are both silent, enveloped for a moment in their individual sadness and frustration. He wants to say something to comfort her, to help her see this trauma for what it is.

— Ginny. I talked to Sam a few minutes ago. He said you were very brave.

— I tried to find you, she says, not moving or facing him, her voice a flat monotone. — I talked to three or four people at the office. They were all looking for you. Finally one of them, somebody in maintenance, said he thought you were out on the floor of one of the mills, but he didn't even know which one.

She spins around, questioning, accusing.

— How could you, Ted? How could you disappear like that when you knew it could happen any minute? Her voice is softer, more pained, not so fierce, the Scotch and the fatigue muting her fury, however slightly.

— I'm so sorry, he says. — There was a crisis at the #2 plant. An electrical line break. I had to go. They couldn't locate anyone to fix the damn thing and I lost track of time. I should have let you know. I'm so sorry I wasn't there with you and Sam. I thought there was more time …

He reaches toward her again, thinks better of it, pulls two stools from under the counter.

— Here, he says. — Sit down, He opens an overhead cabinet, picks out a package of her favorite peanut butter crackers, opens it, and hands one to her.

— Have you had anything to eat?

She tastes the cracker, puts it down on the counter, makes a face, and shakes her head.

— Doesn't go with Scotch, she says. — I ate something. I'm trying to think ...

Frowning, trying to recall, she answers like a dutiful child.

— Sam brought me some coffee when he came to the hospital, she says, — and a doughnut. She speaks slowly, as if recalling what happened a few hours ago had happened last week or last year and she has trouble remembering. But she is responding, facing him, looking beyond him. He holds his breath.

— She was never in a coma, you know. Just sleeping a lot. The pain meds probably. The nurse called about two. She said Dolly's breathing had changed, that it sounded labored and she was calling the doctor. He waited 'til I got there. He said there was a fruity smell to her breath, a sure sign. He said he could give her some morphine to ease the breathing. She was making these awful wheezing noises like she couldn't get a breath. I said yes, please.

Suddenly she looks directly at him, grabs his arm, pleading.

— O God ... Teddy ... did I kill my mother?

— Of course not. You helped her. She needed you and you did the best thing you could do for her.

Her grip relaxes. Her gaze returns to the rain-streaked windows. It's as if she is watching a film projected against the blackness, looking beyond him, describing what she sees.

— Go on, he says, not moving, not taking his eyes off of her face.

— She seemed to relax after that. By the time Sam got there, she was sleeping again and then all of a sudden, she just stopped breathing. I didn't see at first. I was looking out the window at the clouds, watching them build up in the west like all hell was about to break loose. Sam called my name and I turned around and the nurse was hunched over sobbing like her heart would break. She had no right to that! She hardly knew Dolly.

Ted lets the thought lie. He's breathing at the top of his lungs.

— And then? he says in a whisper. — Tell me the rest.

— And then I went out into the hall to find the doctor who came in and listened to her heart and said she was gone. Sam wheeled over to the bed and held her hand. I didn't feel anything, because she was still there somehow. I wanted to get out of that room and leave her in peace. I didn't feel anything. Just a need to escape. And then, once I was on the road in the car I was — relieved. Isn't that terrible?

— No, it's not. It's normal.

Pushing the glass away, she turns, rests one hand on the counter. He covers her hand with his. She doesn't seem to notice, staring into the middle distance, seeing what he can't see.

— Sam said he had to sign some papers to release ... the body ... and then he said he'd bring me home but I had to find you first and tell you Dolly was dead so I could finally tell you about the divorce, and that I've been thinking about it for months. I couldn't just sit there and wait and wait and wait any longer.

— I understand, he says.

Her voice is much lower, calmer. He is not so concerned about the divorce talk as he is about her general state.

— I'm tired, she says. — I'm going to bed.

— Do you have anything to help you sleep?

She doesn't answer, slides off the stool. Pulls herself up the stairs as if she weighs twice her one hundred twenty pounds. The conversation is over.

— I'll be up in a minute, he says, as if she hears. As if it matters. He sees her up the stairs, then calls the dog.

— C'mon Beau.

He lets the golden retriever out the mud room door, watches as he scurries across the apron in front of the garage, raises his leg, and scoots back beneath the overhang, shaking the water off his coat. Ted grabs a kitchen towel and wipes his paws.

— There you go, he says, opening a can of dog food and spooning it into Beau's bowl. If he can't help his wife, at least he can take care of the dog. The rain that cleared briefly begins again, harder this time. He hears it battering against the southwest side of the house, a sign the storm is renewing itself. He checks the locks, turns off the lights. When he goes upstairs, he finds a lamp turned on in the guest room. The door to the master bedroom is closed.

Sam calls late the next morning.

— I got the boys, he says. — They've agreed to postpone their hunting trip for a few days. Nice of 'em.

— What else would you expect?

— Dolly wouldn't like this obit. Ginny won't either. I thought we had something on file at the office.

— We do. No way to get it to the paper in time to make the deadline last night. How bad is it?

— Well it defines her in the first sentence as the widow of deceased textile magnate Ben Ward. And it goes into some detail about their wedding and how they were distant cousins and about his tragic death at age forty-five. Four children, three grands. Spelled all our names right. Doesn't say anything about her role in the industry, the first woman CEO thing.

— Too bad. The one you put together is stronger, Ted says. — More business oriented. It goes out first thing this morning. Maybe the regional papers will use it.

— This piece of crap doesn't do her justice, but the Big Five will love it, which reminds me, I got them all lined up to be honorary pallbearers. So Dolly gets the last laugh. They finally have to accept her.

Not the most sensitive crowd. I don't think they even noticed how she used their attitude toward her. Remember the first time OSHA got on us? She kept quiet and Ward Mills wasn't tainted by the protest. She made us look better than we were.

— Always, Sam says. He coughs. Ted can't tell if it's emotion or Sam's usual difficulty getting sufficient air into his lungs. — They got the part about the DAR and the Junior League right. If they'd left that out Dolly would really be pissed off. How's Ginny?

— Don't know. I guess she's down at the barn. She left before I woke up, but the car's still here. She was in a state last night. Mad at the sitter, the weather, mad at Dolly for dying before they settled their differences. And she's mad at me too for something, but I'm damned if I know what it is.

—Give her some space. She's never seen anybody die before.

And neither have you, Ted thinks. Well, almost.

— Are you up to coming into the office this afternoon?

— No. Bad night. Tell Ginny I'll call her later. We've got a lot to talk about.

Ted lowers his voice trying to maintain control.

— You don't know the half of it.

And so it goes. Once again the Wards will turn to him, lean on him, expect him to organize for them and protect them from intrusion and lead them out of the shadow of the valley as he has done over and over for the last thirty years. He's sick of being their front man, their patsy, their guardian. Sick of running their company and now, with Dolly gone, maybe he doesn't have to, or want to, or need to anymore.

Ted catches Virginia before she leaves for the barn.

— I thought I'd call Billy about being the lead crucifer, he says.

— What are you thinking? With that cast on his arm? He can't possible carry the big cross.

— I know, but he should have the right of first refusal. She was his grandmother. Does he have a sports coat with him?

— I doubt it. He may not be able to get it on over the cast but I'll take one this morning. And a clean white shirt and a tie, she says.

— He can borrow one from Sam, Ted says, but she doesn't hear. She is already out the door.

An abrupt, point of fact conversation, he thinks. No emotion. Hell of a way to run a marriage.

2

Monday, October 22, 1988

Virginia calls from the kitchen.

— Ted? They're here.

From his office Ted watches the limousine wind its way up the curving driveway. After two days of rain the front has blown off to the east, clearing the air. The ginkgo trees that line the drive are at their most glorious, brilliant and golden in the October sun. Fall in its glory. Dolly's favorite time of year. Virginia had wanted crepe myrtles or Bartlett pears but Ted and Dolly had objected. Under protest Virginia agreed, although it had never been easy for her to capitulate where Dolly was concerned.

A shaky equilibrium exists between Virginia and Ted. They are speaking rarely and only when they must. Virginia and Sam have juggled the problems concerning the service relying on Dolly's written instructions. Chip and Warren have not interfered. As Sam says, she didn't leave much to chance now did she?

Only small things. Where to seat the senators if both of them come. What flowers to put on the altar and who will serve as acolytes, details conditional on the time of year and availability, issues that even Dolly could not predetermine. Ted deals with the accumulating pile of medical bills and with the immediate legal necessities with help from their lawyer, John Reece. Sam is handling the publicity as it relates to the company.

Virginia comes into his office, elegant in a black suit, her only jewelry small stud earrings and a strand of pearls, a gift from her grandmother.

— Are you all right?

— Have to be, she says. — And you?

He knows he looks rumpled, distracted.

— As you say …

He rises with effort, flicks his computer off, sending a jagged white light diagonally across the screen. As the computer screen flashes and dies, he turns, sees Virginia's face pull apart vertically and come together again out of sync, Picasso-like. In his left peripheral vision an irregular wiggling line floats, throbbing and translucent.

— Aura, he says.

— That front that came through last night?

— Probably. Damned October weather. The pills …upstairs. My bathroom cabinet.

— I'll get them.

— Dark glasses, he says.

She is already halfway up the stairs and doesn't hear. He shades his eyes with one hand and gropes his way to the mud room closet where he finds the glasses in the pocket of his wind breaker and fumbles them onto his face. He has time, five to ten minutes, before the pain sets in. The aura hangs in the upper quadrant of his vision, crinkling in an arc of brilliant colors, growing larger with each breath and sliding toward the center of his visual field. It pulses forward, expanding and intensifying as he eases his way across the kitchen, reshaping itself into a blinding neon zigzag. He clutches the granite counter top, his depth perception destroyed. Virginia meets him at the sink, handing him the pills and running a glass of water.

— Jesus, Teddy, she says. — Lousy timing. Outside the car horn sounds politely.

— Can you make it?

He hears the sympathy and appreciates it.

The sunlight hits him in the face, closing his vision to a squint. The reflection off the shiny black automobile blinds him. His stomach heaves as the aura retreats and a knife-sharp pain jabs above his left eye. He can't feel the ground under him, feels as if he is walking on air. The dark-suited driver holds the rear door open as Virginia guides him into the car.

— Where's Volly? he asks.

— Meeting us at St. Luke's, she says.

Sam is in the limo waiting for them.

— I thought we were picking you up at Montvue, Virginia says.

— Some sort of mix-up. They sent two cars to the house and Volly wanted to drive Jesse and Annie and Billy, so I figured I might as well have a nice little ride in the country before the big show. Sam signals toward Ted. — What's wrong?

— He's got one of his headaches.

The driver has pulled down a seat for her in the middle of the car beside Sam's wheelchair.

— Jesus, Teddy, Sam says. — Lousy timing.

A half dozen other limousines are parked outside St. Luke's stretching up the street like a line of giant beetles. As soon as their car pulls up in front, a man in a dark suit opens the door, reaches in offering his hand to Virginia. She takes it, steps out, and looks around for the family. Volly and Billy are coming around the corner of the church from the parking lot. Virginia hugs Billy, notices he smells like Sam's shaving lotion. Volly looks past her into the limo, sees her father in dark glasses.

— Dad? Volly leans into the car, reaching for Ted's arm. He responds with a weak smile.

— Hey, sweetheart, he says. It's the best he can do.

The man who tried to help Virginia turns his attention to Sam. Moving around street side, he pulls Sam's chair out, opens it, and positions it close to the car door. Virginia nudges Billy, who follows, steadies the chair while Sam slides the transfer board under one side of his buttocks, lifts himself out and settles into the chair. Readjusting his clothes, he lifts his legs one at a time by the fabric of his trousers, manipulating his feet onto the metal footrests.

— We'll have to go around to the side, Sam says to Billy, as if they haven't done the same thing a dozen times. Billy nods, maneuvering the chair onto the sidewalk with his free hand, steadying it with his cast. Virginia thinks how handsome her son looks. And her daughter? Nice dress. Long sleeves, high neck, burgundy. A good color for her. The diamond and ruby circle pin a bit much for the time of day even if it was a gift from Dolly.

Virginia looks up the street, sees her older brothers and their wives coming toward the church. In the opposite direction, Ward cousins are climbing out of Cadillacs, Lincolns, and a few BMWs, all with Georgia plates. Warren steps forward, reaches to embrace his sister. She raises her hand to his chest, blocking him. Chip, a few steps behind, catches her arm and leans in to kiss her on the check. She stiffens, pushes him away with her elbow. Moving between Chip and Virginia, Ted nods to Callie, Chip's wife, takes Virginia's arm, signals Volly to step in at the other side. They follow the brothers up the steps into the familiar dark-paneled warmth of St. Luke's foyer.

Coming inside Ted is momentarily blinded, but as his pupils adjust, he sees Dolly's casket to the left, flanked by Jesse and Annie Owens, the couple who have served the family for forty years. He thinks how big the casket looks, so large for so small a woman. The cover, white silk with a large gold embroidery cross, shimmers in the sunlight. An arrangement of white seasonal blossoms and roses perfumes the foyer. He tightens his grip on Virginia's arm unconsciously and she looks at him, questioning.

The young minister, blond like the Wards, robed in white with a gold stole, greets the family members one at a time, his smile vague but beatific. He has been at St. Luke's less than a year, but he has been attentive to Dolly.

— If you'd prefer to wait in the sacristy? The minister signals toward the side door. He assumes they will want to enter the front pews as discreetly as possible, but Virginia declines.

— We will follow Dolly, she says. It's what she wanted.

The minister marshals the acolytes who light their thick white candles. The crucifer, the youngest son of a Big Five member, a young man who has grown up with Volly, nods in her direction, lifts the cross. The solemn processional begins, led by the minister intoning the opening sentence, his voice commanding but compassionate.

— *I am the resurrection and the life ... he that believeth in me, though he were dead yet shall he live ...*

Dark-suited attendants move the casket around the corner and into the nave of the church. The immediate family follows. Jesse and Annie hesitate, but Sam, who has joined them via a ramp on the side of the foyer, signals them forward beside him. He reaches up, touches Annie's hand. Jesse takes the push handles of the wheelchair from Billy who falls in line with his sister behind their parents. As they move slowly down the center aisle, Ted hears their footsteps magnified a thousand times on the polished flagstone floor.

— *I know that my redeemer liveth, and that he shall stand at the latter day upon the Earth ...*

Slowly, slowly, Ted's head throbbing with each step, they proceed toward the front of the beautiful old church, where they were married, where their children were christened, where they have celebrated Christmas and Easter, attended the weddings and funerals of friends together as a family for thirty years. Colored light pours in through twenty stained glass windows, the largest two given by the Wards. He sees the Big Five across from the family pews, recognizes the senators with them. He nods to them as he and Virginia reach the front of the nave.

Chip leads Callie into the vacant front pew, followed by Warren and his wife, then Virginia and Ted. Jesse wheels Sam into place beside them directly in front of the casket and joins Annie in the second row with the grandchildren where John

Reece, the family lawyer, has been seated. Behind them, half of the left side of the church fills with Wards.

— *Blessed are the dead who die in the Lord; even so saith the spirit, for they rest from their labors ...*

Once they have taken their places, a blast from the antiphonal trumpets announces the first hymn. To Ted's heightened senses the organ sounds an attack. "Onward, Christian Soldiers" assaults him, militant and too triumphant, the full choir, full-throated, everything as Dolly specified.

For Ted the sounds have blended into a painful cacophony. He hardly notices the faint buzz, the comments sotto voce, drowned out by the choir and the less than sonorous singing by the assembled congregants and notables. The hymn is endless.

At the beginning of the last verse, the organist takes the pitch up a whole step, soprano voices ringing clear above the melody in descant.

— *Like a mighty army, moves the church of God ...*

Finally the choir reaches the last line. The organ pronounces a great amen. Ted feels the vibration of the giant bass pipes throughout his body.

Light-headed from the drug, and welcoming the cessation of sound, Ted hands Virginia a prayer book. She drops it into the rack in front of her without opening it.

When the music stops, a shuffling noise rises to replace it as hymnals fall into racks and people thumb through prayer books, directed by the minister in search of page 469, Burial of the Dead: Rite One.

The service is mercifully brief. No communion. After the introductory prayers, Chip mounts the pulpit where the Bible lies open, ready for his reading from the Old Testament Book of Isaiah. His voice is strong and steady. He reads deliberately, dividing his attention between the family and the honored guests across the aisle. The congregation joins in the responsive psalm, Dolly's favorite.

— *I will lift up mine eyes unto the hills ...*

Warren stumbles climbing the steps to the lectern. Without looking up he reads a short passage from Corinthians. The minister presents a brief eulogy, approved by the deceased, delivered by this nice young man who hardly knew her. One more hymn, "O God, Our Help in Ages Past," and they are ushered out as they were ushered in, by strange men in dark suits who seem to be in charge.

Ted appreciates again as he did at his wedding how conveniently elastic Episcopalians have made things, short and sweet or long and dramatic, both options open and anything in between. One small blessing of the new prayer book. I'll tell Ginny later. Might make her laugh. He looks to his left, notices how pale she is, how the creases at the corners of her eyes have deepened. Her face is a mask, unsmiling. She has not spoken a word since they entered the church.

Afterwards the family receives at the City Club two blocks away. The buffet is generous, the bar open. The two senators are first to greet Dolly's four children who form a receiving line just inside the ballroom, all very cordial and civilized. Just as Dolly would expect. When the last of the guests depart, the immediate family members are driven to Dacus for the interment. Someone explains to the young minister that the lake near Dacus has been the summer home of Wards' for three generations. Again, the service is brief. A half hour later it's over.

— Thank God it didn't rain, Virginia says.

From her seat in the limo she watches the cemetery recede around the curve. She catches a last glimpse, the brilliant spray of altar flowers, white lilies and gigantic chrysanthemums, which will cover the raw earth of Dolly's grave. The length of wrought iron picket fence hanging on the down slope of the wooded hillside. The two men with shovels waiting respectfully until the family is out of sight. Ted appears to be asleep.

The limo lurches onto the paved road, bouncing Sam off balance. He grabs the hanging hand strap to stabilize himself. Virginia, watching, has the sensation of going up in a fast elevator, the response she experiences whenever she sees Sam helpless. If, in the twenty years since the accident Sam has learned to be a cripple, Virginia has not learned to accept him as one.

— Thanks, she says.

— For what, baby sister?

— For coming up to the farm this morning.

— No problem, he shrugs. — We're paying for the seat. Might as well use it. Sorry to be late. Volly's fault. Your daughter didn't like my tie. I told her she was damn lucky I was wearing one. He looks in his brother-in-law's direction.

— When are you gonna tell me what's going on between you two?

— The club did a good job with the reception, she says, looking away. Sam shrugs, changes the subject.

— Warren and Chip behaved, he says. — Ted held it together.

— Everyone thought it was grief. The two continue talking quietly as if Ted were not there.

— I'd kill for a cigarette, she says, fidgeting.

— By the way, Sam says, — the minister asked me why we call Dolly by her name. I told him it was her idea. He noticed the boys still call her Mother. Pretty observant. He spent a lot of time with her the past few weeks.

Virginia snuffles disdainfully. — The bishop told him to.

— I figured maybe it made her feel younger having us call her Dolly. Don't think she enjoyed mothering a lot. I mean, it's not like she beat us or anything; she saw to our needs or saw to it that somebody did. She just wasn't around all that much, always off doing good and distributing, like the church says.

— Convincing yourself or me?

— Forget it, Sam says. — None of anybody's business what we call her. Too bad the governor couldn't make it. Must have run out of hair spray. Got both senators, though. Not a bad catch for short notice.

— Dolly told me about sitting next to the senior senator at a luncheon once. She said she couldn't keep his hand off her knee. The other one's charming, but I can't understand a word he says.

— That's the way they talk in the low country. I was surprised she decided to be buried in Dacus. The rest of the Junior League's at St. Luke's.

— I know. But even after all these years it's where she wanted to be, in Dacus beside Big Ben. Not to mention thirty or forty other Wards. You stay in touch with the Georgia branch better than I do. Any of them use their lake house this year? They used to come every summer, don't you remember? Virginia is beginning to worry about Sam's memory lapses, but the problem may be that she remembers too much.

— The church up here does a good job with the cemetery, Virginia says. — I think those were good times for them when they'd come up here. When we were little. Out of habit, she glances at Ted, slumped in the corner of the huge car, a hand over his face. — Jesse told me Dolly used to come here when she first found out about the cancer. He said they'd stop at the cemetery and then she'd walk through the lake house to make sure the boys were keeping it up to suit her while he checked the boats. Jesse said she liked to sit on the front porch and rock and look at the lake.

— Ginny, why did she put Chip in charge of the lake house instead of us? Sam's brow furrows as if the thought has only just occurred to him.

— All part of the plan to lure him back to Parkersburg to run the mills.

— So he showed up once a year for a weekend and that's it?

Virginia sighs. — The jerk, she says. Not angrily, more as a statement of fact.

— Speaking of the Wards, Volly says Ben's portrait in the library is really awful. Chip asked if he could have it, when all this is over. How 'bout that?

— I don't think Dolly would like that at all, Virginia says. — You're not going to let them go, are you? Jesse and Annie?

— After Dolly rescued them from that white-trash trailer park? There's an Indian legend about how if you save somebody's life they are yours forever. Couldn't dig 'em out with shovel now. Besides, who'd iron my shirts and make me pecan pie?

Sam does not mention the other things. How Jesse drives him on long trips to the beach because he tires so easily. How Annie cooks his dinner every day and leaves it in the warmer. How they tend the house and gardens, knowing on his bad days to leave him to himself.

— Can't fire somebody that's been with you for forty years, Sam says.

Forty years. Virginia remembers. She stares out the window, thinking about the chickens.

The family lived with her grandfather in a gray stone three-storied house across the street from John Wesley College six blocks away from downtown Parkersburg. St. Luke's was three blocks down and two blocks over. The house was four blocks from the drugstore where she and the boys were allowed to charge cherry Cokes and read comic books off the rack without paying because they were Wards.

After school she played dolls in the shade of the car port, the *porte cochere* as Dolly called it. Or she went to Brownie Scout meetings at the church or downed milk and cookies in the kitchen where Miss Ida Stout, her grandfather's housekeeper, reigned supreme from seven in the morning 'til four in the afternoon. Miss Ida was a true Southern cook famous for her biscuits and pound cake, and all in all Virginia liked the arrangement.

She especially looked forward to that time in the evening when her father came home from the office. After listening to *The Lone Ranger*, Virginia would go to the front parlor and stand in the bay window watching for him, trying not to touch the lace curtains because Dolly said her hands were always dirty and she would make a mess. He honked the horn when he turned onto West Avenue. When she heard it, she ran through the house, scooted past the kitchen table where Chip and Warren were supposed to be doing their homework, fast as she could so they couldn't pull her sashes. Big Ben parked his Chevrolet in behind her grandfather's big black Cadillac and called to her, "Where's my baby gal?" She'd come running down the back steps and he picked her up in a big swinging hug. She shrieked and squealed, loving it.

They had given the chickens Old Testament names, Delilah and Jezebel, the white one named Bathsheba, and Virginia's favorite, the littlest one, Jaelie. Her father told her to think about the bad ladies of the Bible and what happened to them because they were sinners and broke the Ten Commandments. The five-year-old Virginia was disinclined to think much about sin, since the nature of their wickedness was never fully described, but she liked the way the names sounded.

That summer she perfected a pantomime of the rooster, King David, tossing her head from side to side, her elbows out and her wrists turned in on her hips, wiggling her fingers like feathers. Her father laughed and called it her chicken strut.

Walking back to the house they always sang. She chose "Yankee Doodle" hinting for a real live pony. He favored "She'll Be Comin' Round the Mountain" with sound effects. Dolly stood on the back porch, calling them, telling them to hurry and wash up, the food was on the table. But he never rushed.

By July the humidity intensified making it too sweaty to skate. Daily afternoon thunderstorms kept her indoors, where she and Sam were plagued and teased constantly by their two older brothers. The new pool at the country club was open in the mornings but Dolly was too busy to take them, absorbed as she was with supervising the construction of Montvue, their future home, in a newly opened, very private section of College Heights.

Late one August afternoon, Virginia had climbed into the willow tree hunting a breeze. She was humming "Hush Little Baby," rocking back and forth waiting for the sound of the car horn which signaled her father's arrival. Afterward when she thought back over the way things happened, she wondered if she might have been singing so loud she didn't hear, but when she reasoned things out, she knew. He drove slow, coasting down the driveway so she wouldn't know he was home. That night he never blew the horn. Instead he surprised her, separating the willow branches and calling her name.

"Virginia," he said. "Time to wash up for supper."

"Hey Daddy. I didn't hear you." She reached out for his arms but he was too far away so she jumped down, hurrying toward the chicken yard. He caught her by the shoulder.

"Already fed the chickens," he said releasing her.

"You fed them without me?" She looked up at him for an explanation, but he didn't respond. She thought of Jaelie, the littlest one, and of how the others bullied her.

"But Jaelie won't get a bite. The others won't let her. Daddy! She'll starve."

"No she won't. She'll learn to fight for what she needs. It's time you quit feeding the chickens anyway. It's no chore for a young lady. Come on. I told you it's time to wash up for supper." He turned and started toward the back porch.

"No!"

He stopped but didn't turn around. "Don't sass me, Virginia."

"Why won't you let me feed anymore?" She held her ground belligerently.

"I told you," he said. "For the last time, it isn't proper for a young lady to be feeding chickens."

"But I don't want to be a young lady. I want to be your gal baby and feed the chickens with you." Her voice rose to a wail.

"I don't want to hear another word about those chickens. Now get up those steps before I switch you good."

"Please, Daddy, please! Just let me make sure she's all right."

Virginia started toward the chicken yard again but he caught her arm with one hand and broke off a willow whip with the other. She heard the crack and swish. The wand whistled through the air biting into the soft skin behind her knees. She cried out more from surprise than pain.

"I will not have a child sass me," he said, switching her twice more. She fought tears, too angry to give in to expectation and too proud to let him see her cry. To her mortification, her brothers and Dolly had assembled on the back porch.

They moved into the new house a month later, surrounded by four acres of prime real estate. Enough space for the children to build their own homes someday, Dolly said. She got some men from the mill to build a shed out back, bought Virginia a white pony, and signed her up for the pony club. Two months later, Ben Ward died, struck down by a sudden massive heart attack. What Virginia remembers of her father derives from the chicken story. About her favorite Jaelie, he had said, "She'll learn to fight for what she needs."

3

Friday, October 26, 1988

Four days after the funeral life at the farm has gradually resumed a more normal routine. Ted rises early, goes for his accustomed run, down the drive, over a short stretch of asphalt to a three-mile flat on the old River Road. The sky is clear and vibrant, an intense color, real Carolina blue. A steady breeze from the west rustles the browning foliage of the oaks that grow along the water's edge, creating lacy shade patterns on the gravel road. Yellow maple leaves swirl around Ted's ankles. Beside him the Cowee River burbles clean and sparkling, shallow over a bed of smooth stones, wider here in the valley, but not much deeper than upland where it borders the farm for several hundred feet before veering off to lower ground.

Ted processes while he runs, organizing the day ahead, assessing everything from labor disputes to ideas for Virginia's birthday present. He misses Beau, his usual companion, a mute and therefore congenial audience for his daily monologues. Beau is on kennel rest for hip problems. It seems to Ted that the ageing process is suddenly impacting everything: his older friends, the men at the club where he plays golf, the dated equipment of Ward Mills, Inc., and now even his dog. Knees and hips, knees and hips. Can't go to a party these days without hearing a litany of aches and pains. People don't take care of themselves.

Ted is no exception. Not until he hit forty and gained an extra ten pounds had he started running, but he needs to be more consistent.

John Reece, the family and corporate lawyer, comes to mind as a role model. Ted smiles to himself, thinking of Reece who has taught him so much. Fifteen years Ted's senior, he is a dedicated rower. He lives on the lake, rows every morning. The effort has done little to balance Reece's natural physique, heavily muscled through the chest and shoulders, slim in hips and thighs. Virginia had described him to Ted early on in their relationship.

"There's something slick about him," she said, "like a big fish." Between the two of them he officially became The Porpoise.

"The Porpoise says if we don't clean up those spinning rooms we're going to hear from OSHA." Or "The Porpoise says Dolly isn't paying Social Security on Annie and Jesse and he wants you to talk to her."

Out of loyalty to Dolly, Reece scheduled occasional meetings with Ted, in part to check on his progress and get to know him better, but primarily to help him understand the Parkersburg code of behavior. At one of the meetings after a lengthy discourse on the significance of the Big Five, Reece made an interesting point.

"You need to understand," Reece said, "Ward Mills, Inc., is privately owned, governed by the board made up of Young Ward, Dolly, and her children. Dolly and her brother Young are the majority stock holders, with three hundred shares each issued by their father before his death."

Running in the valley, white-fenced pastures on either side, Ted remembers those first unofficial conversations with gratitude. He was young, just beginning, working in the lower echelons of the company in an extensive personalized training program. Prompted by Dolly, Reece was trying to help him gain perspective.

He stops for a water break, stretches his hamstrings, and takes a minute to think backward, recalling how Reece's talk about racial discrimination surprised him.

"For the Big Five," Reece said, "the concept of equal employment opportunity threatened the way things had always been.

The highest paying, most skilled jobs—weaving, loom fixing, and so forth—had belonged to white men. Blacks worked outside, on the loading docks, or as janitors. Menial, out of sight. I am proud to say only Ward Mills accepted the change and voluntarily complied. And I am happy to think I helped influence Dolly and Young to break ranks that way."

"What about the other companies?" Ted asked him.

"Never underestimate the ability of human beings to find a way around an obstacle. They just let their government contracts expire without a whimper and kept to the old practices."

Twenty years later, Ted saw that Reece wasn't just giving him a history lesson. He was giving him valuable clues about how to deal with the Big Five.

Reece proved to be as good a corporate lawyer as anyone the Big Five ever employed, as well as a solid, if somewhat formal, older friend. Ted realizes that he and Reece were bound by the commonality of having been born somewhere other than Parkersburg from the beginning. That they were forever outsiders in a small, tightly held world, a fact which neither of them is ever allowed to forget.

Two riders canter toward Ted. He doesn't know their names but they look familiar. Possibly classmates of Billy's at the academy? Probably children of the Big Five who stable their horses at nearby farms. Slowing to a trot, they smile and speak as they pass.

— Morning Mr. Brunson.

— Great day to be out, he says. He picks up his pace, straightens his posture, waves as they go by.

On the way home, he stops at the bottom of the hill to admire the farm, thinking how well Virginia has executed the restoration, the rings located across the driveway from the barn virtually hidden from the house, the pastures fenced in white, marked by cylindrically rolled bales of hay ready for storage, their home, nearly invisible from this angle through the avenue of trees that flanked the drive. The buildings have settled well into the land. Early on he had driven up from Parkersburg with the architect to check the axis of the house. He wanted the primary living spaces to capture both sunset and sunrise. Partial to the latter, he likes the idea of a fresh start. As he continues the climb, the gentle ancient mountains of the Blue Ridge rise into his line of sight beyond the roof, flowing northeast by southwest in perfect alignment with the house.

He towels the sweat off his face and walks toward the barn, discouraging the three resident cats who wrap themselves around his legs, meowing.

— Scat! he says. — Go 'way! He doesn't care for cats. He's a dog person.

He hopes to find Virginia inside. He is tiring of his guest room exile. She has not invited him to return to the bed they have shared for thirty years. He heard her leaving the house early this morning, assumes she is avoiding him on purpose, but he remains optimistic. The few times they have been together, sharing a meal or discussing some aspect of the funeral plans, she appears more resigned than angry. She has not mentioned the divorce again.

Ted hears the handyman's truck chugging up the hill, goes out to greet him and inquire about his wife who is ill.

— Morning Wilson. How's she doing?

— No better, Mr. Brunson. No better, but no worse. I'll tell her you asked. What are you doing down here? Don't see you around much.

— Waiting for Mrs. Brunson. You know how it is.

Or as Dolly used to say, 'Twas ever thus. His public life in good shape, his private life a mess. Ted walks away to discourage further conversation.

It's not the first time Virginia has broached the subject of divorce, but the vehemence of this current announcement was so uncharacteristic it pushed him into silence, partly out of surprise and partly out of empathy for the trauma she has suffered. He has watched her through the ordeal of Dolly's diagnosis and the frustration of her treatment, offering hope and having it snatched away when each new treatment failed, first radiation, then chemo. He has seen how the uncertainty and the waiting have drained his wife. She has developed a chronic edginess, a dread, like the attitude of earthquake victims expecting unpredictable aftershocks. He wants to help her, but has not found a way satisfactory to either one of them.

The funeral and his own gnawing sense of loss, which he has suppressed, have filled the intermittent days, but there is still the matter of the stock and the imminent sale of the mills, which he cannot engineer until Dolly's bequest becomes public knowledge. He would prefer to have Virginia and Sam support him, although it may not be legally necessary, but he has not mentioned the bequest to anyone. He promised Dolly. Time has weighted the burden. The boys left for their annual week-long trek to the hunting camp in Canada immediately after the funeral, so the reading of the will has been postponed.

Walking through the barn he checks the stalls, sees that Virginia has taken out the youngest horse, Sandlapper. This new horse has thrown Virginia twice balking at a fence. Last time she broke her wrist. Odd, he thinks, that Billy has suffered a similar injury while swinging from a rope in the garden at Montvue. The same rope his mother and uncles played on when they were children. Perhaps Billy has inherited some congenital skeletal weakness from Virginia, or more likely he is simply clumsy, like most boys his age whose feet have outgrown their bodies. Ted is leery of coincidence, but it seems to him that nothing happens without echoes.

He stops to speak to the gentle bay gelding Virginia bought for him a few years before, encouraging him to take up trail riding for exercise and distraction. The horse has a nice personality.

— Oh Henry, Ted says. — How's my literary horse today? Ted wishes he liked to ride more because Henry seems to enjoy having him around. Virginia says horses have definite likes and dislikes and behave differently depending on the mood they are in and the people they are with. Ted admits to being prejudiced in Henry's favor because the horse has behaved like a true gentleman, patiently suffering his learning curve as an inexperienced rider, never nipping or bucking.

— Good boy, big boy, Ted says, patting his neck. The horse nuzzles his shoulder, searching for a treat.

— Yes, well, I like you too. Maybe we'll have more time later. If and when life slows down a little. Ted strokes the swirl between Henry's eyes, pushing his forelock to one side, knowing the prospects for any slacking of his responsibilities is little more than an optimistic illusion. — Your girl's coming soon. She'll take you for a good long run. Seems to be a new girl every year, right old man? They outgrow horses or they go off to college or they discover boys.

Ted steps out of the breeze into the tack room to avoid cooling down too fast. The fragrance of treated leather engulfs him in a wave of nostalgia. He inhales deeply, rubs his hand over the surface of a fine English saddle, remembering the feel and the smell of his baseball glove. The sensory cue opens a mental slide show of his childhood and adolescence as scenes and people from the past rush by in his mind's eye. The kids from his neighborhood, his teachers, his parents. He thinks how far he has come since those days when belonging to a baseball team was the single most important goal of his life.

He and John Reece had first compared their formative years on a trip to New York a year after he and Virginia were married. Offered a drink, both asked for Scotch and water. A small commonality, their preference in alcohol, but one that set them apart from the bourbon drinkers of the Big Five.

"How did you happen to come to Parkersburg?" Ted asked. "You're not from around here, are you?"

"No. I grew up in Columbia, graduated from Princeton, came home to the university for my law degree, and went to work for my father," Reece said. "When Ben Ward died, my father was one of the first people to contact Dolly and ask what he could do to help. She told him she needed a good lawyer, so he sent me to Parkersburg on loan to help her straighten things out and I never went home again."

"You grew up in Fort Hill, didn't you," Reece said changing the subject. "It's a different place today from the town you knew, I suspect."

"And how," Ted said. "When I was growing up it was another middle-sized Southern city with wide streets and big churches." The stewardess interrupted, bringing the drinks he and Reece ordered.

"Cheers," Reece clinked his glass against Ted's. "Here's to the future of Ward Mills, Inc. Now, tell me more about young Mr. Brunson."

"A pretty dull story," Ted said. "My parents moved to Fort Hill from South Carolina and opened a hardware store in the Plaza neighborhood when I was five.

Ted looked out the window at enormous fluffy white clouds piling up, thinking of the way events in his own life have built, one on top of one another. Judging from the distant look on his face, Reece got the impression that Ted had not been asked often about his origins.

"Dolly tells me you had a full scholarship at John Wesley. Golf, right? It has served you well?"

"Got me into John Wesley," Ted said, "but baseball's more my game. I fell in love with baseball when I was a kid. Did you play ball, Mr. Reece?"

"Call me John, and no, I'm afraid not. I had asthma as a child and I was near-sighted.

"Do you hunt? Virginia's brothers hunt a lot."

"Not my sport," Reece said. "I went with the boys once at Dolly's insistence. I nearly froze in the blind and the smell of dead birds made me nauseous. Contrary to your mother-in-law I find that Southern boys are not all born hunters. May I assume you played baseball in high school?"

"Four years, and American Legion ball in the summers. You could say baseball got me where I am today. I played for the Ward Mill team a couple of summers in Fort Hill."

Ted's hand tightening on the arm rest as the plane began its descent, the sure sign of an inexperienced traveler.

"And I don't know much more about you than when we took off," Ted said.

"There's plenty of time," Reece said. "I think the Wards plan to keep us both around for a while."

Ted hears a Jeep pull in. It's the current "stable boy," a girl, coming in to muck out the stalls and exercise the horses. She has brought a younger girl along, a friend or possibly a sister, who looks to be about fourteen, the age he was when he got his first paying job. As Ted had told Reece on that first trip to New York, Ted's uncle introduced him to a pharmacist who hired him to work the soda fountain on Saturdays. By then he had reached a sufficient height to control the milk shake machine and toast the chicken salad sandwiches, delivered daily, packaged in symmetrical clear plastic triangles. He loved those sandwiches but found the work boring. He kept at it because his mother insisted that dealing with the public strengthened his social skills.

Ted steps out of the tack room to speak to the two girls. Thinking that his unannounced appearance might frighten them, he coughs politely.

— Oh hi, Mr. Brunson, the older one says. — What are you doing down here?

— On my way back from a run, he says. — Did you see Mrs. Brunson on your way in? I've been waiting for her.

— No, she says, looking around. — She's got Sandlapper this morning, hasn't she? It'll take a while to tire him out.

— You know her mother died, he says.

— Oh gosh, she says. — I'm sorry. I remember her. She came to the pony club shows when your daughter was riding. She was a nice lady.

— Yes. She was. Ted feels a lump rise in his throat. He goes into the tack room to cover the dampness gathering behind his eyes and to retrieve the towel he carries on his runs. It is moist with sweat, reminds him of the first time he worked for Ward Mills, Inc., at the end of his junior year in high school. His college fund was still short so he applied for a summer job on the third shift at one of the two Ward Mills in Fort Hill. He put in eight hours a night in the lint-filled, poorly ventilated spinning room, lifting one hundred-pound warp-beams, one end at a time, off enormous looms and cleaning the grease and residue that accumulated behind them. He went home filthy and exhausted, slept until one and worked the rest of the day at his parent's store.

Halfway through summer he had gained considerable muscle and a new supervisor, who, as the most recent hire, had been put in charge of recruiting for the company baseball team. Approaching a sweat-drenched Ted at the end of an eight-hour shift, he asked, "Son, have you ever played any baseball?"

For the rest of that summer and all the following one, Ted pitched for the Ward Winders and got paid for it. His natural ability and modesty gained him the notice of his bosses who offered to recommend him for the management training program once he finished college.

Not that it mattered, he thinks. By then he had met Sam and Virginia, and felt that he had impressed Dolly enough to gain her support if he had asked for it, but that was the kind of favor Ted never would have asked. He always credited his summer supervisor with the opportunity to begin his career. Of such personal kindnesses bank presidents and textile CEOs are made, a life lesson Ted never forgot.

Naïve perhaps, but genuine.

Reminiscence isn't helping him to defer unpleasant realities. He needs action, wants to get on with his day. By eight Virginia is still nowhere to be seen. He gives up, goes to the house, showers, shaves, makes his usual breakfast, a bowl of corn flakes and a mug of coffee, and takes his food into his office. He sees Mary Helen's note in the stack of condolences yet to be answered, lavender among the ecru and white stationary, and has a sudden sensual recollection of her long slender fingers tracing down his chest to his stomach. He looks at his own hands, broad, stubby fingers, a laborer's hands. Not thin and supple like Mary Helen's or small and busy like Dolly's, always in motion with their rounded nails and genteel Windsor Pink polish. Virginia's fingers he visualizes curling inward, reins running through them, small surprisingly strong hands with clipped nails. Good hands, as they say in the horse business.

He stretches his fingers, blunt and strong, like his mother's. Ted loved her, admired her, felt he owed her so much. She had invested heavily in his future, living modestly and continuing to run the family hardware business alone after her husband died.

"It's a good business," she told him, "but your world will be bigger. Don't worry about me. I've got everything I need right here — my garden and my church."

The women he has known. Any one of them, including his ever-so-smart daughter, Virginia Dorothea, far beyond the most imaginative fantasies of the teenage soda jerk and amateur baseball player he had once been.

Life has been kind. Surprising. Lucky.

The dancin' man catches his eye, lying on top of the gun cabinet. One of the maids has moved it from the window sill. He puts it back where he likes it, framing one side of his mountain view. The toy, a classic Appalachian antique, had been a Christmas gift from Dolly. When Ted opened the present, Virginia had slipped her hand beneath the wrapping paper on his lap.

"You work too hard," she said. "You need more recreation."

Embarrassed that Dolly might see what Virginia was doing, Ted jumped up so quickly the wrappings fell to the floor. He stood there, blushing, clutching the three pieces of wood, soliciting Dolly's help in a pinched voice while Virginia chuckled.

"How do you make him dance?" he said.

"Put the dowel in the back," Dolly explained. "Now sit down. Put one end of the balance board under the side of your leg, that's right, and stand the dancin' man on the other end. Hold him steady. He dances when you thump the board with your free hand."

"You're a fast learner. You're gonna be good at this," Virginia said, enjoying Ted's embarrassment at the double entendre that had sailed over Dolly's head. "You play well."

The expression became a private signal between them, a password for sex. She would come out of her shower fresh, relaxed, wrapped in a white terry robe that smelled like it had been air dried outdoors. Walking up behind him, she would encircle his waist with her arms and ask in a whisper, "Wanna play?" He never turned her down. He misses touching her, holding her.

He picks up the toy, its jointed pieces clapping against each other, feeling the smoothness of the wood, caressed by many hands before his. Retreating to the sofa, he plays the toy across the coffee table. Awkward at first, he regains the skill quickly to his surprise. A thought occurs. He drops the toy. Too many metaphors.

— This is my day for postponing the inevitable, he says aloud. There is no one to argue or agree. He has wasted the morning, knows he has blocked the last few days by focusing on the past, pasting together fragments of his life, trying to find connections, to rediscover the path that has lead him here, the situation he finds himself in. His career in jeopardy, his wife angry and distant, his children living away from home. Coincidental? Perhaps. Or the result of his ambition and the cumulative decisions he has made. He wonders how he can maintain a sense of order, regain his balance, push through without Dolly. He wonders if he should even try.

Enough, he tells himself. He has to go. If he hurries, he can get to the office and still make time to stop off at the club for lunch. Might even catch Reece there if he's lucky. After that he'll stop by Montvue to see if the kids need anything.

He misses them both. Billy sleeps in town because of the swim team. Sam says there's no problem. Annie feeds him and Jesse gets him to school every morning in time for the six o'clock practice.

Volly had gone to Montvue as soon as she arrived from Los Angeles. She will not come to the farm because, she tells him, she and her mother are having a difference of opinion that Virginia has not mentioned. Something about a man Volly is dating, a foreigner. A French artist doing a residency at UCLA.

When Ted told Sam, he huffed, the hollow coughing sound he made when he laughed. "Like mother, like daughter," he said. "Dolly took out after Virginia about some older guy who came to call. Virginia made the mistake of telling Chip, sort of bragging about how she was dating a graduate student at Chapel Hill while she was in high school at St. Mary's. She invited him to the beach house that summer. Poor bastard! He arrived out of the blue, a hippy type with a beard and a backpack, driving a beat-up old junker. Must have been in his thirties. Dolly met him at the door and threw him out."

Insofar as Virginia and Volly are concerned, Ted doesn't ask for details and he doesn't interfere. From what he has observed, there are always tensions between mothers and daughters. He considers the conflict natural, part of the maturation and individuation process. He finds the discord unpleasant, but defers to Virginia on most child-rearing subjects, rather than create a fight that could alienate Volly permanently.

Driving past the barn — still no sight of Virginia — he thinks how Volly managed to get past her equestrian phase before she finished at the academy. Despite a clear talent for exhibition and a way with horses, Volly was done with competition by the time she hit sixteen. Ted asked her why.

"Mother expects me to win every time. It's a given. There's no excuse. Some days I'm tired or I just don't care, but she's always on point, after that blue ribbon. Even on my good days, I can't please her no matter how hard I try, so I'm quitting."

Virginia complained to him that Volly was lazy. He didn't try to explain. He thinks now perhaps he should have.

Meanwhile Dolly was delighted. She envisioned Volly as the debutante of the year, even the Cotton Queen. The first step that next year was to tour Volly around to high status balls in both Carolinas. That plan drowned when Volly, in full debutante regalia and in the company of her two marshals, drove her new Saab into a fire hydrant in downtown Raleigh on the way to the Assembly Ball. Laughing hysterically and soaking wet, the whole crew was arrested for drunk driving.

"Like mother, like daughter," Dolly said.

On the way to Raleigh to spring the reluctant and contrite debutante, Sam informed Ted of Virginia's colorful past.

"Virginia broke every rule at St. Mary's. Sometime she got caught, sometimes she didn't. She didn't seem to care either way. Dolly sent her to prep school in the tenth grade to get her away from a big ole country boy football player she was chasing.

Yessir, I'm afraid my baby sister had more than her share of unsavory playmates. We both did."

"Funny," Ted said smiling, "she's never mentioned that part of her history."

"Rules never bothered Virginia," Sam said. "Why should we expect Volly to be any different?"

When Virginia goes to Montvue that afternoon, she finds Sam and Billy watching a show about the World Series. She hugs Billy, gets no response as expected.

— I'm going up to check on some things in Dolly's room, she says.

Hesitating at the door she takes her shoes off like a suppliant on a pilgrimage.

The room has always intimidated her. Dolly had it done by an Atlanta decorator for the Christmas Home Tour years ago. In the English country style popular at the time, chintz drapery was matched on the slipper chair and the dust ruffle of the high mahogany canopied bed. As Virginia looked around she realized how well it has aged. Mellowed, that's the word. Everything in perfect proportion, the room is painted a deep Williamsburg blue. The white wool carpet floats like an island over dark hardwood. A beautiful, restful room. Feminine but not soft, assertive in the use of color. Sad today as the blues and whites paired together remind Virginia of other blues and whites, of IV bruises and hospitals walls.

Dolly's intimate personal possessions crowd her. The silver dresser set, the worn black leather prayer book on the night table, the subtle mixture of scents — *L'air de temps*, her mother's perfume, combined with the smell of freshly laundered linen and the slight tang of potpourri. Virginia feels she is intruding in a private space, Dolly's space, her presence still powerful, nearly overwhelming.

Off limits. Virginia and her brothers restricted from entering. As children they were none of them welcome here with their sticky fingers and dirty feet.

Standing in the middle of Dolly's room, Virginia has an aching sense of loss, a pang of regret for never having known her mother except as the stern uncompromising parent. Her things, this room where her presence lingers, presents another side of her, an obsessive side. In the carefully arranged perfection, Virginia perceived the demands Dolly must have put on herself as well as her children. "People are watching us," she told them. "We must set a good example."

She finds the diaries easily. They fill the book case of Dolly's English secretary. A tasseled key ring hangs from the upper glass-fronted cabinet. Matched volumes bound in blue and dated annually line the shelves. She wonders why she had not noticed them before. Unlocking the beveled glass doors she sees her own reflection and is chilled by the thought of Volly coming into her bedroom on some distant day, searching for her journal, the one she has just begun in the red spiral notebook. The idea of reading her mother's diaries generates a sudden sense of betrayal. She can't do it, not yet.

She tells herself the hour is late for beginning such a serious task, that she is too tired, that this would take more time than she can spare. Instead of starting in on the diaries as she had planned, she takes down a packet of letters, tied with a white grosgrain ribbon. They appear to have been handled frequently, the top one addressed to Sissie, Dolly's first cousin, who had died in 1972. The handwriting, a small tight cursive, perfect Palmer Method script, is Dolly's.

Wondering how they came to be returned, she closes and relocks the bookcase. As she leaves the room, she reaches down and smooths the footprints she has left on the white carpet.

4

Tuesday, November 1, 1988

Ted hears Virginia's voice as he comes downstairs. She paces back and forth in front of the sink, which she does habitually when she is on the phone. This morning she is flipping the white spiral cord in circles as if it were a jump rope. Irritation radiates from her, tangible as heat from an open fireplace.

— Hang on, she says into the phone. — Ted just came down.

— It's Chip, she says, putting a hand over the mouthpiece. — He wants me to make reservations at the Wade Hampton for Friday night. They're bringing Mimi. Please tell me what his wife and child have to do with reading Dolly's will?

Ted knows from experience that anything to do with Chip irritates Virginia. Best to keep things as matter of fact as possible.

— We'll book them a suite. I assume Warren's coming too. Where are they? Are they still in Canada?

— Sounds like it. This is an awful connection.

Ted retrieves his coffee mug from the sink where he left it an hour ago when he had come downstairs to watch the sunrise. He thinks of Dolly, who used to say the early bird catches the worm. This morning he has apparently caught a bucketful.

Looking toward Virginia he sees her stiffen. She is listening to her brother on the phone again and doesn't like what he is saying.

— You've talked to Sam? she says and Ted knows the conversation has turned to Billy.

— He's sleeping out at the pool house. There's plenty of room upstairs. It's silly to stay at a hotel. Okay fine. Whatever you want.

Ted watches, hearing an unusual wariness in the tone of Virginia's voice.

— Yes, they do have a special relationship. We couldn't do without him. He's wonderful with both our children. Before Billy broke his arm Sam was going to his swim practice at least once a week.

Ted feels an involuntary sting of reproach, as if she is rebuking him again for not doing enough as husband or father. Virginia has stopped pacing. He sees that she is concentrating on the conversation, her eyes narrowed.

— Yes, I'm sure we're doing the right thing, she says. — What do you mean Sam's too involved? We have *not* imposed. Billy's starting physical therapy this week. She looks to Ted, frowning, gripping the phone cord as if she had a snake by the neck.

— The therapists are satisfied with his progress, but they want him to take it slow. Sam's getting a heater put in the pool so Billy can work at Montvue. She has dropped the phone cord and begins flexing her free hand, loosening the tension in the swollen joints of her fingers.

— Of course he doesn't make eye contact. He's a teenager. None of them make eye contact. You just wait 'til Mimi ... His school work? It's okay. He only missed a few days of classes after his fall. Actually the swim team is keeping him in school. It's the only thing he likes about the academy. He'll be back with the team sometime next semester. Why are you so interested in Billy all of a sudden?

Virginia is quiet, listening intently. When she speaks again, her voice takes on a saccharine sweetness.

— Of course. How could I forget? You were there. We're SO grateful for that!

Ted catches the sarcasm in her voice, wonders if Chip hears it too.

No. No after effects. Some bruises and a mild concussion, and there was a crack in the ulna they missed on the first x-ray.

The break is slow healing. You know how it is, a major bone like that. We did thank you, didn't we? For what you did? Getting him to the hospital so fast? Yes. You remember correctly. It was the same rope swing where I broke my collar bone forty years ago. Dolly should have cut that tree down years ago.

Suddenly she freezes at something he says.

— What do you mean 'the other thing?' she says. For a moment she doesn't answer. When she does, her voice is as hard as the granite countertop. — My son is not retarded if that's what you're implying. He has some learning disabilities but he will graduate from the academy just like you did. She slams the phone down and turns to Ted, red in the face.

— He said there has always been something 'a little off' about Billy. He wanted to know if the accident has had any further effect on his cognitive ability. That bastard! She storms off up the stairs.

An hour later, Ted is finishing the morning paper when he hears the buzz of the intercom from the barn. The handyman says Virginia is needed. Something about a shipment of hay that has been delayed. He calls upstairs to her.

— Ginny! Problem at the barn.

— Coming, she says.

— What's this Montvue scenario? About the swimming pool?

— Sorry. It just came up yesterday. When I took Billy for PT after school yesterday, Sam was at the gym working with a trainer. They want Billy to use the arm as much as possible but they're way on the other side of town, so Sam's going to hire someone to work with Billy at Montvue, short term. Gotta run. Call Sam if you've got a problem.

Volly is still in town, at Montvue for the rest of the week. Just the day before, Sam has reminded him how she and Virginia treat one another when they are under the same roof. Ted is relieved she is not at the farm adding to the tension, but he hates missing the time he might be spending with her, with both his children. When he calls, Sam says Volly is sleeping in.

— Duke changed her, Sam says. — And now she's living in Lalaland. Los Angeles is no place for human habitation. You should pass through and keep on going. Sam makes a deprecating sound.

— I don't like this new attitude of hers. She scorns everything Southern, like nicknames. She says they demean women and that Southerners suffer from terminal cuteness where names are concerned, Chip being a prime example. I had to laugh at that one.

— She's outgrowing us, Ted says. — Living in California, studying art, she's … he hesitates a minute, searching for the right word. — She's more worldly.

Ted has reservations about her choice of graduate school, frustrated by the distance between them. When he called with the news of Dolly's death, her machine answered in unaccented syllables: "You've reached Dot. Leave a message." He gets it. Dot. George Seurat. He learned antiques from Dolly. From Volly he is learning art history.

Ted misses her and he still pays the bills, so he decides to stop off at Montvue for a visit. He hopes he can have the necessary chat with Sam about the will, too. He thinks he might include Volly, if she's interested.

Ted is about to leave for Parkersburg when Virginia comes up from the barn, still annoyed with Chip.

— I'm surprised they're taking Mimi out of school again so soon after the funeral. Callie was out of town a lot when they were first married, but Sam says she isn't traveling so much lately, probably ageing out of saucy ingénues. Maybe that's why she spoiling Mimi. Compensation for being away when she was little. Must come from her side. Indulging children doesn't run in this family.

What runs in this family, Ted thinks, is an overarching ability to mold reality into whatever shape best accommodates the current situation, to see only what the Wards want to see. He has come to think of the brothers dispassionately, learning to manage them early on while they still worked for the company. He is civil for the sake of peace in the family, and the chunks of stock they own. But since Dolly's diagnosis Chip has taken an unwelcome interest in Ward Mills. Along the way, Ted learned to decode the siblings' conversations and the way they turn on each other, squabbling like a bunch of hungry monkeys. All except Sam and Virginia, who never argue. They are in touch in a more profound way. It has taken Ted years to understand that symbiosis and it still surprises him on occasion.

— Don't be too hard on him, Ted says. — Remember how he handled the situation when Billy fell. I was telling Volly yesterday.

— That was to be expected, Virginia says, pouring herself another cup of coffee. — Billy is family. I would have done the same for Mimi if the situation had been reversed. I mean we were just lucky he was there in the first place, passing through, so he said, on the way to call on a customer in Fort Hill. He says he stopped to check on Sam.

— You don't believe him?

— I think he was here for a reason.

— Does it matter why he was there? Ted says. — Look, Virginia. He got Billy straight to the hospital and stayed with him until Sam found us and we got there. And by that time he had arranged for the best neurosurgeon in Parkersburg to see Billy and already had the CAT scan done. You should be grateful. I am.

— I'm telling you Chip didn't do anything so exceptional, she says. — The point is that Billy's going to be fine. It wasn't a big deal.

Ted hears the message. No one knows what's best for Billy except his mother. It's Dolly all over again.

Virginia grabs her denim jacket from the mud room closet and the keys to the pickup off the cork board by the door.

— Can you call the hotel this morning? she says. — I'm renting two stalls to a girl from Columbia for the show this weekend and she should be pulling in right about now and then I've got to get Beau from the vet's before lunch. Oh and the maids should be here around ten.

She is gone before he can reply. Business as usual. She has managed once again to avoid the issue, covering with fierce activity. Last night she was on the phone returning condolence calls until ten o'clock. Then she had disappeared upstairs with no explanation.

If that's the way she wants it. He tastes his coffee, finds it bitter and cold, and dumps the residue in the sink. Going into his office to gather some overdue business correspondence, he can't avoid seeing Mary Helen's lavender note card. He has reached the age when nothing comes into his life free of encumbrance. Letters, songs, seasons arrive smudged with the fingerprints of cumulative memory, marked so clearly with telltale evidence he wonders Virginia doesn't notice. But Virginia has been otherwise occupied. With the horses, then with the children and Dolly.

He had admired Mary Helen years before when she flirted with him at country club dances, and again at Dolly's party during the 1969 Hilton Head trade meeting, but his memories of the accident blocked it all. That one day changed his life, scarring him inside and out. He became more solemn and introspective, struggling with strong emotional reactions to commonplace events. He got teary over sentimental television shows and furious at political ones. He was haunted by the knowledge that he had escaped death by a matter of inches, saved by the width of a bridge abutment.

Ted's physical injuries had not been major, more superficial than permanent. Without Sam at the office, his workload doubled, a good thing, a distraction from thoughts of his own mortality. Within three months he appeared healed, except for the scar on his cheek. He thought he had put the worst behind him, but no matter how hard he tried, the image of Sam, trapped forever in the wheelchair, served as a constant reminder. The tick-tick sound of the wheelchair rolling down the hall at the office, his hollow cough, any contact between them touched a deep spot in Ted's being which he fought to suppress. Dolly never blamed him. His pain and remorse were as evident as the scar on his check.

Preoccupied, Virginia didn't notice. Like Dolly, she was grateful Sam was alive and credited Ted with saving him. When Ted was alone, driving back and forth to work or running in the mornings, questions about the chain of events that particular awful day surfaced unsolicited from his subconscious. The lives of the people he loved, his own life, had suddenly become infinitely more precious.

Once Sam was out of danger and his recovery began, Dolly took over. She added a spacious room and bath behind the kitchen at Montvue, fully outfitted and equipped for a paraplegic. She extended the deck, adding a ramp to give Sam easy access. When he came home from the rehab facility, she greeted him with a new car, a big heavy Buick, with hand controls. By September, all of their lives had fallen into a more predictable pattern and Ted was eager for the long weekend with his wife that lay ahead, an ATMI conference on imports and tariffs at the Homestead.

At the last minute, Virginia decided against making the trip. She was too busy running her first three-day event, she said. As Ward Mills Marketing Director, Mary Helen's husband had gone on ahead. Mary Helen was to ride up with Virginia and Ted, but when Virginia announced she couldn't make it, Ted and Mary Helen were thrown together alone for the six-hour drive. That's how it began, a temptation too obvious to be ignored.

Ted felt rejected and determined to enjoy himself over the weekend with or without his wife. He had his golf clubs and here he was in the car with a beautiful woman. The possibilities made him reckless. He had always found Mary Helen attractive and he told her so.

Six months into the affair, he realized how expensive it had become. He was intoxicated with the look of her, the scent of her, some exotic perfume she wore, the sensual way she moved, her slender pale body, the texture and color of her hair, thick and curling into ringlets but so soft and the most luscious shade of mahogany red. He knew he was obsessing, losing work time, feeling guilty about cheating. Still he might have gone on with it for years, but Mary Helen showed signs of a more serious intent. He was ready to break it off when Warren preempted him.

On a sunny spring afternoon in April of 1971, Warren saw Mary Helen and Ted leaving a motel together, or so he claimed. He called Virginia the next morning.

"I want you to see my new office," he said, "but don't bring Mother. We want to surprise her at the official opening next month."

"Warren, for heaven's sake," Ginny said, "I do not have time to drive to Atlanta for the sole purpose of seeing your office. What's going on down there?"

"I, uh … Chip and I, we have something important to discuss with you."

"Okay. Just tell me." Virginia was accustomed to Warren's self-dramatizations.

"Not on the phone. Chip and I think you should hear this in private."

"If you two have screwed up Dolly's investment portfolio and you want me to cover for you —"

"No. It's personal. Very personal. I'm serious, Virginia. You need to come."

"Oh all right. But only because I need to find a dress for Chip's wedding. Maybe I can catch a sale at Lennox Square while I'm there. Your office is around there somewhere, isn't it?

"Right across the street. You can't miss it. There's a big sign that says Ward Brothers."

"I'll be there tomorrow about ten," she said. "You have to buy me lunch."

For Virginia, the three-and-a-half-hour drive to Atlanta was sport. As competitive on the highway as she was in the ring, she actually enjoyed the traffic on the interstate, pushing beyond the speed limit and maneuvering to get to the front of each successive gaggle of southbound cars. She found the newly expanded office of Ward Brothers with no trouble, but had to pass inspection by the receptionist and Warren's secretary before being ushered into his office. She didn't like being jerked around, especially by her older brothers' minions.

When she came into his office, Warren was standing behind his desk, dwarfed by the ten-foot ceiling, the oak paneling, and the array of preserved animal heads mounted around the walls.

"You could have met me outside," she said. "Phew! This place looks like a taxidermist's office."

"I saw Ted yesterday afternoon over in Anderson," he said without preamble.

"Oh?" she said. "Ted didn't mention it but he doesn't always tell me where he's going or where he's been." She pretended to admire the reddish brown skin of a preserved impala head. "Where's Chip? I thought he was in on this too."

"He's tied up right now. He wanted me to talk to you first anyway."

"He got most of these, didn't he? On the African trip?"

"Yeah, but I got the buck," he said. "An eight-pointer."

"At a trophy farm."

"What?"

"Nothing. What is it you want to talk about, Warren? "

The pitch of his voice rose with nervousness. "Like I said, I saw Ted yesterday ... at the Holiday Inn ... right there off I-85?" He paused between phrases, pumping significance into each revelation, watching for her reaction. "I was coming home from a Board of Governor's meeting at Clemson."

"We all know how important you are, Warren," she said.

"It was sheer coincidence."

"You make it sound like an act of God," she said. "So you saw Ted at a motel near Clemson. So what?"

"There was a woman with him. He was helping her into her car."

"And?"

"It was that redhead Chip used to date. Mary Helen Bruce."

Reflex tugged at her scalp and flattened her ears. She shifted her attention to the next trophy in line, a boar, pretending to study the curving tusks and bristled snout, buying another minute to steady herself before continuing in the same casual mocking tone.

"You couldn't stop and wave and say, 'Hey Ted what are you doing over there with that woman Chip used to date?'"

"Under the circumstances..."

"I'll bet you Dolly was around there somewhere. Didn't that woman's father die right after Christmas?" She moved on to take a closer look at a springbok with long pointed horns. "He had lots of farm land on this side of the county, if I recall. You know how Dolly and Ted wander all over looking for property. I'll betcha' that's what they were up to."

She turned to face him, dropped her purse on his desk.

"Well?" she said. "Is that it?" She watched the possibility dawn on him that he was making a fool of himself, enjoying the signs of his discomfort, a slight reddening of his cheeks, his left hand toying unconsciously with the pen on his desk.

"I didn't see Mother anywhere," he said.

"That doesn't mean she wasn't there. She was probably in the ladies room fixing her lipstick. I'll bet they met Mary Helen there for a late lunch and some negotiating. That makes sense. That motel has the best buffet in the Upstate."

"Well I wouldn't know about that," he mumbled. Warren sat down in the high-backed executive office chair, trying to re-establish his authority, but Virginia leaned across the desk, glaring, her voice gruff and low.

"You're accusing Ted of screwing that bitch because you'd like to be doing it yourself."

"I am not!" He spoke too fast, giving his doubt away. "I just thought you ought to know the kind of scum you've brought into this family."

"You are one sorry excuse for a man," she said. "That scum, as you describe my husband, is the reason Ward Mills, Inc., is making enough money to finance your trips to Africa and pay for your hunting lodge in Canada. You ungrateful little toad!" She picked up her purse from the corner of his desk where she had left it. "I've got to go, but I really appreciate your keeping an eye on Ted for me. He's gonna love it when I tell him what you've been up to." She started toward the door.

"Blood's thicker than water," Warren said, jumping up so fast his chair slid backwards, banging into the credenza behind it.

"Not in this case."

She wanted to tell him how much she loathed him, how he disgusted her, what a disgrace he was to the Wards. She stopped with her hand on the door knob.

"I don't know why Chip puts up with you," she said." You must have something really awful on him."

She slammed his door on the way out, bumping into Chip, who grabbed her by the arm.

"Ginny," he said. "I'm so sorry."

"Take your hands off me!"

Engulfed by waves of hurt and near nausea, she jerked free. She had to get away from that terrible stuffed animal smell or throw up.

Virginia stopped on her way out of town to buy a pack of cigarettes. Just one, she told herself, lighting up, but by the time she crossed the state line, she wanted another. Three hours later she turned off the paved road into the gravel driveway. The farm … home … never looked so good. She passed the barn, driving up the hill and pulled directly into the garage.

Upstairs in the master bedroom, she kicked off her shoes and sprawled across the bed. She was still there, curled into a fetal ball, when Ted pushed the door open at six thirty.

"Oh," he said. "What are you doing sleeping at this hour? I thought you were at the barn. Did I send my good blue suit to the cleaners?"

"Last week," she said.

"Everything all right with the horses?" Ted changed out of his suit into an old pair of shorts and a tee shirt.

"If the new girl keeps showing up."

"I thought she was supposed to be reliable," he said.

"As reliable as any."

"What's wrong?" he said. "You don't sound like yourself."

Virginia stretched, feeling the pain of muscles knotted from driving and emotion.

"I just got back from Atlanta. My brothers had some news for me," she said. "Warren saw you and Mary Helen Bruce leaving the motel in Anderson yesterday."

In the few seconds that it took for her to say the words, the balance in their marriage pitched out of kilter. Ted felt a jab of pain in the same way he might feel the discomfort of a tetanus shot. He hesitated a moment, considering his options.

"I'm sorry you had to find out this way."

Over the next few days, Ted made the mistake of trying to explain. Virginia had not expected such horrendous crushing honesty. To her it seemed he had torn their marriage apart the way a person might tear a photograph in two, separating the subjects forever.

"I was about to break it off," he said. "I've hardly seen her lately. It's been a couple of months."

"You make it sound like a business proposition. We've got this beautiful child, these years together. Oh God! You've been faking it, haven't you? All this time?

"No! No, no."

"You're lying. You married me because I'm a Ward and you had wormed your way into Sam's good graces. You saw a good thing and grabbed it."

Ted moans. "Oh no. Virginia. I loved you from the first time I saw you. This … this thing … it just started after the accident," he said. "It had something to do with survival, about my being alive. When you have to face your own mortality, it makes you do crazy things. I don't love her. It doesn't touch what you and I have between us. It doesn't matter."

"If it doesn't matter, why did you do it?"

"I'm telling you the truth," he said. "I want to put it behind me. Behind us."

"Shut up, Ted. I don't want to hear it!"

In desperation he said, "I could have lied."
"God," she said. "I wish you had."

Ted had rationalized. He felt legitimately neglected, thought that these little meaningless affairs infiltrate every marriage and do precious little harm. That's what he had learned from his Big Five associates, his golf friends in Parkersburg, the people Virginia and Sam had grown up with who spoke casually about their liaisons. He assumed she would think the same thing, but he was wrong. The conversation resumed downstairs as she prepared dinner and he made drinks.

"How can I make this up to you?" he said.

"By giving me a speedy divorce."

"You don't mean that. Maybe if we go away … how about that trip to Vienna. You've always wanted to go there."

"You've already given me a lovely present," she said. "I think I'm pregnant."

"Oh my God …" He crossed the room, reaching out to her. She turned her back to him.

"Go away," she said. "Just go away."

5

Thursday, November 3, 1988

Ted finishes some routine business at the mill office, signing letters, reading a weekly report on the health of the industry. As president of Ward Mills, Inc., he is a part of the Big Five, essentially a lobbying group for the industry. He learns from them and participates as time allows, enjoying the ability to influence legislation and the opportunity to work with a group of local mill owners, but they have never made him feel completely accepted. Nor did he care to be.

He stops by the City Club for lunch and as he had hoped, he spots John Reece at the far end of the dining room. Reece sits alone gazing through the spotless arched windows at a cascading fountain just outside. As Ted knows, Reece has a passion for water. His house at the lake lies within sight of the Ward family compound. Dolly treated him like a member of the family, as Sam explained.

"Reece was Dolly's confidante from the day our father died," Sam said. "Dolly never suffered from lack of advice, most of it patronizing, from the members of the Big Five. She needed a buffer."

Reece was another generation, from an old respected Columbia family Dolly knew through church circles, the Upper Diocese of South Carolina being a relatively small arena. There had been questions from time to time about a more personal relationship between the two, but Sam judged otherwise. Although they enjoyed each other's company, Dolly and Reece kept their dealings strictly professional.

"She was a widow with four young kids and a husband who had died without a will," Sam said. "He was fresh out of law school, a young man she identified as a fine Southern gentleman, a good role model for us."

Ted approaches respectfully. He understands that John Reece knows more about the Wards than any other living soul.

— Are you waiting for a client or may I join you?

— By all means, Reece says, gesturing to a chair at his right.

— You look tired. Reece signals one of the waiters. — Would a martini help?

— It's Thursday. I'm resting my liver.

— Moderation in all things. Admirable. Well then. The Crab Louis looks good.

Ted realigns the silverware on the heavy white cloth. Without looking at the menu he orders the crab.

— Trusting your judgment as usual, he says. His smile is quick and more reflexive than sincere.

— Funeral went well, Reece says. — Dolly would have approved of the turnout. I chatted with both the senators. How is Virginia holding up?

— Don't know. We aren't talking a lot … too much going on. Ted looks directly at Reece. — She's had a rough year.

— Certainly no worse than yours, my friend.

— She keeps things to herself.

— That's not healthy. Maybe she should see someone? Didn't you tell me Dr. Mason had been helpful with Billy at one point?

Ted snorts. — Do you want to suggest it?

Reece shakes his head and chuckles. — No, I don't think so. Virginia doesn't believe in asking for help, does she?

— Never. She's very busy right now hovering over Billy paying him more attention than a broken arm deserves. And she's training two horses by herself, working nine or ten hours a day.

— Some of us tend to take on more than we can handle, Reece says. — As you see, life gets more complicated as we grow older. It was easier in the good old days when I first came to work here. Young Ward was totally in charge then.

— And none of us realized he'd take early retirement and leave Dolly to run the business, Ted says, not in the mood to rehash familiar Ward family history or provoke another time-consuming Reece Lecture, so he closes the conversation politely. — It's a good thing you moved here when you did, he says.

But Reece will not be denied. — Dolly never liked being the boss. I watched her push you and Sam as hard and fast as she could. She insisted she had no aptitude for management and that being a woman in a man's world made her uncomfortable. As you will recall, she used to take me along with her to the Big Five meetings and she insisted that I prep her beforehand, not that she needed it. Dolly did her homework. Funny, but in these last few years, I would have sworn she was beginning to enjoy herself. She began to appreciate the fact that she was good at it. Most of us enjoy doing what we are good at, especially when the odds are against our accomplishments. Reece blinks, returns his attention to Ted, smiling to confirm the rather oblique compliment.

— She was at the top of her game when she got sick, he says. He clears his throat, brightens his tone. — And Billy? How's he doing?

— I'm not sure, Ted says. — You know he spends most of his time at Montvue. Comes home on the weekends occasionally. The arm is healing fast enough and the concussion isn't having any secondary effects, but he doesn't seem to have any friends. His only extra-curricular is the swim team. Frankly it's hard to connect with him. He's got his own routine and he isn't very interested in the rest of us. Teenagers. What can you do?

Unwittingly Ted's voice has risen over the clink of silver and glassware and the rumble of male voices, expressing more concern than his words imply. He looks over his shoulder to see if anyone has overheard, but no one has taken notice. Reece leaves his fork on the side of his plate, giving Ted his full polite attention.

— You know Billy has some learning disabilities, Ted says. — It may be some form of autism. He needs a lot of help with his school work, but I don't think he cares much about whether he gets out of high school or not. In fact I don't know what he cares about except swimming and tropical fish.

Reece senses Ted's frustration, but doesn't flinch, letting Ted vent his feelings.

— Dolly mentioned the problem, he says. — Only a slight handicap. She said he'd grow out of it.

— One of Dolly's classic self-delusions, Ted says. — College isn't likely. He may well need moderate custodial care for the rest of his life.

Reece's eyes never waver but his tone softens almost imperceptibly.

— You know there are special schools …

Ted shakes his head again.

— I've accepted it but Virginia's still in denial. Now she's probably blaming the concussion. I may need to set up a trust. Ted takes a deep breath, sighs.

— Of course. Whenever you're ready. Poor Dolly. She couldn't accept Billy's problem as a deficiency. She had her heart set on passing the mills down to him, the fourth generation.

— I told her about the situation as gently as I could, Ted says, — but without specific diagnosis, she refused to face it. That's why we took him to Mason in the first place, but he wasn't much help. It's funny looking back now. She was so obviously disappointed when Volly and Mimi both turned out to be female. She would never have considered either one of them running the company despite the fact that's exactly what she did.

— Dolly didn't discount the girls because of their gender, Reece says. — She was being protective. She believed it would be as hard for them as it had been for her. I'll tell you this: It will be another ten years before these fine Southern gentlemen accept a woman as CEO of anything and they will probably underestimate her just as they underestimated Dolly. Don't you make the same mistake, Reece says. She was smart enough to make you her successor.

— Not so flattering when you consider her choices. Chip's lazy and Warren's short of brains and balls. Virginia's not interested although she'd be great if she set her mind to it. Sam has the brains but his physical capacity is so limited, no stamina. So, there's no backup, even if things were going our way, which they are not. Ask the business analysts. They'll tell you that when Reagan blew off the tariff bill it was the beginning of the end. Times are bad for the whole industry and they're going to get worse. But I'm not telling you anything new.

Ted pauses while the familiar waiter lowers his plate in front of him.

— Here we are, Mr. Brunson. Extra remoulade, the way you like it.

Reece picks up his fork again once Ted is served, but Ted ignores the food and continues in the same elegiac tone.

— The Big Five persist in thinking salvation lies in modernization. New equipment, fewer workers, state of the art production. It's futile. Some of the larger companies have already started sending work overseas. This whole industry is going down the drain. I'm glad Dolly didn't have to see it. We've got to act if we're going to save our shirts.

— There's time yet, Reece says.

— Not a lot, Ted says.

— What do you have in mind?

Ted looks around again. No one is near, but he speaks quietly.

— I want to sell.

Reece drops his fork. It bounces off the table cloth, clanging loudly on the parquet floor. Ted leans to his left, picks it up. Reece is frowning. He turns his head to one side as if he hasn't heard correctly. Reece raises his right hand, signaling to the waiter.

— You know that was the last thing Dolly wanted.

— I do, Ted says. — I wish there was an alternative but I don't see one at the moment. Between the external and internal pressures, we're running out of time. I enjoyed working for Dolly but I won't work for Chip and Warren even if they are only minority shareholders.

Their waiter approaches, glances at Ted's plate and asks if anything is wrong with the crab.

— No. Thank you, Ted says. — But Mr. Reece needs a fork. And while you're at it, I'd like some more tea, please.

Sensing Reece's concern, Ted continues to explain his case.

— With Young Ward gone, we're all even at one hundred shares each. So if Virginia and Sam vote with me, with what Dolly gave me when I made vice president and what she left me in her will, I've got enough to sell. Unless Chip finds out about this and tries to organize the outside shareholders like yourself. Or worse yet, if he plays the family card. At this point I haven't even got a buyer.

— Are you sure Chip and Warren would oppose you? From what Dolly told me, they have a very nice setup in Atlanta.

— But this is their family's business. Has been for two generations. Ward Mills, Inc., has been their cash cow, doing exactly what their grandfather intended it to do, providing them with generous annual dividends as the profits rolled in. They're too far removed to understand what's ahead, and on top of that they don't like me. The fact that it's my idea would be enough to sour them both. If they knew about it, they'd want to dump me and bring in management from the outside. That would only postpone the inevitable.

— You don't seriously think Sam and Virginia would vote against you?

— Not Sam. I'm going to see him this afternoon. But Virginia? No telling. She says she's divorcing me.

Reece looks pained, makes a tsk sound, shakes his head.

— That's not good news. Virginia's too impulsive. Can't you talk her out of it?

— She got over it last time because she was pregnant with Billy, but with things the way they are now …

Ted samples his lunch, eats one bite. — You knew about that, didn't you? I figured Dolly told you.

— I'm sure she'll reconsider when she's had time to digest some of what's happened. Virginia will want to protect the children. This divorce business will blow over when she calms down.

— Maybe, maybe not. Once Virginia enters the field she plays to win. I'm going to stall her as long as I can.

— This isn't a horse show, Reece says. — One more thing. Have you thought about taking the company public?

— Who'd buy stock in a textile company right now? Anyway it's too complicated and it takes too long and I doubt the boys would go for it because the stock value would drop at least temporarily. Ted stares out the window at the endlessly cascading water. Reece touches his arm.

— Ted, selling may not be the answer. Certainly it is not as simple as it looks. There's more that you need to know. I have notes at the office. You should come by in the morning.

Absorbed in his own process, Ted misses the gravity of Reece's tone and the emphasis of his touch.

— I hate going against Dolly's wishes. She was so good to me. I admired her style, the way she moved people and things around always in the best interest of the company and the family. That had to be more than luck. She had great instincts even if she wouldn't admit it. It's the kind of confidence Ginny has with horses.

Leaning forward, Ted puts one elbow on the table and faces Reece. — Present company excluded, Dolly taught me all I know about this business. She trusted me with the future of Ward Mills, Inc. I owe her. I don't want to fail either her or the family, especially my family, if I can help it, but I'm tired of managing the Wards as well as the company … all these complications …

— Between Scylla and Charybdis, as my Greek professor would say.

— Or Catch-22, Ted says. — I'm damned if I do, and damned if I don't.

In the parking lot, Ted realizes that it is only one-thirty, too early to show up at Montvue. Sam sits up half the night watching old movies on television and naps for at least two hours every afternoon. After the accident, once Sam was mobile he came to the office once or twice a week, recalling for Ted that one day in his life he would most like to forget.

Sam said he only came in to get away from Dolly's tender ministrations, not to mention thoughtless intrusions, but the pattern changed during the summer. He appeared more debilitated by the heat this year, his breathing more difficult and now his routine rarely varies, dominated by the paralysis which orders his existence. As Virginia told Ted, nothing and no one could have accomplished the kind of consistency that dominates Sam's life but a near fatal accident.

Ted can think of no better way to pass an hour than to drive through Parkersburg. During the years since the federal government imposed cotton dust standards, he has done his best to persuade the power brokers who finance the Chamber of Commerce that economic diversity is no longer an option but that it has become a survival strategy. Most of his efforts have been ignored but a few new industries have come on the scene. He's curious, wants to check them out.

Late ride through Parkersburg. Sounds like the title of a bad Western, he says to the radio announcer who has introduced Handel's *Water Music Suite*, one of his favorites. The title reminds him of the funeral, recalling the line of the hymn Dolly loved: "Time like an ever rolling stream bears all who breathe away . . ."

Once on the interstate he passes the obvious exits and drives farther out, turning at a cloverleaf to approach the city from the west. He takes a two-lane road, soon to be widened, that leads past a sprawling new mall under construction. In an act of what Ted views as madness, the city fathers last year eliminated automotive traffic for six blocks downtown, creating a pedestrian area. Once prosperous businesses are closing already and the new mall will finish off the rest.

Ted thinks the town was so much more alive in the fifties. The recession of the mid-seventies hit small businesses hard and in the interim the core rotted.

Look at this! he says to himself. Nothing has grown downtown but the churches. They've spread outward in every direction with multi-purpose activity buildings, church schools, and parking lots. They've cannibalized their own lawns and looted the city tax base.

Passing the single black neighborhood inside the city limits, a narrow fortress of low-cost apartments circled by bare earth, Ted feels anger and guilt. Virginia's grandfather once owned six blocks here, the ones nearest the original Ward Mill. A sprawling automobile dealership has replaced the shacks of the mill village where owners kept rents low as long as there was no talk about unionizing.

Depressed by what he sees, Ted realizes he should have been more involved. He had abandoned the town for the disassociated life of a country squire, turned away from the community whose citizens put bread on his antique mahogany dining room table.

Forgive us things done and left undone.

Cutting north he sees that a diesel haze has settled over the interstate corridor. He eases down the ramp and rolls up his windows. Passing mile after mile of corrugated tin boxes enclosing textile machinery plants and truck terminals, he could be on the outskirts of any of a dozen Carolina towns. The buildings are horizontal, long and flat and low and indistinguishable from one another. The newer companies, perhaps a dozen, he thinks, have popped up like mushrooms each with bright green lawns and flag poles and multisyllabic nonsense names in discreet low plastic signs, a ground-hugging monotony like the development that surrounds Atlanta or Fort Hill, only not so much of it. If he drives on twenty miles, he will be in Gaffney in the shadow of the infamous Peachoid, a water tower contoured and painted to replicate a ripe peach. He smiles thinking of Dolly and the first time she saw it.

"Oh my," she said. "It's lewd!"

Approaching Parkersburg from the northeast, he takes the old two-lane road into town. When he first saw the land as a college freshman, peach orchards rolled across the hills, gone now before a vanguard of housing developments, strip malls, and apartment villages. Parkersburg has grown unevenly, by jig and jot, too fast here, too slow there, always outward, a city spread in all directions randomly, like the tentacles of an octopus, alternatively nurtured or ignored by a power structure that dealt with progress in the framework of enlightened self-interest. They have protected their own lifestyle against the infusion of competitive industry. Meanwhile the young, not so enthralled by tradition, have gone elsewhere seeking jobs and newness, a sad commentary on the way Parkersburg, like the industry he has devoted his life to, and like the Ward family, lives in the past.

At first Ted had been enchanted. The close community, the stately homes, the implied camaraderie of the profession, a make-believe kingdom with its own court.

And they were kind. He was overwhelmed by their kindness. His upbringing left him ill-prepared for their lifestyle and their graciousness and he misread their courtesy for sincere appreciation. He was young, unschooled in hidden agendas and ulterior motives. What he interpreted as genuine concern was an ingrained manner of behaving that insulated and protected, the upper class Southerner's idea of what Dolly called *noblesse oblige*.

Ted liked living in Parkersburg until he realized the inward focus of the power structure was a kind of sickness, every bit as paralyzing as the accident that left Sam immobile, stuck for the rest of his life in a wheelchair at Montvue.

At one time Ted had coveted the house, could have had it for himself and Virginia, could have it still. The thought amuses him as he turns into the asphalt driveway that horseshoes in front. It's where she first kissed him, at the front of the steps.

In a self-deprecating mood, Ted wonders how she chose him. He has never asked her, only accepted the fact that she did.

After three. Sam will be done with his nap.

Ted parks in back near the ramp. Sam has rolled onto the rear deck and sits with his head thrown back like a zoo bear basking in the afternoon sunlight. Staying warm is a problem for Sam. Without moving he acknowledges his guest.

— Afternoon, brother. Leavin' work a little early, aren't you?

— Not really. Where's my beautiful daughter?

— Gone to the club. That bikini of hers should be against the law.

— It's the first of November. Why is that pool still open and what's wrong with the pool here?

—Can't answer your first question but the second's easy. No sweaty old golfers to ogle her and buy her gin and tonic. We don't drink at Montvue before five, man. We got rules around here.

Ted laughs. If ever there was a person who broke rules, it is his beloved brother-in-law, Sam.

— Thanks for taking her in, Ted says.

—She's damn good company even if she is a little liberated for my taste. Are you here to tell me what's going on with you and Virginia?

— She hasn't talked to you yet?

— Nope.

— Don't take offence. She's not talking to me either.

— So. What brings you to my humble barracks?

— Came to see you on company business, Ted says. — Hope I'm not too early?

— Not too early, brother. Maybe a little late, but not too early. Chip called this morning. About our stock.

The "our" stings. Whose "our" does he mean? His and Virginia's? Or his and Chip's and Warren's? The possessive. Always the possessive plural. The way they talk about themselves. The Wards. As if they were a small autonomous European principality.

6

Friday, November 4, 1988

Early morning, Ted showers, dresses, makes coffee. Dreading his meeting with Reece, he fears he is in for one of Reece's soliloquies. He calls up to Virginia when he hears her stirring.

— I'm leaving, he says. — Reece has a bee in his bonnet and wants to see me. I've put him off for two days and I can't stall. Virginia? Did you hear me?

— Another one of the Reece Lectures? She appears at the head of the stairs with a towel wrapped around her. — I'm just getting in the shower. Meet you at Montvue?

— No. I'll come back for you. We should arrive together.

Thirty minutes later, Ted enters Reece's office.

— Morning, counselor.

— Ted.

Reece is not smiling. This time Ted gets the frostiness. He has made a mistake in putting this conversation off.

— I have been remiss in bringing this up, Reece says, — which I realized when you expressed an interest in selling the company. Speaking as your corporate lawyer I feel you will need to read the information in this file before you reach a conclusive decision. Reece hands Ted a legal-size folder.

Ted opens the folder and scans the first page, skimming the history of the original thousand shares chartered by William Warren Ward, Dolly's father, in 1946.

Reece can't resist explaining.

— This traces the divisions and subdivisions of the stock, ending this year with the current number of shares held by each member of the family as well as the two of us. In 1947 just after Ben and Dolly moved into Montvue, old Mr. Ward gave one hundred shares to Ben, which Dolly inherited in 1948 when Ben died. When the old man died in 1955, he left six hundred shares to his two children, Dolly and Young, divided equally, three hundred for each. Since Young had no children, the old man insisted that Young's shares go eventually to Dolly's boys. Young Ward agreed. In writing. Otherwise he'd have gotten no stock at all. The document wasn't legally binding, but Young didn't know.

Reece notices Ted checking his watch.

— We're not due at Montvue until noon.

— Right, but I need to go to the farm and get Virginia. This is not a good day for her to be driving on the interstate.

— I understand. You can read up on the details later. The crux of the matter is that out of the original and single issue of one thousand shares, two hundred remain unaccounted for, not a viable situation if you continue with your plans.

— I respect your opinion, but I disagree, Ted says. — We should talk this out at a board meeting. Right now I have to get going. Thank you, Reece. My apologies for postponing this meeting.

— Not entirely your fault. I should have pursued this with you sooner.

— See you shortly?

Reece nods. — After all these years, my various multiple visits to Montvue … this one … such a sad occasion.

They have agreed. They will hear Dolly's will at Montvue as she requested. More like demanded, according to Sam. Nevertheless he has ordered traditional arrangements from the florists — fall flowers and autumn leaves for the wine cooler on the round table in the front hall. Jesse has arranged the bar in the butler's pantry as usual at family gatherings and Annie has set out a light buffet.

A ripe pumpkin surrounded by gourds and wheat stalks rests in the center of the dining room table. Virginia opposed any table decoration but Sam and Volly ignored her. Twelve Tiffany sterling luncheon forks are aligned with an equal stack of Limoges dinner plates. The monogrammed linen napkins are dinner size, as Dolly would say, the only acceptable napery for lap food. At the other end of the table, a rectangular silver tray holds a crystal pitcher of sweet tea, a silver ice bucket, and twelve silver tumblers. Eleven people are expected, but at Montvue the buffet is always set with one extra place, a sign of hospitality and abundance and in case an unexpected guest appears, unlikely in this case, given the occasion. Regardless, at Montvue, tradition is tradition. Annie has ham biscuits warm under a foil cover. A cranberry Jello mold perfectly turned out, as per all family gatherings, serves for color. There is a round silver platter, circled with Bibb lettuce and centered with a mound of the inevitable chicken salad, a smaller sectioned tray containing homemade bread and butter pickles along with pickled cauliflower and artichoke relish. On the sideboard Annie has set out dessert — a three-tiered coconut cake, a tray of pecan tassies, and a footed cake plate piled with her special brownies.

The menu is standard Ward fare except for the molded salad, a fall complement. During the warmer months, the salad would be tomato aspic.

The Atlanta contingent is due around one. When Virginia and Ted arrive at twelve thirty, everything is in order. Volly comes down the stairs just as her parents walk in.

— Tell me one more time, she says. — Why are we doing this? It's medieval.

— Because Dolly asked us to, Ted says. He hugs her and kisses her on the cheek. — Mmmm, you smell good and you look good.

Virginia hugs her daughter and then holds her at arm's length, looking her over.

— Aren't you chilly in that sundress?

— Showing off my tan, Volly says. — I've been working on it at the club.

— You're not wearing a bra these days?

— Come on, Mother.

Ted hears and ignores, and moves to greet Sam who is rolling in from the sunroom.

— Where's Billy? Virginia says.

— He's in my room watching television, Sam says. — He'll be out as soon as Annie rings the dinner bell.

The other men will be dressed as Ted is, in coats and ties. Sam wears a blue sweat shirt emblazoned with the seal of the University of North Carolina at Chapel Hill. Ted notices and smiles. The choice is a deliberate gibe at Warren and Chip, graduates of rival N.C. State.

— I hear a car, Virginia says. — They couldn't be here this soon.

She crosses the hall, opens the heavy front door and steps outside to meet John Reece who is coming up the steps carrying a large black briefcase. Linking her arm through his, she ushers him toward the living room where Dolly's larger than life-sized portrait hangs over the mantle. Reece pauses in the doorway, looks up.

— A superb likeness, he says. — She was … what? . . . in her early thirties? About the time I first met her. My father used to say a woman is in her prime at thirty. We were all in love with Dolly. Taking Volly's hand, Reece pats it with avuncular affection. — You favor your grandmother more every day.

She looks up at the portrait, smiles.

— Thanks. That's some compliment, she kisses him on the cheek, looks over her shoulder at her mother as if to say, I'm like her. Not like you.

— The others? he says, settling into one of the wing chairs beneath Dolly's portrait.

— Chip called just before they left, Virginia says. — They should be here shortly.

We're going to get a bite of lunch first. Annie's outdone herself.

— Coconut cake? Reece says, looking hopeful.

— And a box for you to take home for supper.

— Good morning, Sam, Reece says. — Ted tells me your boarder's going to stay awhile.

— Always glad to have company, Sam says. — Besides I can use the help. Cleaning the fish tank in the sunroom is a bitch.

Reece hears the sarcasm. In Sam's condition, cleaning the fifty-gallon fish tank is a virtual impossibility.

— Fish tank? Reece says, both skeptical and curious. — Why a fish tank?

— Treat for Billy. He loved the one at the hospital and he's been working hard at therapy. Why not?

— You haven't seen it? Virginia says, obviously less than charmed. — It's in the middle of the sunroom. You can't miss it. Changing the subject, are you still rowing every day? I imagine it's pretty cool on the lake these mornings.

— We never know what to expect, do we? Reece looks pointedly at Ted, who misses the cryptic message.

The five of them engage each other in ritual small talk for the next twenty minutes until the sound of two cars out front interrupts them. Virginia and Ted greet the brothers and their wives formally, as if they had not been together a week before at Dolly's funeral and interment.

As agreed Volly takes charge of her twelve-year-old cousin, Mimi, while Virginia directs Callie and Pat, Warren's new wife, to Dolly's bedroom to freshen up. She thinks Pat's beige pantsuit matches her personality and that Callie's fitted black dress has far too deep a décolletage for the reading of a will. Dolly would not approve.

The group reassembles in the living room and the hall, Warren and Chip with martinis in hand, the women sipping kir royales, passed by Jesse. The hall clock announces the half hour as Annie appears from the kitchen. After removing the foil from the ham biscuits, she rings a small silver bell. Its refined overtones have summoned Wards to the dinner table for fifty years. Down to this last small detail, the function is progressing exactly as Dolly decreed.

Everyone serves themselves and the group disperses as expected. Billy fills a plate and disappears without speaking to anyone. Virginia tries to catch him, to encourage him to interact with the rest of the family, but he is gone before she can get to the end of the table. Sam takes his plate and his beer into the sunroom followed by his older brothers. Within moments they are in a heated discussion over whether or not Duke and Carolina will be making it to the Final Four in the spring. Warren and Chip have left their wives to fend for themselves, not unusual at a family party, but which Ted perceives as awkward under the circumstances.

Ted and Virginia chat with Reece and the women in the living room. Listening to their conversations — gardens, Atlanta boutiques and fashions, trips to Europe and beyond — John Reece marvels at how graciously Dolly's daughter manages this most awkward, stressful responsibility.

Pat looks uncomfortable, but Callie, ever the diva, has taken the wing chair opposite Reece and is telling him about her latest appearance in St. Louis at the summer opera festival in *La Boheme.*

— There was some confusion with the agents, she says, and I ended up doing Musetta instead of Mimi. My Marcello was a total hypochondriac, which was such a surprise because baritones are so much more normal than tenors. Anyway, he ate raw garlic for breakfast and smelled like an Italian restaurant all the time. I'm telling you, the duets were painful. The conductor's boyfriend was coming on to the tenor when nobody was looking. It was a madhouse.

Reece appears dutifully amused. Virginia smiles, passing the tray of brownies.

— Warren, Chip, she calls to her brothers. — Let's get this over with.

They bring a restlessness in with them, charging the room. Reece, who hasn't seen much of the boys since their move to Atlanta, notices their edginess. Warren appears impatient, checking his watch and tugging at his shirt sleeves. Taking a close look at Chip, Reece gets the impression he isn't ageing well. His once blond hair has faded to ashen, receding on either side of an already high forehead. There is a puffy look about both of them, typical of men who drink too much too often. Sad, he thinks, in light of Dolly's expectations for them, especially Chip.

Virginia winces as Sam shifts his position lifting his right leg with both hands and crossing it over the left. She wonders how they will react to the news that Dolly has left Ted a substantial number of shares in Ward Mills, Inc., a fact Ted finally got around to sharing with her last night, after he had talked with Sam.

— Coffee anyone? she asks, but has no takers. — A drink then? Callie accepts a glass of wine and Sam takes another beer.

— We cancelled the hotel reservations, Chip says. — We can get back to Atlanta before seven and Callie hasn't been feeling well.

Although, Ted thinks, she looks perfectly healthy and she's drinking in the middle of the day. As Virginia observed at the reception following Dolly's funeral, if she were married to Chip she'd drink in the middle of the day too.

Volly and Mimi help Annie gather the plates and drift upstairs toward the doll collection. Reece begins the proceedings by clearing his throat to get their attention. He stands, shifting his weight from one foot to the other.

— Dolly requested that I meet with you to explain the details of her will, he says. — I've sent copies to each of you. I hope you've taken time to read it.

Both Chip and Ted nod. With no mention of the stock in the document, Ted assumes Reece has handled the transfer another way or that the process is taking more time than he imagined.

— The first page contains standard provisions. Item I includes the payment of debts, expenses, taxes and names the executor, a responsibility Dolly asked me to assume, which I accepted. Reece clears his throat, waits a moment for a reaction, gets none, and proceeds.

— Item II concerns the disbursement of tangible personal property, most of which Dolly distributed prior to her death. As you know, she set up a trust fund for the church in Dacus and one for Jesse and Annie as well when they retire. The remainder of her jewelry, clothing, and the furnishings in her bedroom are left to her daughter Virginia to be distributed as she sees fit. Reece quotes directly from the document in his hand, reading the next item verbatim.

— Montvue and its contents are left to my youngest son, Samuel Alexander Ward. At his death the house and property shall pass to my granddaughter and namesake, Virginia Dorothea Brunson.

A rustle of shifting postures announces the mix of curiosity and tolerance with which this last item is acknowledged. As everyone in the room knows, certain properties, like the land where Montvue stands, traditionally pass down the female side of the family. Being a Ward and naturally acquisitive, Virginia is puzzled to be skipped. More hurt than angry, she masks her reaction. Reece continues quoting from the will.

— I have not provided for nor made any bequest to my two older children, Benjamin Franklin Ward, Jr., and William Warren Ward, as I feel they have been adequately provided for during my lifetime.

Chip scowls. Warren looks toward Chip, who raises a hand in his direction, silencing him.

— The next items are standard provisions, Reece says. Not tarrying over the obvious, he flips some pages and continues. — There is a codicil.

Ted leans forward, surprised. He has no recollection of a codicil in the original will that he witnessed three years ago, nor is there any hint of an addition in the document he holds in his hand.

— I have not circulated copies until today because there wasn't time, Reece explains. — Give me a minute. He shuffles through the suitcase-sized leather case beside his chair and pulls out a handful of stapled pages, which he passes out, one to each brother, one to Ted, and one to Virginia. They stir and settle once again, restless now as a flock of finches.

Ted sees that the codicil is dated September 14, 1988. With increasing uneasiness, he realizes that Dolly changed her will a month before she died. Reece begins again, reading directly from the document.

— I hereby give and bequeath to Samuel Alexander Ward, John Beauchamp Reece, and the Atlantic Bank and Trust Company all of my stock in Ward Mills, Inc., to be held in trust for the beneficiaries as set out below.

Ted experiences one of those electrifying moments when events move in slow motion and at the speed of light simultaneously. Reece's voice echoes in his head. All of my stock in Ward Mills ... all of my stock ... He holds his breath, hoping for some qualifying phrase. "Except for," that's what he wants to hear, but there is no "except for."

Virginia, sitting beside him, feels his body tense and moves a hand to his knee. Although it is the conciliatory gesture he has hoped for, he misses it. Along with the others, he turns the page of the document he holds. His palms are wet but his hand is steady.

— I think it's best if I explain this simply without the legal jargon, Reece says. — On the tenth anniversary of Dolly's death, the share of the trust will be divided equally among as many of her grandchildren as are living at that time. Any grandchild who has reached the age of twenty-one at that time shall receive his or her shares outright free of trust. As each remaining grandchild attains the age of twenty-one the trustees shall convey their shares to them. When all the shares have been distributed to the grandchildren, the trust shall terminate.

Looking up quickly, Reece speaks parenthetically. — Dolly stipulated that the preservation of principal and the best interests of the beneficiaries shall be weighed in guiding all investment decisions.

Once again there are no questions. Reece resumes reading.

— It is my hope that in structuring the inheritance in this manner, I have secured the future of Ward Mills, Inc., and given my grandchildren the opportunity to work together for the greater benefit of the company.

Reece pauses once more, looks around the room. Nothing.

— There is further information concerning the appointment of successor trustees in the event of the death of one or more of the original trustees as designated by Mrs. Ward, which is of little interest at the moment.

Ted's brain races ahead, ideas and questions bouncing together like balls in a spinning wire bingo cage. Even if he has enough stock without the promised shares from Dolly to accomplish a sale, it is as Reece said this morning, the ownership of the remaining shares will be of concern to any potential buyer. Later, he thinks. Later. But why? Why did Dolly do it this way with no warning or consultation when for the past twenty-five years, they have made all major and most minor decisions concerning Ward Mills, Inc., together?

— Well that's that, says Warren standing up and jingling the keys in his pants pocket. On his third marriage and not likely to have any children at his age, he has had enough.

— Sit down, Chip snaps.

— Any questions? Reece asks.

— The other trustee, Chip says, prompting from across the room. Reece will not be rushed.

— Ah yes, the other trustee. Reece glances at Ted as he replaces extra copies of the codicil in his briefcase.

— As noted, there are the three of us. Someone from the bank — an investment advisor, I presume — is the third party and will be representing the beneficiaries.

— I see, Chip says, clearly irritated. —Who's this banker?

Reece remains unruffled, responds quietly. — That's up to the trust department. When I know, you'll know.

— I see, Chip says again. — And the real estate company? There's nothing in the will about it.

— Dolly turned that over to Ted last year, Reece says.

— What a surprise, Chip says, sullen and sarcastic. — I guess that's it then.

As if on cue, they stand, ill at ease, moving forward to leave, mouthing small proper thank yous. Virginia struggles to behave in an appropriate manner but cannot decide exactly what that might be so she covers by playing the good hostess.

— You must take some of this food with you or Sam will eat all the cake by himself. Here, Pat, let me get Annie to make you a little care package. We really need to eat this chicken salad. Just give us a minute and you can take some home. Sandwiches for supper, everybody! Oh and some brownies for Mimi. Warren, I know how you love Annie's brownies.

She is babbling and she knows it. The group is dispersing too abruptly.

Chip nods to Ted and Reece, makes one last crack to Sam about his shirt, edging Callie none too subtly into the hall where Volly is waiting with Mimi. Callie thanks Virginia over her shoulder as they go out the door. From Warren Virginia gets only a hasty nod as he hustles Pat out and into their car.

— Ginny? Sam touches his sister's arm. — I'm gone. Call you

tomorrow. Sam wheels himself through the sunroom toward the deck and his quarters beyond.

Virginia turns to Ted who is standing in the hall, staring at Dolly's portrait, looking up at it as if willing it to speak. Reece has closed his briefcase, but is evidently waiting to talk with one or both of them privately. The door closes. Reece steps forward into the hall.

— I must caution you not to jump to any conclusions. This situation is more complicated than it appears and it will take us some time to develop a practical strategy, but it has some interesting possibilities. Ted finally speaks.

— What the hell just happened here? Did Chip do this? Did he come up here in September and coerce Dolly into doing this?

— You know I can't answer that question. Ted looks at Reece, clearly disappointed.

— When we talked at lunch on Tuesday and this morning, you knew all along, didn't you?

— On both occasions I spoke as your corporate lawyer and your friend. Until the day she died, I was first and foremost Dolly's personal lawyer. I'm sorry to be the bearer of bad news, but I must counsel you to think this through before you do anything. When you're ready, we'll talk again.

Reece kisses Virginia on the cheek, thanks her, and, as is his habit, pauses for a moment looking up at the portrait of Dolly before he leaves. Ted regains his composure but can't bring himself to be pleasant. He can however be polite.

— Let me take that to the car for you, he says, picking up the small chiller Annie has left by the front door as Virginia promised.

— The file I gave you, Reece says. — You will read it?

— Of course, Ted says. He doesn't say when.

7

Parkersburg S.C.
Friday, September 7, 1957

Ted Brunson stood in the dean's office at John Wesley College looking out the open window. The summer had been miserably hot and humid, but a thunderstorm the night before broke the pattern and the morning dawned dry and clear. The lawn rolled out before Ted glowing with the same emerald intensity as the fairways of the Fort Hill Country Club, within a few blocks of the house where he had grown up. It was thanks to those fairways that he was admiring the turf before him today. "The Club," as its members called it, had been built on the east side of town in the twenties by an over-eager developer. The depression put an end to his dream. Except for a narrow section of spacious houses directly fronting the golf course and a few blocks adjacent, the enclave he had envisioned never became a reality. For no apparent reason, business executives gravitated toward the south side of town. The rest of the community went to smaller post-war ranch houses. Anchored by several churches, one Baptist and one Methodist, the neighborhood was stable, the population consistent. A two-block stretch of small businesses grew up along the divided avenue known as The Plaza. Brunson Hardware was one of them.

Ted's parents, owners and operators, had never inquired about joining The Club. They were not society people, unlike Ted's uncle and namesake. Uncle Ted and his associates loved the Donald Ross course and the columned Southern-style architecture of the new postwar clubhouse, so elegantly suited for their wedding receptions and debutante balls. Above all they loved the exclusivity.

A successful real estate broker and the father of one child, a daughter, Uncle Ted enjoyed the time spent with his nephew, encouraging him, agreeing with his sister that her son "had potential" as he liked to say. He argued that his teenage nephew give up baseball. He should master a gentleman's sport like golf or tennis where he would meet "the right people," and so on occasion he took Ted along when he went out to The Club for an afternoon round of golf. Ted and his uncle so obviously shared physical characteristics that they were frequently mistaken for father and son. Both over six feet tall with thick dark hair, they had the same intense brown eyes and olive complexion that, according to Ted's mother, appeared every generation or so in some Brunson male because an American Indian had once long ago scaled the family tree.

Ted enjoyed taking a few drives or putts when the course wasn't crowded and his uncle noticed he showed a natural aptitude for the sport. Once Uncle Ted stood him for a couple of lessons with the pro, he was quick to learn the layout of the course. So quick that Uncle Ted gave his nephew his old clubs when he bought himself new ones.

Ted saw golf as a head game. He loved it for its combination of athletic skill and mental challenge. Although baseball remained his first love, he made the Plaza Midway High School golf team as a junior, the year his father died, killed by a drunk driver in an automobile accident. Uncle Ted did his best to compensate, increasing the number of times he included Ted in golf outings at The Club.

"Some of the men you're meeting, they're fellow alumni of mine." Uncle Ted said. "These men are the lawyers and bankers who run things in Fort Hill. If you're ambitious and if you work hard, you could be one of them. You should consider John Wesley College when you are looking at higher education. You will go to college, right? No more of this nonsense about trying out for a minor league baseball team."

Ted disliked his uncle's attitude, but his devotion to his mother quelled any complaint. He would go to college. He would get a good job and take care of her.

Ted hoped for one of the two highly coveted appointments to West Point or Annapolis, but John Wesley was only a few hours away, and with his mother alone in Fort Hill, it became a reasonable alternative, provided he got financial aid. Once Uncle Ted suggested the possibility of a scholarship, young Ted became attentive to any mention of John Wesley in the newspaper or when they were on the course. What he learned was not particularly useful — the men talked mostly about football — but he heard nothing to discourage his interest, and he grasped the significance of being recommended by an alumnus who was a successful businessman. Uncle Ted had stressed his point: who you know is as important as what you know. The idea was beginning to sink in.

Ted kept his grades up with little effort, never quite at the top of his class but always in the upper third. Through his involvement in a church project building a playground at a day care center, he became an Eagle Scout. He made time to write editorials for the high school paper and dabbled in student government, running for class president and winning two years in a row. Between playing baseball, helping at the store, and maintaining extracurricular activities, he didn't get much sleep, but he was vindicated when the promised assistance came through as expected. He would have preferred a baseball scholarship, but those were many and small. The golf scholarship was one of only two and it was inclusive.

He took a day off and drove to Parkersburg in advance of freshman orientation to look the school over. At his uncle's suggestion, he stopped by the dean's office to make a courtesy call. He had just turned eighteen, but he was perceptive enough to realize that knowing the dean personally might come in handy at some point in his college career. His uncle's alumnus status, augmented by a generous donation to the dean's pet project, a new dorm for upper classmen, had been well received and reciprocated. The bounty was delivered by the dean's secretary.

"Ah Mr. Brunson," she said. "I'm afraid Dean Whitman is tied up this afternoon but he arranged for your big brother to show you around. Freshmen are assigned big brothers as you probably know to help with any little problems that might arise, like homesickness or getting around town." She offered him her most patronizing smile, opened the file folder she was holding, raised her eyebrows, and lowered her voice as if she were conveying a wonderful surprise.

"Well aren't you the lucky one," she said. "Sam Ward is your big brother. You know the Wards, the textile family? Well Sam is over at the KA house right now. He came by to pick up some registration forms and told me he was going to check in at the house and see if anybody had come in early. I'm sure he'll be back eventually or you could go over to the house and introduce yourself. You'll like Sam. Everybody does." She pointed toward the window as if the decision was settled. "Fraternity Court is at the end of the quad down that little lane to the left."

Ted was not familiar with either the Wards or with the KAs, but the secretary's remark conveyed an air of privilege. Besides, he had taken time off from the store to get this preview. He figured he had nothing to lose.

The seven houses edged a shady semi-circular drive where only one car, a new white Thunderbird convertible, was parked in front of the KA house. The front door stood open. Ted walked into an empty room, full of hot, heavy air. It smelled of cigarettes and stale beer. Large ordinary furniture crowded the room. Of the three leather sofas, one sagged in the middle. On another, Ted noticed a wad of dirty gray stuffing seeping out of a split in one cushion. His mother, a meticulous housekeeper, would not have tolerated the tables, marred by scratches, cigarette burns, and interlocking bleached circles, the telltale prints of damp beer cans. The rug was disgusting, marked by a variety of unidentifiable stains. Multiple ashtrays, all full and overflowing, offended Ted's sense of order and his nose, exploding his fantasies about the glamour of fraternity life. The house was quiet except for the gravelly voice of Fats Domino drifting in from outside.

As I was walkin'
One early mornin'
I met a woman.
We started talkin'.

Through the open patio doors Ted saw a boy and girl dancing. Continuous, graceful, and sexy, the shag was as hot as the sand at noon and cool as the night breeze off the Atlantic. The pavilion at Ocean Drive where it had begun was the acknowledged summer hangout of boys and girls from the Piedmont who had created a mating ritual of their own from the languid beat of rhythm and blues. Watching them made Ted feel big and awkward and envious, the way he felt when he had tried to shag at high school dances. The shag required a looseness his body didn't have. His self-consciousness kept him from relaxing into the beat. He couldn't get it right — the pure Southern, slightly suggestive, flirtatious kind of male-female interaction the style required.

They were so smooth, these two, and graceful. The girl, she was beautiful. Sunlight glinted off of her ID bracelet. She wore the golden tone of a girl who spent the whole summer in the sun. Most of Ted's friends were lucky to join a one-week family beach vacation. This girl looked like she lived at Myrtle Beach or Pawleys Island. Her white shorts were neatly cuffed and hugged her bottom without a wrinkle. She wore a close-fitting white tee shirt with the sleeves rolled up, cutting across the fullest point of well-defined biceps and breasts. A white grosgrain ribbon circled her blonde ponytail. She made him feel like he did when he saw Grace Kelly in *Rear Window* or *To Catch a Thief*. She was classy.

The boy, just as tan and blond as the girl, wore a white Oxford cloth shirt with Madras shorts and penny loafers. No socks. Ted felt self-consciously over-dressed in his khakis and his dress shirt and his graduation necktie.

Watching, reluctant to interrupt, Ted sensed a connection between the girl and her partner. They moved as if they had grown up dancing together. He was mesmerized by the way their feet moved over the flagstone pavers, shuffle step, shuffle step …

Ted had heard it was all in the hands. The boy held the girl's right hand in his left, fingers loosely laced, only tightening his grip when they balanced against one another, bodies apart, arms fully extended. The motion flowed continuously without any visible directives, the signals working as precisely as traffic lights. Ted could see the dance existed on a horizontal plain with the couple balancing backward on their heels at the farthest extension of the step, coming toward each other, then past, heads turned aside, brushing shoulders, or skimming hip against hip only to spin out again. He had never seen it done better.

Without realizing it, he had inched forward into the doorway. The boy noticed, pulled the girl into his left side and caught her, holding her around the waist.

"Hey," he said. "You must be Ted Brunson. I thought you might show up early." He nudged the girl gently. "Say hello, Ginny."

The girl smiled and Sam Ward grinned, a smile as wide as a slice of watermelon. He reached forward to shake Ted's hand, keeping one arm around the girl as she pulled the ribbon off her hair. It fell to her shoulders in a perfect shining golden cascade unlike anything Ted had seen before, even in the movies.

She was a princess, one of the girls who had looked right through him in high school, but with one big difference. This blonde was looking straight at him, appraising him openly. He felt a blush rise to his cheeks.

"Right, hi. Nice to meet you. You're my, uh, big brother, right?" They were still shaking hands. Ted tried to focus on Sam but his eyes kept cutting away collecting details, the deep vee of her tee shirt, the diamond dinner ring on her right hand.

"Yeah," Sam said, breaking the handshake and grinning again at Ted's obvious awkwardness. "That's me. Wanna see where you're gonna live this year?" His voice was smooth and easy, like his dancing. When he turned the girl loose, Ted saw a pack of Camels stuck in the fold of his sleeve. Where Ted came from nice boys carried their cigarettes in their pockets. If they smoked at all.

Sam looked fondly at his partner.

"Scat," he said, giving her a generous pat on the rear. He slicked his hands back through his hair cut in a stylish duck tail. Ted got a last look at the legs as she walked toward a low brick wall where they had set up the 45 record player. She leaned over, reached down, and turned it off without bending her knees. Ted caught his breath. Sam noticed.

"She rides horses," he said. "All the time. Great, uh, legs, huh?"

Sam led the way through a hedge and down a well-worn dirt path to the quad.

"The freshman dorm is old but handy," he said. "You can sleep late and still make an eight-thirty class at Old Main."

Ted didn't care about any of it. He wanted to know more about Ginny, but didn't ask, thinking she was Sam's girl. Trying to impress Sam, he tried to sound more sophisticated than he was.

"So what are the drinking rules around here?" he asked.

"Surely you know the Methodists are teetotalers. Now, I myself am a Whiskey-palian. No rules to speak of. All you have to do is show up twice a year, once at Christmas and again at Easter, and they guarantee your salvation with no questions asked. Do you go to church? This place is famous for turning out preachers and college professors."

"Not so much," Ted said. "My parents worked six days a week and they usually didn't make it out on Sunday mornings, but my Mom's made up for it since my father died."

"What did your old man do?" Sam asked.

"They owned a hardware store. My mom runs it now. We carry everything from Allen wrenches to riding lawn mowers. I worked there on and off since I was in fourth grade. I went in after school every week day 'til I was big enough to get a paying job as a soda jerk."

"You're here to play golf, right?"

"Rather play baseball but it doesn't pay as well."

Sam backed off and looked Ted up and down.

"You are sure one big son of a bitch not to play basketball," he said.

"I played a little in high school, but I wasn't very good at it. Not very good with girls either." He was thinking about the one he just met, embarrassed about his awkward introduction.

Sam chuckled. "Not to worry," he said. "You'll do fine."

"For what?" Ted asked. "Intramurals?" He hoped Sam wouldn't make basketball a condition of their friendship.

"For my baby sister," Sam said. "She's coming down from St. Mary's for homecoming the first of October with my car, which she is driving very carefully until then. Hers is still in the shop. Nearly totaled it this summer. Some drunk rear-ended her. Ruined her tan. She had to wear one of those padded neck braces for a month."

Ted winced at the mention of a drunk driver, thinking of his father.

"Well this is it," Sam said, gesturing toward the three-story red brick story building in front of them. He dropped down to sprawl on the front steps, pulled the pack of cigarettes out of his rolled shirtsleeve, and offered one to Ted.

"Thanks, but I don't smoke," Ted said.

"Boy Scout?"

Ted looked down and laughed. "Is that bad?"

"Not at all. You might even be a good influence. See, I got in a little trouble last semester and I can't keep my car on campus 'til mid-semester break, which happens to be homecoming weekend. Things work out, right? I've got the tickets for the game and the dance already. You got a tux, kid?"

"No." Ted looked away, embarrassed at the apparent inadequacy.

"No big deal. We can rent you one." Sam looked across the green expanse of the quad. "It's not so bad here. Think you'll like it?"

Ted shrugged. "I wanted to go to West Point," he said, surprising himself at sharing a confidence with someone he had only just met.

"West Point," Sam said, investing the name with a touch of wonder. "My choice was the Air Force Academy. I could see myself in that uniform. Really gets the girls."

"What happened?"

"Astigmatism," Sam said, "and they don't offer management or marketing courses. I've sort of got this job lined up when I get out of here. Look, I've got to get back."

Ted lumbered to his feet, realizing the interview was over. "About homecoming. I'm on a full scholarship and I can't afford —"

"Forget it," Sam said. "Everything's covered. My mother will be so glad I've got a keeper for the weekend she'll probably pay for the whole thing herself."

"But the date with your sister?"

Sam interrupted again. "The girl at the house," he said. "What did you think of her?"

"She's a knockout," Ted said. "You're a lucky man."

Sam's face split open into his widest grin. "You kinda got things wrong there fella, but I'll tell her you said she was hot stuff. Ginny's my twin, born fourteen minutes after I was. Big brother, baby sister, get it? Like I said. Things work out."

The next week when Ted arrived to begin his freshman year at John Wesley College, he found a note stuck on the door of his dorm room.

Little Brother, You got the A-OK from the princess. Time to meet the queen. Sunday lunch. 12:30. Pick you up in front of Main.

"Ginny?" Sam said, answering Ted's question before he asked "Sorry. She's already left. But she'll be back as often as she can get away. She really hates St. Mary's. She wanted to go to Virginia Intermont and take her horse, but Dolly wouldn't hear of it. Said she wouldn't study at all. They won't let her keep her horse in Raleigh."

The car was a red Austin Healy. "A loaner from my brother Chip," Sam said. Ted was impressed with the car until they arrived at Montvue. Then he was overwhelmed. By the long drive, the landscaping, the gardens, the house, everything including his hostess.

Sam's mother came out to meet them. "Did you ever see such a beautiful day?" she said. "Ted! How nice to meet you. Sam has told us all about you. Come in. Come in. Annie's got dinner on the table."

She was small like Virginia. Ted thought she looked fragile, understood why she was called Dolly. Her skin was as pale as Ginny's was tan but he could see the resemblance. She was gracious and attentive. Elegant, Ted thought, in her tailored suit the same china blue as her eyes. And like her daughter, a little flirtatious. She took his arm and led him in through the front door.

"I'm sorry Chip and Warren aren't home this weekend," she said. "They've gone to Fort Hill to meet some school friends and see a movie. Something French with this new girl, Brigitte Bardot?"

"*And God Created Woman*," Sam said, snickering. "Not your kind of movie, Dolly."

"That reminds me," she said, "next time you'll have to come early and go to church with us." Ted caught the meaningful look directed at Sam.

"Yes, ma'am," he said.

The first of October brought a perfect weekend for football, crisp cool weather, tangy air redolent of damp leaf piles and wood smoke from the first fires of the season. Virginia arrived in town for the homecoming festivities late on Friday, in time for a quick meeting over hamburgers and beer at the KA house, where Sam made a futile attempt to monopolize his date, a May Court beauty Virginia had brought home with her from St. Mary's.

"Man those guys need to get their own women," Sam complained to Ted. "I am sick of this bird-doggin'. Keep Ginny on a short leash."

As if there was any danger of Ted letting her out of his sight, even though he soon realized that Ginny would take care of herself. She knew all the brothers, introduced him around. He expected her to flirt but was delighted that she didn't. Among Sam's friends she was comfortable being herself, a little distant, but one of the guys.

Slow-dancing on the patio he savored the touch of her from the soft fragrance of her hair down the length of her body. She was light in his arms, nestled against him, her head on his shoulder. When the music resumed at a faster pace, she pulled away.

"These parties are all alike," she said. "It's getting too loud. Let's cut out." Ted was glad to oblige. He wanted more time with her, wanted her to himself, and he had the clear impression that she felt the same way.

On the way to Montvue, he tried to find some soft music on the car radio.

"I like the Four Freshmen," she said. Ted had never heard of them.

"The drive from Raleigh wore me out," she said." I'll be more fun after I get some sleep."

"I'm looking forward to the dance tomorrow night," he said.

"More than the game?"

"More than the game."

"Me too," she said. Leaning across the space between them, she kissed him on the cheek. "Hmm," she said. "Old Spice. My favorite."

"Too much?"

"Just enough."

Back at the dorm he checked Sam's room and was surprised to find him.

"I got a wrist corsage," he told Sam. "Will that be okay?"

"No place to pin anything," Sam said. "She's gonna wear one of those strapless things with the big skirts. You can't get close enough to hang the corsage on her even if there was someplace to put it. Hoop skirts, chastity belts. One and the same."

Ted struggled into the rented tux, arrived at Montvue early in time for Sam to manage the bow tie. Sam was working on it when Virginia floated down the stairs in a wasp-waisted pale blue tulle gown, the skirt a mass of ruffles. She had wrapped her hair into a French twist with one soft wave on the side. He realized the corsage shouted high school, presented it sheepishly. She took the box, dismantled the corsage, and pinned the gardenia in her hair.

"It's just right for this dress," she said, looking in the hall mirror. "It's different. I like it."

Dancing with her enchanted him. He held her at a distance at first, but she moved closer.

"Sam teach you to dance?" he said. "You're so much better than I am."

"You're doing fine. People are watching," she said. "We look good together."

"Simple jealousy," he said. "They're looking at the most beautiful girl on the floor."

Sam got a call from Virginia the next day.

"Who is this Ted person?" she said.

"You like him?"

"Don't know yet. He's shy, isn't he?"

"Just not as pushy as the crowd you're used to."

"Tell me more," she said.

"He's not rich if that's what you want to know. He's got one of the two golf scholarships John Wesley offers. His father's dead. Mother runs the family business in Fort Hill, a hardware store. Solid people. Uncle's in real estate. Very successful. Ted's mentioned joining him someday."

"Not a lot of family, I hope."

"Wanna know what I think?" Sam said.

"Do I have a choice?"

"You've hung around with this crowd — the boys' friends and mine — too long. They'll never take you seriously as a person. They think of you as the little pest that followed us around all the time."

"And beat you at your own games," she said.

"Yes, that too. One of them — I'm not saying who — asked about you last week. Wanted to know how you were. He said you sure were lots of fun and he wondered if anybody would ever tame you."

"I know who it was," she said. "We got very drunk together the night he got kicked out of the university."

"I know. And so does everybody else in town.

"Bunch of loud-mouthed sissies."

"Okay. He's around and he's interested. You graduate next year. Is that what you want?"

"Your friend Ted. He's sweet and sort of innocent?"

"He's stronger than you think. And Dolly likes him."

"That's not a plus."

Sam could hear her drumming her nails on the phone box.

"What does he want?" she said. "An in with the Parkersburg crowd? A job?"

"A chance," Sam said. "All he wants is a chance."

For two people with so little in common, they talked a lot.

"When I'm on my horse, I get this feeling of independence and freedom. It's like flying or dancing, only better because you're in it with the horse and you have to know each other. There's nobody else, just you and this beautiful, powerful animal who wants to please you," she said. "It takes all your concentration and every muscle in your body."

"But it's dangerous," he said. "Don't you ever get thrown off?"

"Not often and not far," she said. "The jumps are only about three feet or so. It's more about pacing and timing. You'll have to come and watch me."

"Baseball's the same kind of feeling. It requires that same concentration. I like being a part of something, of coordinating and anticipating, of learning your teammates, what they can do or can't do. Taking up the slack. Golf's so individual. It's okay. I mean, I get my tuition paid, but I miss the fellows I used to hang out with."

Ted thought Virginia could replace any sports excitement he had ever known. Virginia thought she wanted to go to bed with Ted. They saw each other as often as possible during the school year. He followed her to several horse shows that spring.

Over spring break they went to the lake house, properly chaperoned by Sam and a date and by Annie who also did the cooking. Being together so constantly increased the intensity of their relationship, the physical side pushing them into frustration.

"You know you're making me crazy," he said.

The dorms at John Wesley didn't reopen until the following day so Ted was staying at Montvue. They ate dinner with Dolly and Sam, went downtown to see *Bridge on the River Kwai*. They return to Montvue, find it awash in floodlights.

"Let's stay out here where it's private," Virginia said.

"No way," Ted said. "I saw the gun rack in the back hall." Inside, the house is silent except for the ticking of the hall clock. They could see Dolly's bedroom light on, the door ajar.

"Goodnight, children," she called out to them as they passed. Virginia giggled.

"She's checking up on us," she whispered.

He kissed her lightly at her bedroom door.

"See you in the morning," he said and went down the hall, forcing himself not to look back, making more noise than was necessary closing the door to the guest room.

Ted rested uneasily, finally got to sleep, awakened in the middle of the night. He must have been dreaming of her, didn't want to open his eyes, the vision so intense it pulled him into consciousness. Virginia stood beside the bed, wearing a white silk nightgown. Suddenly fully awake, he pulled himself up on one elbow, realized he was shirtless, clutched the covers, embarrassed at the situation as much as the condition he found himself in. When she knew she had his attention, she slid the spaghetti straps down off her shoulders, first one side, then the other. She dropped the gown, pausing a moment, brazenly showing him her naked body, and slipped in beside him. He tried to call her name but the touch of her drove every other thought from his head and a low animal groan was all he could manage.

He had never been in bed with a woman before. He was disarmed by her eagerness, the smoothness of her skin, the curves of her as he ran his hands up and down her body, trying to contain himself, to be gentle. All he could think of was a way to fit the two of them together, to surround her and mark every inch of her as his. Inexperienced as he was, he spilled himself on her thighs, gasping and apologizing. She took his hand in hers and kissed his fingertips.

"No harm done," she said. Rising from the bed, she walked into the bathroom.

"We'll try again later."

It was the best night of his life.

8

Friday, April 18, 1958

"Can you write?" Sam said.

"What do you mean? Of course I can write," Ted said.

"No, I mean, can you write sports?"

"I guess so. Why."

"Got you a summer job, big fella. You'll play ball for the mill team and write the games up for the in-house paper. Won't pay much but you can still go to summer school. How's that for a deal?"

"I don't know what to say. I … thanks."

"Ginny will be in and out of town following the show circuit. Probably more in than out with you hangin' around. Dolly's taking Annie with her up to the lake. My brothers will be home, working at one of the mills. Montvue's gonna be like a big frat house."

Ted had pledged KA that spring, because he couldn't afford it any earlier. Sam was his sponsor, indoctrinating him into fraternity rituals and Ward rituals as well. Over PBRs on the KA patio, Sam briefed him on a choice piece of Ward family history.

"You know they were cousins, Dolly and Ben," he said. "Second or third. At least not first. It's a wonder we all aren't simple-minded."

Ted didn't know whether to laugh or not, so he helped himself from the bag of chips Sam offered.

"Why do you and Virginia call your mother Dolly?"

"She told us to. Ginny said she wants us to feel like her pals instead of her kids. We'll grow up faster. One of those crackpot parenting ideas she read about in *The Ladies Home Journal.* I understand why she didn't enjoy us as children. We were a pretty scrappy bunch."

"From what I've seen you still are."

"Stop interrupting," Sam said. "Like I was saying, Ben's timing was perfect for Dolly. He showed up at the exact right moment. He was one of the Georgia Wards, graduated from Tech but didn't fancy going into banking, which was the family industry in Columbus. Give him credit, he tried it for five years and finally begged off. His daddy called our grandfather and asked if he might find a place for a bright personable young man with some good financial experience.

"According to Aunt Sissie, Ben Ward succeeded with Dolly where others had failed by ignoring her. He was eleven years older than she was, already running the purchasing department after six months on the job. And he was family. Nothing was more important to Dolly, so she decided she'd have him. I've often thought Granddaddy set the whole thing up, but who knows? Big Ben's family summered at the lake in Dacus like the rest of us and Virginia thinks Dolly had her eye on him from the time she was twelve or thirteen. Anyway, you'd think Dolly would have had enough to do what with all of us being born so close together, but no, she kept her hand in things on West Avenue too."

Sam paused long enough to take a good long swig of beer. "Help yourself to the chips and sit back and listen. It's time you learned some of the more sordid facts about the Wards.

"The story began when Gramma Ward died in '46. Dolly got her nose out of joint when Old Man Ward moved the housekeeper, Miss Ida Stout, into the downstairs guest room. More convenient, he said. He liked his breakfast early. Well, Dolly didn't think that looked right, the two of them living under the same roof. It was not a good situation, she said, so she decided to move herself and Ben and all four of us into the big house."

"From what she's said later, Big Ben thought it was a bad idea, but he had his hands full with the mills. He was more or less in charge by then, but Uncle Warren — Young Ward, they called him — Dolly's brother, was pressing Granddaddy to expand and Ben thought the old man was getting a little dotty, so he conceded to keep the peace."

Sam stopped long enough to fish two more beers out of the chiller, cracked them, and passed one to Ted.

"Granddaddy Ward didn't argue because he knew there wasn't any use. I figure he'd decided to let the situation play itself out. Which it did about a year and a half later and Jesse saw the whole thing. He was in the vestibule locking up for the night when Dolly came in from a meeting. She was vice president of the Junior League that year and president designate. I remember because she made such a big deal out of it afterwards. He said she must have tiptoed in through the kitchen and had started up the stairs before he noticed her. He was about to speak to her when she stopped suddenly and looked to her left, toward Miss Ida's room.

"Jesse said he froze. He knew what was coming. He heard the sound of a doorknob turning and here comes Granddaddy cool as you please, amblin' out of Miss Ida's room in his underwear. Of course Dolly saw him too. Jesse said she gasped like she'd been hit in the stomach. Granddaddy just kept on going, passing her on the steps.

"'Playing a little gin rummy,' he said. Lordy, but that man had a fine gift for understatement.

"'Looks more like strip poker to me,' Dolly said not moving an inch. 'This is not good for the children.'

"'Aren't they all in bed? Isn't that where you ought to be too, missy?'

"Jesse said he liked to fainted out there in the vestibule for fear one or both of them would see him. Well, Granddaddy went on up to his room like he always did after his gin rummy games with Miss Ida and Dolly went to bed I guess, but not before giving Big Ben an earful.

"Nobody mentioned the situation and we wouldn't have known what they were talking about anyway. We were way too young to pick up on subtleties, but I figure the atmosphere got a little frosty. Jesse said the dinner table was mighty quiet there for a couple of weeks."

Sam paused. "Gotta wet my whistle," he said taking another swig of beer.

"Anyway, a month later, Dolly showed up with the plans for Montvue. Her momma had left her this five-acre piece of land over in College Heights. Dolly described it as an act of divine intervention. Just perfect, she said. We could walk to the country club and there was plenty of room for all of us to build our own homes there when we grew up and went to work for Ward Mills, Inc. 'And such a fine view of the mountains,' she said. 'We'll call it Montvue.'

"When we moved, that's when Chip and Warren took up tennis and Virginia got her first pony. Named it Snowball. Snowball from Hell if you asked me. Meanest damn horse I ever saw. Bite you quick as she'd look at you. But Ginny adored her. Riding that horse got her outdoors and gave her a way to shine on her own."

At the time, Ted made little of the family story, accepting it as another example of how the Wards always managed to get what they wanted. But in retrospect, he came to read Sam's story as it was intended. Sam was describing for him the way things worked in the Wards' world, what behaviors he might expect if he married Virginia. Sam might have been more direct, but Ted would have missed even the most specific warning. He was nineteen, in love for the first time. So enthralled by Virginia and all she represented and by the level of Southern society in which the Wards operated, that he was oblivious to any consequences. Too smitten to even consider the implications, he was made brave and strong and fearless by her attention. Ted would have walked through fire to have her.

Parkersburg Daily News
June 21, 1959

Virginia Dorothea Ward and Graham Theodore Brunson, Jr. were married in an afternoon ceremony at St. Luke's Episcopal Church on Saturday. Mrs. Brunson is the daughter of Mrs. Dorothea Lee Ward, president of Ward Mills, Inc., and the late Benjamin Franklin Ward. Mr. Brunson, of Fort Hill, North Carolina, is the son of Mrs. G. T. Brunson and the late Mr. Brunson. Vows were exchanged before the Right Reverend C. Martin Richards, bishop of the Upper Diocese of South Carolina and the Rev. Robert Louis, Minister of St. Luke's. Mrs. Brunson is a recent graduate of St. Mary's School in Raleigh, North Carolina. Mr. Brunson is a rising senior at John Wesley College.

Given in marriage by her uncle, William Warren Ward, Jr., the bride wore a full-length candlelight *peau de soir* and *alençon* gown with a semi-belled skirt and three-quarter length sleeves. Her short lace veil was a family heirloom, first worn by her grandmother, Virginia Lee Ward, nee Coles, at her 1912 marriage to William Warren Ward. She carried an arm bouquet of calla lilies, a tradition in Ward family weddings. Matron of Honor was the bride's first cousin, Mrs. John Hunter of Columbus, Georgia. The bride's brothers, Benjamin Franklin Ward, Jr., William Warren Ward, and Samuel Alexander Ward served as ushers. Following the ceremony, guests enjoyed a garden reception at Montvue, home of the bride's family. After a honeymoon in St. Thomas, Virgin Islands, the couple will reside in Parkersburg. They will be at home in College View Apartments after the first of July.

"Hey, lover." Virginia met Ted at the door of their apartment, throwing her arms around his neck and kissing all over his face.

"Hold on a sec," he said. "Let me get my jacket off."

"Might as well take everything else off too," she said, unbuttoning his shirt.

The next afternoon, Dolly called him to Montvue for what she referred to as a little tête-à-tête.

"My brother and I agree that it is best if you come to work here after you graduate. You will need to adjust to the typical demands of a family business," she said. "Being married to a Ward, you will be welcomed in our community. We have arranged full memberships for you at the city club and the country club. Consider that a wedding gift. I understand you have some local friends from the golf team at John Wesley. My boys play tennis if that is of any interest.

"As to your future, never forget this is a competitive business. Don't get drunk at the club some Saturday night and start talking about our operations." She paused and smiled. "And don't look so worried. I want you to know the worst from the beginning."

"Are you offering me a job?" he asked.

"Well of course," she said. "We can't have you working for the competition. We will start you out slowly. Give you a chance to survey the operation by working in all the various departments. I understand you have some experience in one of our spinning rooms? Yes, well. We won't have to go that far down the line."

She smiled again and offered her hand. "Do we have a deal, then? As soon as you graduate, you come to work for Ward Mills, Inc. I expect you will find your career path accelerated but difficult, that is, if you can handle the responsibility."

Dolly stood, indicating the end of the interview.

"One last item," Dolly said. "Don't rub yourself raw against Virginia. She drinks like her father Ben who had a hollow leg. Don't try to keep up with her or it will kill you. "And my boys," she continued, "they are the holders of a demanding heritage. The future of Ward Mills, Inc., rests on their shoulders. You will need to find a way to get along with them if you are to succeed here."

Ted had a problem with the boys. It was evident that neither Sam nor Virginia liked their older siblings. An only child, Ted assumed the animosity was a hangover from childhood rivalries and didn't pursue the reason, but he didn't like either one of them either, especially Chip, who was haughty and arrogant.

Ted was surprised one afternoon, when Chip invited him to the country club for a round of golf, even more surprised when Chip's first drive soared in a perfect arch and landed two hundred yards in the middle of the fairway.

"I thought tennis was your game," Ted said.

"I play tennis to win," he said. "Golf is more of a social game."

There was something phony about the remark. Ted's competitiveness kicked in. He played to win. When they made the turn after the ninth hole, he was ahead by three strokes. They were waiting for a foursome in front of them when Chip surprised Ted once again.

"Boy, you have fallen into a pot of jam," he said. "But why do you want to work here? Textile manufacturing is the most boring job in the world. Mother thinks we should love the business just because our name is on the company stationary, but Warren doesn't like it any more than I do. If you asked me, the business would be better off with professional management from outside the family. But don't tell my mother I said that."

It appeared to Ted that Benjamin Franklin Ward, Jr., was not the chip off the old block his nickname implied. He tried to understand Chip's point but felt exactly opposite. The first few months of his training were exhilarating, as he explained to his bride.

"Ginny, I love this!" he said. "Transferring from mill to mill, meeting the people, trying to digest the interrelated nature of the operation. It's hard but it's fascinating! I hope I'm doing okay."

Virginia rolled over from her side of the bed into his arms.

"Believe me, Uncle Young and Dolly would let you know if you weren't. Hush and kiss me."

As if to assuage his concern, Young Ward put him in charge of a recent acquisition, a small plant in Union, South Carolina. In one year he streamlined the operation and raised production levels by fifteen percent.

At the same time, Dolly was becoming involved with day to day operations. She told Ted something about her history the day after she claimed a permanent office next to her brother.

"When Ben came along, I knew I had found a partner who respected my interest. He discussed every aspect of the operation with me, taking me along to international trade shows, even teaching me a short course in accounting. More importantly he demanded respect from the Big Five." Dolly's voice softened, tender with memory. "He was a wonderful man. I wish you could have known him.

"Young has suggested partnering the management chores with me. We'll keep that part of our agreement quiet so that no one feels threatened. I don't know how much Virginia has told you, if anything, but the company is privately owned. Young and I each inherited fifty percent of the stock, except for some shares my father retained during his lifetime. He gave one hundred shares to my husband, which I inherited. If this works out for us, both of us, I will give those shares to you."

Dolly told Ted she never forgot what she had learned from Ben Ward. Rule number one: You will catch more flies with honey than with vinegar. And rule number two: Surround yourself with the smartest, most honest, dedicated people you can find.

Close to the end of his third year with the company, Sam called him in Union.

"You need to get over here pronto," he said. "Dolly wants to see us and she sounds serious as a heartbeat." The drive took half an hour. Dolly's office door was open. She was studying a single sheet of paper on her desk. Sam stood behind her looking out the window.

"Morning," Ted said. She looked up, unsmiling.

"I'm just reading Sam's latest press release," she said. Reading upside down, Ted caught the headline: "Ward Heir Leaving Family Company."

"Chip has decided on a career change," Dolly said, handing him a copy of the press release. "He has been persuaded that he will have more time for hunting and fishing if he takes up a less demanding profession like selling stock." Dolly did not say who persuaded him.

"Young will be turning to you two, I suspect, offering you more challenges and increased responsibilities."

The on-site office was Dolly's first indication that she would be more active in the management of the company. At her suggestion they shipped Warren off to New York to the sales people, but the city was too much for him. After a year he came home. His first wife, Peggy, a local girl from a second-tier family, had a first-tier brain. She preferred New York and told Warren she'd find a job and stay in the city. Sam suggested offering her a spot on the sales staff long before the divorce was final, figuring the gesture would hold Warren's alimony to a minimum. When the Parkersburg pond proved insufficiently large for Chip, he moved his office to Atlanta, taking Warren with him. As expected Ward cousins provided proper social entrees that Chip turned into successful business connections.

Ted never discussed the boys with Sam. If he brought the subject up with Virginia, she was dismissive.

"Chip isn't stupid," she said, "just devious."

During the early years of his marriage, Ted came to realize that Chip protected Warren, but he also used him. He could not see the boys' departure as a great loss for the company, although he felt Dolly's disappointment in the way things had turned out. Virginia told him she was glad they were gone.

Sam was the first to see what was happening in the organization.

"Dolly's movin' in," he said. "Hang on to your shorts."

9

Wednesday, April 14, 1965

"I've been summoned," Virginia said. "Dolly's taking me to lunch tomorrow to plan my birthday party. I don't guess you could talk her out of it?"

Ted and Virginia were having their ritual evening drink, sitting side by side on a rattan sofa, part of the new furnishings on the screened porch of their house. The porch was attached to a roomy colonial with three bedrooms. It overlooked the ninth fairway at the country club. Dolly gave them the down payment on the occasion of their fifth wedding anniversary.

"I'll try if you want me to, but it's a little late to cancel this year. How 'bout if you suffer through this one and maybe next year we'll just arrange to be out of town?"

"You're laughing at me, aren't you?" She poked him in the ribs. He groaned dramatically. "Stop it," she said. "It's not so much the idea of the birthday I hate, it's the conversation. There's been too much talk already. I don't want to hear another word about why I'm not pregnant or when we're planning to have children."

"Look," he said, "we've only been married five years. We're happy, aren't we?" He took her hand and kissed the palm. "You know what the doctor said. It's only a matter of time. It'll happen when it happens."

"Easy for him to say but I'm so frustrated! The routine … it's like putting a puzzle together blindfolded."

"That bad?"

"Yes," she said. "That bad. Taking my temperature to see if I'm ovulating, inviting you home early if I am … We're losing all spontaneity, turning our sex life into a chore. Sex on demand is worse than no sex at all."

"I don't know about that," he said.

"Don't joke. I'm serious."

"Sorry," he said. "I've only been going along because I thought it was what you wanted."

"I do want to have children, your children, but I can't keep doing this stuff. I'm not trying any more of their tricks," she said. "No more fertility tests and absolutely no artificial insemination."

"Fine by me," he said. "We'll wait and enjoy." He put his glass down and stood up. Taking her hand, he pulled her to her feet and into his arms. He nuzzled her ear, whispering.

"I love you. But all this talk about our sex life ... I don't suppose you could keep dinner warm for another thirty minutes, could you?"

Noon, the next day, Virginia waved to Dolly across the parking lot. A light breeze blew a few strands of hair across Virginia's face but didn't move a curl of Dolly's carefully set perm.

"So windy," Dolly said. "Isn't that long hair a nuisance in the summer?"

Virginia smiled, ignoring the inevitable criticism. Inside they were shown to Dolly's preferred table in the far corner, away from the swinging doors to the kitchen. They were served immediately. Dolly had pre-ordered: chicken salad with a pickled peach on the side and cheese biscuits.

"I just don't know when Chip is going to settle down," Dolly said, once they had ordered. "I think he's having an affair with that trashy opera singer."

"She seems nice to me."

"Rather big boned, wouldn't you say?"

"They say she looks great on stage."

Dolly disagreed. "Too much hair and all that makeup in the daytime. They won't be here for your party. She's singing at some opera gala in Atlanta. It's just one little song, but it seems to be more important than your birthday."

"You don't like her. What do you care whether she comes or not."

"It's family," Dolly said. "If she wants to be a Ward, there are certain obligations."

"I doubt they'll marry," Virginia said. "She's very serious about her career."

"Career? What career? Singing in second-rate opera companies in places like Houston and Seattle? What does he see in her?"

"Glamour by association," Virginia said. "You know how vain Chip is. They make a very handsome pair. However, Dolly dear, it's none of your business whether or not they are sleeping together."

"Don't be vulgar, Virginia." Dolly took another sip of sweet tea. "I suppose you've noticed Warren and Juanita show no inclination to have children. It's her, I'm sure. I don't think she even likes children. But Sam is engaged again. My last hope for grandchildren. Another Miss Something-or-Other. I assume you and Ted do not plan to have a family?"

"That's none of your business either."

"Well it most certainly is! I'm your mother. You're almost twenty-five. I have hesitated to bring this up," — Virginia could hardly keep from laughing — "but I think I'm entitled to know if something is wrong with you that you can't have children. There are specialists, you know. Have you seen a doctor?"

"There is nothing wrong with either of us and I'm not talking to you about this." Virginia managed to remain more amused than irked, but Dolly couldn't resist one last nudge.

"I don't see why you can't tell me what's wrong."

"I'm leaving now," Virginia said, pushing her chair back and standing up. "You can call me about the party later."

The conversation reminded Virginia of the red sneaker. She had picked it up in the front yard this morning on her way to get the mail. It belonged to the skinny little boy who moved in with his parents across the street and who was running barefoot in the spring grass playing fetch with a small fuzzy white dog. He stopped when he saw her cross the street.

"Where are your babies?" he said. "Everybody on this block has babies. Are your babies grown?"

"I don't have any babies," she said. "Not yet."

The paraphernalia of parenthood strewn around the neighborhood rebuked her. The swing sets and doll houses, tricycles abandoned randomly in the middle of the sidewalk. Holding the single shoe, its tongue hanging loose, one string knotted where it had broken, she felt that something inside her was broken too.

Driving home from the club she acknowledged the truth. She didn't care much for her designated lifestyle. The small circle of friends from childhood, the ritual patterns of behavior like the Saturday night dances at the club where the men drank a little too much and held her a little too close on the dance floor. The worst part of it was the way they condescended to Ted because he attended John Wesley instead of an Ivy League school or the university.

"They're so obvious," Virginia told Sam, "and it goes right over Ted's head. He doesn't hear it. Like last weekend, at the dinner dance Saturday night. The band was taking a break and the group at our table drifted out onto the terrace. Ted and I decided to leave and started walking to the car. We hadn't gotten out of sight before we heard this huge burst of laughter behind us. I knew somebody, probably Chip, had made a crack about us. I told Ted what I thought and he said I was paranoid, but I'm not. I know what they're doing. I've seen it happen before when someone new marries in from the outside. I can't spend the rest of my life going to useless meetings and throwing charity balls with the same people over and over."

She was sure of one thing: she wanted out. Out of the club, the ladies' lunch scene, out of her mother's microscopic interest, and out of Parkersburg.

On her birthday Ted left her in bed lolling in the afterglow of love making. A tender and generous lover, always waiting for her, he coaxed her along with gentle hands. Not that it took much. She enjoyed sex. Since that first time, long before their wedding night, it had been the same. As if he could not deny her and as if she could never get enough of him.

He was also a thoughtful roommate. He made the coffee, left her a bouquet of red roses on the kitchen counter, and went to an early meeting at the office without disturbing her.

Red roses. Not the most imaginative gift, but the safest. That's Ted. Thoughtful, reliable. She smiles, stretches, relishing the way things have turned out.

Virginia showered, dressed in her new pale blue pantsuit and left the house around ten. She bought a chicken salad sandwich at a small tea room on the old highway, ate it in the car and arrived for her appointment on time, meeting the master of the Leesville Hunt, who also happened to be a real estate agent.

After showing her two pieces of property in a new equestrian development east of Leesville, the agent suggested a drive-by at an estate in the old hunting country held in trust by a quarrelsome family group. She recognized it instantly, knew it was exactly what she wanted, and called Ted from a pay phone at the gas station.

"I'm in Leesville," she said. "There's a farm I need you to look at."

"You're where? Leesville? Sweetheart, I can't get up there right now," he said. "My day is packed and I'll have to leave a staff meeting early to make the party as it is. Can't it wait 'til tomorrow?"

"No. I don't think so. This place isn't on the market yet, but it will be very soon. I'm getting a sneak preview. Look, I don't want to make a decision like this alone but I've hunted with the Leesville Hounds all around here and it is choice. Please? I'll make it worth your while."

"What the hell," he said. "It's your birthday."

"Thanks. I love you."

She couldn't say it often enough for him. He left his calendar and his papers scattered across his desk, got as far as the car and remembered, went back for the velvet box, a diamond broach, her birthday present. He wanted something lasting to show her that the babies didn't matter. That he intended to stay whether or not they had children. He told her he was part of the problem but she wouldn't believe him. Having a farm might be good for her, a small place where she could train a few horses.

Ted didn't know much about Leesville, a one-stoplight town in the middle of a modest horse industry. Not so moneyed or as historic as those colonies to the north, the area was open enough to support several hunts. Riding trails crisscrossed the county and the Blessing of the Hounds was an annual Thanksgiving Day event. Virginia had ridden there since she was a child. He timed the drive to Leesville in case she wanted to relocate. Thirty minutes outside. Not bad. He met Virginia and the real estate agent at the gas station by the interstate exchange.

"My wife's the expert on horse farms," he said, shaking hands with the agent, whose trim moustache and sharply creased khakis marked him as retired military. "In fact her grandmother's middle name was Lee, so there's probably a family connection. Come ride with me, Ginny. You can bring me up to speed." Once in the car, she reached for his hand.

"Well," she said, "it needs some work. And it's not exactly a farm."

"What exactly is it?" Ted asked.

"A two-hundred-acre estate," she said.

"You couldn't find something smaller?"

"It's three miles as the crow flies from the interstate and just a few minutes away from Leesville and they've got grocery stores and a dry cleaner and a couple of drug stores, so I wouldn't be running back and forth to Parkersburg all the time."

"Did you ask about the taxes? Have they set a price yet?"

"I didn't get any details," she says. "Don't make up your mind 'til you see it. Please?"

Ted's first impression was that Virginia had understated what the place might need in terms of rehabilitation. The rutted entry road dipped and climbed dangerously toward a dilapidated stable halfway up the hill. The one-bedroom house was little more than a shack, on a par with one of the mill houses her grandfather disposed of so many years ago. Its roof sagged from years of marginal upkeep. But when they surveyed the land in its entirety from a higher perspective, Ted had to admit it had potential.

"Wow," Ted said. "This is gorgeous."

The front acreage rolled down from a cleared ridge through virgin woodlands to the Cowee River on the south. To the northwest, pasture land fanned out across the valley toward the Blue Ridge escarpment where the mountains began. Seven ridges away, their peaks, rounded by centuries, the mountains rose one behind the other, a gentle semi-circle broken only by the incursion of the interstate. They were old mountains, shaped by time and erosion to hard rock in places and streaked with waterfalls from hidden springs. With no hotels, no condominiums, they carried old names like Horner's Bald and General Green. April colored them with a hundred different shades of new foliage and splashes of white dogwood, signs of a new season beginning.

At four-thirty, Ted guided the agent toward the cars.

"If you could give us a few minutes," Ted said.

"Of course. If you'll just lock the gate when you leave? You have my card," he said, climbing into his Jeep and starting the engine. "Call me when you decide."

Ted caught up with Virginia coming out of the barn.

"We're in North Carolina, right?"

"Yes. Why? What difference does that make?"

"I don't know, but living in one state and working in another ... Are we going to actually live here? It's too big for a weekend place. And if we do move, where will our children go to school? We'll be paying taxes in two states instead of one. Where do we vote? Do we keep a residence in Parkersburg? We need to think this through."

"We'll worry about those things when we get to them," Virginia said.

"What worries me the most is the size of the property and how much work it needs."

"I know, I know, but it's a once-in-a-lifetime opportunity. This place could be so perfect! We could put the new barn down low close to the road with the rings across the driveway. And there's a stream we could dam for a pond in the west pasture. Of course, we'll need fencing and we'll have to grade the road. We can straighten out a couple of the worst curves, I think. And a house. Oh Ted! We could build such a wonderful house on that ridge. Just imagine seeing all this first thing every morning! Please. Please say it's okay for me to buy it. I've got some stock I can sell so we won't need to get rid of the house in town, not right away. I haven't ever wanted anything as much as I want this." She took his hands, lacing her fingers in his. "Except maybe the first time I saw you at John Wesley. And I'll bet we can get it for three hundred an acre."

"Maybe," he said, "but let's wait a couple of hours. You don't want to seem too eager." In the interim he hoped to talk her down at least a little.

Virginia climbed the ridge to get a better look. She stood with her back to him facing west.

"This is where the house should go to take advantage of the view," she said. He wanted to prolong the moment, took the velvet box from his pocket and walked toward her.

"We could be happy here," she said.

"Aren't we happy where we are?" he said, encircling her from behind, his arms clasped around her waist. She leaned against him, her head on his chest.

"You are," she said without resentment. She turned, kissed him lightly.

"Maybe this will help," he said handing her the box. She opened it, gasped, recognizing the simple elegance and quality of the gift, a horse head pavéd in diamonds.

"Ooh Teddy," she said, "this is six months' salary."

"Eight," he said. "Try it on."

"Did Dolly—"

"Dolly had nothing to do with it."

"My hands are shaking. You do it for me," she said.

He reached one hand inside her jacket and with the other, slid the broach into place above her heart. She took a deep breath, pushing her breast against the back of his hand. They were standing very close, looking at the pin as he threaded the pointed platinum bar through the fabric, closed the clasp, and slipped on the safety. He took his time.

"I love you," he said. "More than anything."

He removed his hand slowly as he felt himself stirring and wrapped his arms around her. They kissed like teenagers, hungry for each other. He pulled away, took her hand, and led her down the hill and into the barn. Bales of hay lined the walls floor to ceiling. One had fallen and split open.

"This suit," she said hesitating. "The straw … we'll have to go home and change."

"Worry about that later," he said, dropping down to a convenient pile of loose hay and pulling her down on top of him.

"Virginia is always late," Warren fussed.

"No one is always anything," Juanita said, eyeing the pack of Winstons never out of her husband's reach. "We're sentient beings. We have the capacity to change."

They were sitting on the deck at Montvue with Dolly, drinking gin and tonic and waiting for the party to begin.

"Something you learned in your psychology class, dear?" Dolly said. "I'm so glad you're getting that degree. It will give you so much self-confidence."

"And a job, I hope."

"You could do wonders for those poor children out at The Oaks," Dolly said. "I don't think they have a staff psychologist. I know the director quite well. If you'd like, I could talk to him."

"Thank you Dolly," Juanita said, "but I'm more interested in substance abuse."

"Drunks and druggies," Warren said. "That's all she talks about."

"Oh well, it's too soon to decide now, isn't it. You've got what? Two more years?"

"One more semester and a practicum," Juanita said.

Not charmed with the idea of a Ward doing social work, Dolly did not care to pursue the nature of a practicum, although the word was unfamiliar, so she changed the subject.

"Aren't the azaleas gorgeous? Jesse and I have to prune them back every other year to keep them looking so compact. I do love those purple ones. They're so fragrant. And the new fountain? It's a copy of one I saw at a chateau outside of Paris."

Warren mixed himself another drink. "Which one of the beauty queens is Sam bringing tonight? The tap dancer or the clogger?"

"The born-again Christian."

Dolly spun around, hyper alert. "Do I hear a car out front?"

Ted pulled into the driveway just as Sam was getting out of his car. Virginia jumped out and ran to Sam to show off her birthday pin. Sam hugged his sister, shook hands with his brother-in-law, and introduced his date, a striking brunette as tall as Ted. Dolly came out and stood at the top of the steps to greet her guests. Her smile faded, but only slightly, when she saw Virginia.

"Wearing pants to a party! Virginia Dorothea Ward, don't you have any skirts? Oh well, happy birthday anyway." Dolly embraced her daughter who had bounded up the steps.

"We're buying a farm," Virginia crowed, excited as a child at the circus.

"A farm?" Dolly said. "What in the world do you want with a farm? And what is that you've got on? Virginia, you are not wearing diamonds on polyester!"

Sam came up behind Ted and picked a piece of straw off the back of his coat.

"Hmmm," he said, flashing his famous grin. "Looks like you've already celebrated."

By Virginia's next birthday, Dolly would be far too busy to plan another party.

In December of 1965 Ted was promoted to Vice President of Ward Mills, Inc., and suddenly, for no obvious reason, Young Ward decided to retire.

"I've had enough," he told Dolly. "I'm going to Hilton Head and play golf for the rest of my life."

Dolly heard something suspicious in the phrase "for the rest of my life" but she didn't pursue it. Assured by her brother that his plans were irreversible, she went home to Montvue and called Reece. He heard the tension in her voice and cancelled the rest of the notations on his calendar, leaving his office without explanation. Dolly met him at the door, wringing her hands.

"May I offer you something to drink?" she said, ever the perfect hostess. Reece shook his head.

"Perhaps later," he said.

"Then let's go into the library."

Dolly closed the door behind them. She walked to the window, looking out on the perfect garden she had created.

"I don't want this job, Reece. I could kill Young for leaving me like this."

Reece read her hesitance as a need for reassurance, but couldn't resist a small joke.

"You could call Warren and Chip," he said. "Or would you prefer to hire from outside? We could get a professional search firm or steal a young hotshot from one of our competitors."

"This company is my responsibility, but the job is going to ruin my life. I'm not cut out for this. I was raised to be a wife and mother, not a cotton mill executive."

"Dolly," Reece said, "You'll be wonderful. The people who work at Ward Mills love you already. We'll all be behind you one hundred percent."

"It's simply not my *milieu*," she said, crossing the room to stand in front of Ben's portrait.

"I'll be out of place. The women I know, my friends, none of them work. Women are supposed to stay home if they can afford to. The Big Five won't make room for me in spite of what Young said. I'm falling into a position that threatens them all. They'll treat me like I'm a dumb little girl. I'll lose all my women friends because I'll be too busy for garden club or bridge. They'll think I'm Miss High and Mighty. I won't fit in anywhere.

"You'll make a place for yourself," Reece said. "I've watched you learn from Young. You don't have any trouble telling him what you think."

"He's my brother," she said. "That's different." Dolly turned to face him. I'm fifty years old," she said. "I should be playing with my grandchildren, not running a textile company."

"Plenty of time to worry about grandchildren when you have some. You've got back-up, you know. I'll be right there at your shoulder whenever you need me, and I won't let the Big Five intimidate you. You've also got Ted and Sam coming on fast."

"I shouldn't have let Chip go," she said.

"Frankly, Dolly, Ted's a better bet," Reece said. "He actually likes what he's doing."

Dolly took a deep breath, which became a sigh. She looked at Reece. Her voice took a softer, more uncertain tone.

"So many people will be depending on me. It's too much."

"Not for you, Dolly," he said. "Maybe for some other woman, but not for you."

"Are you sure?" she said. "I can't try this job on and then quit, as if it were a dress I took out on approval and then returned. Changing my mind would cause too much damage to our image, our customers. Once decided, there's no turning back."

"I cannot think of a better person to protect the company," Reece said. "Why don't you sleep on our conversation? We can talk again tomorrow. In the meanwhile, if I might suggest a time table? Ask Young to keep quiet about his plans for the rest of the month. He owes you that much. Consider going forward with your normal Christmas celebration. We all look forward to visiting Montvue at Christmas, and wait until New Year's Day to tell the family. Your traditional gathering can serve as an impromptu board meeting."

"I've already told the boys they are expected for lunch on the first. They will be spending Christmas with their wives' families. I'll have Virginia and Ted and Sam Christmas Eve. You'll be here too, on the first?"

"Of course. I wouldn't miss Annie's Hoppin' John and collard greens for anything."

Or, he thought, the fireworks likely to follow.

Dolly made her announcement, standing before dessert was served, tapping lightly on her wine glass with a teaspoon for their attention.

"My brother, your Uncle Young, is leaving us, retiring to Hilton Head, where he has found a lovely woman whom he plans to marry. He tells me they will be traveling a good deal. As our father suggested, Young has given his stock to my three sons as of today. I have the certificates at my desk in the study. Reece and I have discussed the alternatives and decided that, with your permission, I will assume the presidency of Ward Mills, Inc., effective immediately. All in favor?

Jaws dropped. After a moment of notable silence, Ted was the first to speak.

"If I get a vote it's yea," he said, smiling broadly. "Great news!" He went to the head of the table and kissed Dolly's cheek.

"Well ... certainly. If ... uh ... that's what you want ..." Chip said.

Ted went back to his seat and nudged Virginia.

"You're serious?" she said. "You're going to run the company?"

"You doubt my ability to do so? I'm not going to be all by myself, Virginia. We," Dolly said, stressing the plural and looking around the table, "we are going to run the company Sam and Ted and Reece and I. And you and the boys, of course. You'll all be members of the board.

"Some of our competitors, and apparently some of my children, think I am unlikely to succeed. Young expects one or two members of the Big Five to see Ward Mills as a take-over prospect, however that is not even a remote possibility. He prepared me and them insofar as he was able and he has agreed to remain available as a consultant."

Sam was smiling, smug in the knowledge that his prediction had come true. His mother had become the first woman to run an operation of comparable size in the textile industry. In the questions and conversations that followed her announcement to the family, Dolly missed Sam's aside to his brother-in-law.

"Sounds like she was just elected Secretary General of the United Nations."

10

Friday, November 4, 1988

In the car on the way home from Montvue, Ted and Virginia share a weighted silence. Dolly's will, Reece's knowledge of its contents, and the strange knowing behavior of the boys has left Ted frustrated, his plans stalled and perhaps derailed. Virginia, hurt again by her mother's apparent disapproval and rejection, resolves to cover her feelings. Ted searches for a way to make it easier for her.

— The will didn't mentioned the other places, the houses at the lake and the beach. You knew about them, didn't you?

— What about them?

— Dolly signed the beach house over to Sam a couple of years ago. I thought surely he'd told you. The lake house is yours.

— Dolly mentioned giving it to me a couple of months ago, but I didn't think she was serious. She was in the hospital and I thought it was the medication talking. Why wasn't that in the will?

— It would have been better for us in inheritance taxes. This way it's going to cost us in capital gains, but Dolly didn't ask Reece. She just did what she wanted to do. She never discussed it with me either, but I think the way she did it tells us something. Dolly felt closer to you than you realize. She left her sanctuaries in your hands. The lake house and her room at Montvue.

— I love the lake house, always have. We used to spend part of the summer in Dacus.

He thought she might be grateful. Apparently she is not. She treats the news as if it were her due.

— At least it's over, she says. — The will business, I mean.

— You're always in such a big hurry, Virginia. The will

business as you call it is just beginning. I should have put the sale together a year ago.

— What sale are you talking about?

— The company. We need to sell the mills and get out of the textile business.

— Are you crazy?

— I know a little more about this business than you do.

— You think so?

— Why are you getting into this? You don't have a clue. You've never taken any interest in the mills or in how Dolly and I ran them.

She is startled, miffed at his anger, hurt by the severity of his words.

— Your snapping at me doesn't help.

He hears, but feels that no apology is necessary. Fatigue and disappointment rise between them like the barren space between the boundaries of a demilitarized zone. His mind is racing. He expected Chip and Warren to avoid him, so their behavior came as no surprise. To a certain extent, they contained their hostility while their mother lived, but made no attempt to hide their feelings today. What hurts him is that Dolly has let him down. She could have told him she had a game plan.

They drive northwest in the midst of heavy Friday afternoon traffic and the direct glare of the setting sun. To avoid further conversation, Ted turns on the radio, its dial set to NPR, at this hour of the day broadcasting "All Things Considered." So close to the election, the pundits are unanimous in their criticism of Dukakis's debate performance, predicting an easy win for George Bush.

Neither one of them is actually listening. The civilized conversation between commentators comes across as shallow compared to the emotions ricocheting around inside the car. The trip home takes longer than usual, or seems to. Ted brakes at the barn to let Virginia out so she can check on the horses.

— I'm getting a headache, he says. — I'm going to try and sleep it off before dinner. Then I've got to talk to Sam. Virginia climbs out of the car.

— You've got to talk to me first.

Once inside Ted goes upstairs and eases himself onto the queen-sized bed in the guest room. His leg muscles have contracted and his shoulders ache more from the tensions of the day than from the tension of the drive home. He has closed the shutters against the late afternoon light, but as hard as he tries to relax, he can't slow the mental treadmill inside his head, pulling him forward but going nowhere. Dolly. Why did you leave me in this mess? Why didn't you listen to me or to Reece? Which one of them got to you? Not Sam. Surely not Sam. What does Reece know that I don't know? Why didn't I ask him this afternoon when I had the chance? Ted answers his own question. Because I was caught completely off guard. He could have given me some sort of clue, damn it. But of course he wouldn't, being the ethical man he is.

Ted hates feeling sorry for himself, considers it a character weakness. He is bone weary, worn down by the loss of Dolly, the pervasive sadness created by what lies ahead, the divorce and the constant friction with Virginia's older brothers. Dolly had warned him. He had laughed the warning off.

Virginia comes up from the barn. He hears her in the shower, rests a few more minutes, and goes downstairs. Remembering the file Reece has given him earlier in the day, he retrieves it from the car, sits at the end of the kitchen counter reading it. Virginia in her robe and slippers makes sandwiches.

— Feeling any better? she says.

— Didn't sleep but the headache's gone. Glass of wine?

— Sure.

— Were you aware of the way the stock has been divided?

— No. Why? Is it important?

— It is now. Reece has gathered some information you should know about. In 1966 when Young Ward left the company, he signed his certificates over to Sam, Warren, and Chip. That was the year Volly was born and Dolly gave me one hundred shares of her stock. When Billy was born in '71, she gave you one hundred shares, reducing her holdings to the two hundred shares. Those go into the trust.

— So?

— When your grandfather divided the stock between Dolly and Young, he kept four hundred shares for himself. He gave your father one hundred shares, which Dolly inherited. In the sixties, Dolly authorized Reece to trace the certificates and buy what he could. Sounds like a clear conflict of interest, but Dolly told him to keep what he'd found, which he did – about one hundred shares. We've lost track of the other two hundred shares.

— Enough to make a difference? she says.

— If we decide to sell.

— I don't want to talk about this right now. Luncheon leftovers on the counter. Help yourself.

Virginia serves her plate, takes it into the den, and turns on the television set. Preoccupied by the events of the day, he joins her, watches the evening news, apologizes for his failure to communicate, and goes upstairs. In bed, unable to fall asleep and without intention, Ted weighs the crisis of the day against the possible loss of his marriage. Of the two, losing Virginia grieves him more. She is strong, beautiful, everything he ever wanted. She needs him, tells him he's good for her. He wonders still after thirty years of marriage why she chose him, how he can repair the damage to their marriage. If he can.

He begins to form a plan. He'll take it one step at a time. Maybe what he needs to do is give in, suggest an informal separation, a trip perhaps to Europe, a new horse, a renovation at the lake house, any sort of distraction. He will find himself an apartment in Parkersburg if that is what she wants. As he told Reece, he will stall as long as he can. His marriage is a part of who he is. He has spent thirty years growing into this place, his place in this world, but he is tired of the conflict. He cannot imagine life without Virginia and the farm, but he can get along without the company, much as he has loved his job, the creative part is behind him. What he treasures most is in serious jeopardy. He can't think straight, takes two aspirin, and turns out the light. Perhaps in the morning … He is almost asleep when he hears the sound of the light switch in the hall.

— Are you awake? she says, pushing the door open. He is as much amused as irritated, thinking of the hundreds of times she has done this when she wanted to talk. He doesn't open his eyes, hoping she will take the hint, but some instinct tells him she's not going anywhere.

— I know you're awake, she says. — Did Dolly know about your plan to sell the mills? Is that's why she amended her will?

— Do we have to do this now?

— Yes.

He opens his eyes, sees her standing at the foot of the bed, her arms crossed. The silky white fabric of her wrap-around robe clings to her hips, outlining her body. He remembers the first night he saw her in white silk, aches to hold her.

He props the pillow up behind his head reluctantly, pushing himself against the headboard into a sitting position, and turns on the bedside lamp.

— Why did I have to learn about all this in front of my brothers? I could tell Sam was surprised but the other two were so anxious to leave. I know them. They know more than they're saying.

— Today … the whole thing. I had never even considered … I've been chasing the stock in my head for nothing. I'm pretty sure the boys will try to block whatever I propose on the grounds that we'd be going against Dolly's explicit wishes, but I don't think they would contest the trust. I had hoped I could get us out of this mess before things got any worse. Now we'll just have to wait and see.

— Can't Reece handle whatever comes up?

— I should have told you and Sam from the beginning what I had in mind.

— Yes you should have, she says. — Why didn't you tell me about the real estate business?

— I did tell you. About the time Dolly started the first round of chemo. You weren't listening. Maybe it was the cancer that motivated Dolly. I'm not sure even Reece knows what she had in mind. Maybe she had a premonition. You know how bad things are in this industry. I only want to protect you and the children.

— You're rambling, she says. — If things were that bad in the industry I would have heard something. Or if I didn't, Sam would know and he would have told me. Even if there is some sort of trouble ahead, nobody else around here is doing anything about it.

— We're ahead of the curve, he says.

— I don't see the Macauleys or the Wrights selling. I see them spending on new equipment, Swiss machines, and efficiency experts and the like. My grandfather started this business. And you're telling me now, finally, you're telling me that you want to sell off the mills he built?

— They aren't as valuable as you think.

Juggling two or three trains of thought simultaneously, he leans forward, rubbing his cheekbones to relieve the pressure in his sinuses. When he looks up, she's standing at the far end of the bed, flexing her fingers, an indication that the arthritis is bothering her. The top of her robe has fallen slightly open. He sees where her tan stops and the whiteness between her breasts begins.

— So you're saying that you're not trying to cheat us out of our inheritance? Dolly knew what you were going to do?

— Not exactly, he says.

— Exactly what then?

— She agreed to look the other way. To set things up so that I could sell the mills after her death if we had to. It's the simplest way, Virginia. Ask Reece if you don't believe me.

— Why did you try to do this behind our backs?

Hearing her align herself with her brothers pains him, but he takes a deep breath and tries to explain slowly and rationally.

— Dolly understood the necessity for containing the plans, he says.

He realizes immediately that he has chosen the wrong words, comparing her comprehension to that of her mother, so he tries again.

— Ventures like this are best kept quiet. The more people you tell, the more you limit maneuverability. If there is any intimation that we're in trouble, and that would be the assumption, the price would tumble before we put any of the mills on the market.

She sits on the edge of the bed, gathers her long silk robe around her legs. He sees that he has her attention but from the set of her mouth, he knows she isn't convinced.

— Look at what's happening in the industry, he says. — First our customers began to realize how much cheaper they could buy from outside this country and get a better product to boot. Then Reagan screwed us with the tariff veto. We all thought your friend, Stan Wright, had some sort of an epiphany when he totaled his Maserati four years ago and started reorganizing. Not so. He's not the playboy people assume he is and he isn't chairman of a Big Five company for nothing. He'd been working on upgrading quality and diversifying for years. The diversity is what will save his operation. He'll go international soon. He's got no debt and he's twice as big as all the rest of us put together.

— We won't let you do what the Martins did, Virginia says. — Sell off the company and pocket the pension plan. We're honor-bound to protect the people who work for us. Some of those families have been with the company since my grandfather's time.

— The Martins had a much smaller operation, but I can't sanction what they did, although it's perfectly legal. Look, Virginia. We're at the end of a sequence. The textile industry as we have known it is no longer viable. Spinning cotton into gray goods is not a profitable venture anymore, and we're actually losing money on the finishing process. We can't keep pouring our resources into newer and bigger machines, because we don't have the income to justify the expense, even when we cut or retrain personnel. Companies our size are going to have to sell sooner or later. If we wait, we lose our shirts and the shirts of all the people who work for us. We can either do it now while there's still a market or wait and get fifty cents on the dollar if we're lucky.

— If things were all that bad, you wouldn't be the only person who knows about it, she says. — I know I'm repeating myself, but you're not answering my question.

— Oh they all know about it. They just refuse to believe that their world is about to collapse. They're like the little Dutch boy sticking his finger in the dike. And even if some of them fold, most of them have already made enough to maintain their lifestyle for a couple of generations.

— So where do you think we should go from here? She emphasizes the "you," still not accepting the idea that he is right.

— There are several possibilities, he says. — If we were bigger we could convert to a more industrial line of products, carpets maybe or industrial fabric or some kind of synthetics. New product opportunities come forward every day, but waiting is chancy. My guess is that only two of the Big Five will come out of this whole thing and they will have to redesign their product and their process. The easiest thing is to simply sell off the mills.

— Doesn't it occur to you that you might be wrong?

Virginia stands, goes to the door, pauses with her hand on the molding and turns.

— I don't see how I can support your plan. Find another way.

He knows she will figure it out, or Sam will tell her. He can put a package together without her stock, but he knows that would mean the end of his marriage.

Although he understands she has not done so deliberately, she has rattled him. She's not being coy. These conversations while she's half-dressed are routine. Virginia is matter of fact about sex; she doesn't tease. She tells him what she likes and what she doesn't. But tonight her behavior, normal and customary as it is, feeds the tension between them. It's painful. She leaves the room but the scent of her remains.

Ted plumps his pillow, lies flat on the big bed, trying to relax. His thoughts drift to the early years of their marriage. So much of what he treasures began when they came to the farm. Real privacy, for one thing. In the apartment they never knew when Dolly or one of the boys would stop by unannounced. It was the same with the house near the country club. In Leesville they made new friends. Some of the horse people that Virginia knew, unpretentious and hard working. The good life. Had it early on. This chaos must be payback. The gods getting even. No use trying to sleep. Good time to call Sam.

For years he has exercised this option; late night conversations with his best friend who became his brother-in-law, or more accurately, his brother-in-law who became his best friend. In college Ted would study in the library until it closed and then check in at Sam's room. Sam was always up, listening to jazz, reading. Ted never heard the true story until they graduated. Sam had gotten caught by the campus police with a beer in his hand and a case in the back seat, which resulted in a semester of room arrest. He never seemed to sweat exams or to devote much time to hitting the books, as they said, but he managed to keep a B average. Ted kidded him about cheating, which Sam regarded as a great joke.

"Ward men only cheat on their wives," he said.

Ted goes downstairs to make the call.

— Hello, he says. He hears a full orchestra in the background. One of Sam's late night movies.

— *Singing in the Rain* again?

— I've been expecting you. Sam turns the music down, but not off.

— I was hoping she'd come to you first, Ted says.

— She did. More or less. But that ain't the half of it.

— No. There's Billy. And there are the mills.

— Okay. I got that one figured out.

— Oh?

— Yup. Here's my theory. Chip got wind of your intentions. My guess is one of the Big Five figured selling out was at least a possibility, what with Dolly on her deathbed. Chip thinks a sell-off of any kind will cost him money and that's all he cares about. In September he called Dolly and told her he and Callie might have another child, maybe a boy this time. He told her it would be unfair to any future grandchildren to leave all of her stock to you. I'm betting he made it dramatic, like he was gonna sire our savior, a Ward male to carry on for the family and take over when we all gave up or died or he killed us off like the Borgias. Sam pauses a minute, coughs his dry useless cough, and continues.

— By then Dolly was pretty much into her drug regimen and had figured out what lay ahead. It's nasty and simple, Sam says. — He played her.

— He manipulated his own mother?

— He's done worse things. Ask Virginia.

— I've never cared much for your brother.

— Me neither.

— I understand why Reece couldn't tell us about the codicil before Dolly died, but why not afterwards?

— Chip played him too. He knew Reece couldn't talk to anyone about changing the will because he's too damned ethical. Man, I'll bet Reece would like to string him up.

— Wouldn't be much left if I got there first. Do you think Virginia . . .?

— She'll get over this, Sam says. — I know her better than anybody, even you. Relax. This whole thing is as much about how she sees her role with us and the boys. She's felt powerless all these years. Why do you think she rides horses? Raw power and control. That and sex.

— How much have you had to drink?

— Think about it. Teenage girls on horses. It's sexual obsession in a socially acceptable form. Parents can only hope they grow out of it or they'll find some big ole stud like you to substitute.

— Come on, Sam. That's garbage.

— Okay, boss, whatever you say. Now, as to the other subject, I know Billy's your son. I'm not gonna forget it and I'm not gonna let him forget it.

— I worry about the responsibility we're asking you to shoulder.

— The kid's got some problems. If I can help, I'm glad to, so forget it. In the meanwhile, your daughter's the one you need to talk to. This business of Dolly's will and the trust has her asking herself a lot of questions.

— I'll call and make an appointment.

— She's right here.

— She's heard this conversation? About sex and horses?

— Just my end. Wanna talk to her?

Ted hears Volly laughing in the background.

— Just tell her I'll be down in the morning. About ten.

— Too early. How 'bout eleven? Annie's off tomorrow. You'll

be at Montvue in time for lunch, so how 'bout pickin' up some barbecue and a six-pack on the way?

— Beautiful day, Volly says. She meets Ted at the door, offers her cheek for a kiss and takes the Styrofoam boxes of barbecue and the beer from him. Walking toward the kitchen she talks over her shoulder.

— You look harassed. Sam told me you expected Dolly to leave you her stock and then she didn't. I don't want to be a part of what's worrying you, so if it's about money, I'm off the payroll after this semester. Dolly sent me a whopping big check as an early graduation present.

— And you're going to use it for a trip to France?

— That's over. He was an opportunist.

Volly puts the beer and the barbecue in the refrigerator.

— What did you do with the money? Ted says. — If you don't mind my asking.

— First I called Sam to make sure it was legit. Then I called Uncle Chip and set up a brokerage account. Well don't look so surprised. You've always said he was smart. You won't have to support me after I finish my class work. I'll find some sort of part-time job while I write the thesis and between that and my investment income, I'll be poor but independent. I suspect that's what Dolly had in mind. Sam says I can always camp at Montvue.

Ted is surprised by her comprehension, impressed with her maturity. Although she has every right to be, she is not the spoiled little rich girl she might have been, the one her mother described to him a few short years ago.

— I've wondered for a long time, she says, — about my grandmother. How she was perceived by the outside world. So I looked her up at the Duke library the day I got that check. There was a big article in the South Carolina business magazine. Very flattering. She was one of a kind, wasn't she?

— In many ways, Ted says.

— About the business, I mean. Her shrewdness. You were there when she took over from her brother. What kind of role did you play?

— My, my. What a politically correct question.

— Don't make fun of me. Yesterday changed everything. I'm not irresponsible. I can see what lies ahead, at least at the end of ten years.

Ted bends down to retie a shoe string, embarrassed that he has underestimated his daughter.

— Basically I did what Dolly asked me to do, he says. — I took the job she offered in the hope of her blessing on our marriage, which she had opposed at first. Between us, Sam and I helped her keep your uncles in line, and for the most part, our collaboration, if you want to call it that, worked well. Dolly had her blind spots, but she was always open to suggestion.

— Wait a minute, Volly says. — Nobody told me. She opposed your marriage?

— Let's go out on the deck, Ted says. — It's too nice to stay inside.

They bring two chairs into the sun from the round wrought iron table. Ted decides telling the truth is the best choice.

— Dolly didn't think my blood was blue enough.

— That's harsh.

— It wasn't personal. She liked me as Sam's friend, but when it came down to marrying off her only daughter, she had other plans, a doctor or a lawyer preferably. Someone with roots in Parkersburg. Give her credit, she adapted once she realized our marriage was inevitable. She gave us a beautiful wedding and reception and fixed up our apartment while we were on our honeymoon, which she paid for. She talked her brother into hiring me, although I've always thought Sam had something to do with that too. Anyway, the more we worked together the better we came to understand each other and the better we liked each other. Dolly respected my work ethic and I respected hers.

— And she knew you were smart, Volly says.

— Smart, maybe, but I was pretty green, Ted says. — I didn't know a thing about manufacturing. In case you didn't know, my degree was in economics.

— So you and Dolly liked working together. I got it. But what did the two of you do? With the company, I mean?

— We made money. But then, everybody else in the business was doing the same. We liked to think we were a little more progressive than most, but to tell the truth, we could afford to think well of ourselves. That was in the sixties and early seventies.

— And then?

— We took some mill profits and our own money and invested outside the industry. We set up the real estate business with our own money. Eventually we had a couple of residential sales people too. I handled the commercial side and we reached further into the upstate corridor as far south as the Georgia border.

— About the mills, wasn't it hard for you, working with Uncle Warren and Uncle Chip?

— Why do you say that? Didn't Chip set up the brokerage account for you? I may not care for him personally but I recognize his talent. He's a smart guy and he honors his obligations. He managed purchasing and distribution for the mills. Pretty complicated and important. We had trouble replacing him when he left.

— Mother doesn't like him, Volly said.

— Has she ever told you why?

— No, but she flinches when he touches her.

— I'm not fond of either one of your uncles, but I feel a little sorry for Chip. He's been in a difficult position most of his life, being the eldest son, shouldering all that expectation. Did Sam tell you? He wants the portrait of your grandfather in the library.

— I say let him have it. No loss there. It's a really bad painting. Would you like a Coke or something?

— No, he says. — I'm fine. Enjoying the garden, the fountain. Thinking of all the conversations that have taken place on this deck over the years.

Volly stares out over the azaleas, quiet for moment.

— You don't dislike anybody, do you? You're calm, objective. Mother has such fierce emotions she scares me. When I was at Duke I didn't think about you and Mother much or the family. I was totally wrapped up in my own life, class of '85, pioneers of the Me generation.

— Understandable, Ted says. — You were on your own for the first time. Small private high school, big university, so many options. I remember those feelings. Try not to be too hard on Warren and especially Chip. He was honest with me from the beginning. He invited me to play golf at the club shortly after your mother and I were married and he told me exactly how he felt about me and the company and the family. His memories of his father were fixated on one conversation.

— What do you mean?

— Think about it, Ted says. — Here's a kid, barely twelve years old, and the last words he hears his father say are, 'Take care of your brother.' Within a year, his father is dead. Then ten years later I come along, marry his only sister, and go to work for the family company. The boys were behaving normally if you ask me. As members of the board, they've been reasonable as long as the business makes money. What amazed me about the Ward boys and still does is that they fought among themselves, angry and mean and just as hard as they had when they were children, according to your mother. Half the time I felt like John Wayne trying to get the herd to Abilene.

— It's hard to imagine all of you young.

— Thanks, Ted says, chuckling.

— Don't be offended. You're just so much a part of the establishment.

— All thanks to your grandmother.

— The parallel between Chip's situation and mine? Is that what you're telling me?

— You mean Billy? Honestly, the situations aren't at all similar. We don't expect you to take care of him. You've got your mother and Sam and a trust fund. And me.

Ted has talked too much, but knowing his opportunities are limited he has plunged on. He is impressed by her interest and attention, grateful for it and for the chance to elaborate his position, but doesn't want to overplay his hand.

— Don't let this inheritance sidetrack you from doing what you want to do.

— But Dolly skipped Mother and left Montvue to me. That's bound to cause more friction between the two of us and I don't want it anyway. Too many ghosts.

— Your mother may have been disappointed, but I doubt that she blames you. When the time comes, you'll find your way. And if you ever feel like you need to talk more or get some good solid advice, call John Reece. That's what I'm going to do tomorrow.

11

Monday, November 14, 1988

Ted is on the phone first thing the next morning.

— John, he says. — I'd like to come in this morning for a private conversation. Would that be convenient?

— Of course. What time may I expect you?

— Within the hour.

Ted leaves a note for Virginia, telling her he will be late. He checks the barn on his way into town but sees no sign of her. He has decided to take Reece's advice about not rushing into any deal. He needs to figure out the best way to leverage his personal position. So far as he knows, the bank has not been heard from. Entering Reece's office, he goes straight across the room, reaching across the desk to shake hands.

— Good morning, he says.

— You seem rather formal today.

— I'm here to apologize. I behaved badly at Montvue. At the reading of Dolly's will. Whatever Dolly intended, however many codicils she created, it wasn't your fault. In your own way, you tried to warn me by giving me the file on the distribution of stock.

— That's quite true, but it doesn't make you feel any better, does it?

— I'm afraid not.

— You understand. She was too sick for me to try and dissuade her.

— Certainly.

— To borrow a sports metaphor, we're in a whole new ballgame now and I can't predict the future any more than you can, but perhaps if we look at the situation together …

— Exactly what I had in mind.

— Here, have a seat. Reece extends his hand to the chair in front of his desk. —First before we even start, are you in this for the long haul? Divorce or no divorce?

— I do not want a divorce but I won't fight it if it's what Virginia wants. Whatever happens, it should not affect my position with Ward Mills, Inc. I have a contract, the one you insisted on, and unless the board wants a law suit, I don't think they will try to fire me. Agreed?

— Agreed. Now, to review. The trust holds two hundred shares of the company stock; each of Dolly's children and you and I each hold one hundred. Two hundred remain unaccounted for. It appears that Dolly's father handed out small parcels of stock, twenty here, ten there, some to retiring employees, some to friends. In 1966, I traced a good many of those shares by researching the annual dividend checks, and bought up what I could with the board's permission. By then it was clear that you would eventually be running the company. I thought you were a good investment and I still do.

— Thank you for that. I couldn't have managed without you.

— Perhaps. Perhaps not, but the problem remains. Over two hundred shares have simply disappeared. Some of the dividend checks came back to us marked undeliverable, some were never cashed, both perfectly understandable. Small amounts of stock in a small privately held company are easily overlooked. The holders may have died without issue, the certificates could have been lost or tossed by unknowing relatives. Whatever happened to those certificates, your hands are tied until we find them or can declare them null and void. Even if you could form a majority coalition, you can't sell the company with two hundred shares outstanding. Nobody will buy a pig in a poke.

— What do we do? If I still want to sell?

— You'll have to form a majority coalition. But first, we call a stock holders meeting. If the named recipients don't respond, we will need to run three public notifications in the *Parkersburg Daily News*. Until the bank appoints a representative, we can only guess at how they might suggest we proceed, but in any circumstance, we need to verify who holds those certificates. We should consider the possibility that Chip captured some of those shares. By the way, I'm sorry I couldn't give you any warning. For what it's worth, I thought you handled yourself very well.

— Thank you, Ted says. — I can't say I'm thrilled with the way things are going. He stands, pushing his palms together, flexing the muscles of his arms. — I was already disappointed. You know how I loved Christmas at Montvue. Fantasy fulfillment for a kid growing up like I did. We sold fresh trees at the store, put up decorations there, but not so much at home. We weren't there except to eat and sleep. Mostly sleep. When the big day finally came we were too tired to care. That first year Virginia and I were married, the Wards' idea of an appropriate celebration bowled me over. I'm going to miss it.

— You'll be fine, Reece says. — This season brings out the best in all of us.

It won't ever be the same, but I hope it gets easier. We just have to plod through this first one without her.

He has no idea what sort of present to get Virginia for Christmas. A car? What's the message there? He already knows what she has gotten for him. New luggage. There will be no party for the lighting of the tree at Montvue. No Christmas Eve dinner with a rib roast and plum pudding, no candlelit midnight communion service with the family. No one has even mentioned the possibilities. He is bewildered, can only hope for a thaw in the pack ice at home.

As Ted predicted, his day turns out to be a very long one. When he comes in from the garage around seven, he finds Virginia sitting at the kitchen counter hunched over a spiral notebook like a school girl taking a test.

— Virginia, what the hell … I thought you must be out. There're no lights on anywhere else. What are you doing?

— I bought a book, she says, — about journal writing. She motions with her head to a paperback lying within reach. Beyond it a stack of newspaper clippings, Dolly's obituary notices, lie unattended. At her feet he sees the cardboard box containing unanswered condolence cards. More have appeared since yesterday.

— I stopped by Montvue, he says. Sam's bought more fish tanks. Says he and Billy are going into business raising and selling tropical fish.

— So?

— It's Billy. When he reels off on one of those extended monologues I don't know how to respond. I can't engage him in any sort of normal conversation.

— Ted, he's a teenager, she says, as if that explains everything.

— It's not that simple.

— Did you know that Dolly wrote in her diary every day? They're stacked up neat as you please in her secretary. I think I'll take a look at them. I'm taking some khakis down for Billy, and I need to buy him some new shirts. It's swimming. All those muscles in his arms and shoulders. Do you think his pants will still fit?

— It's a waste of time, Virginia. He won't wear anything but jeans.

Ted walks around the kitchen turning on lights, wondering if they can get through another evening without mentioning the divorce. He is hopeful that she has changed her mind, but there has been no discussion, no confrontation. The business of death has allowed them to avoid the issue. Still, it wriggles below the surface like worms in a garden.

— Is that what gave you the idea for a journal? Dolly's diaries? Why aren't you using the computer?

— Longhand's better. It's good therapy. You ought to try it yourself.

— What? Therapy? I thought you said therapy was useless. That's what you said before, when you were seeing Mason.

Virginia ignores his response and his churlishness. She slides off the stool and crosses to her desk, leaving the notebook open on top of her calendar. It is as if they are in a play and she is balancing the stage. Gathering up the mail where he has left it, she sorts the bills and drops another handful of notes in the cardboard box. Watching her, he cannot help but think what a long way she has to go. When he is within touching distance he can smell her hair. There's a place at the base of her neck where her hair parts when she leans forward ...

The dog Beau nudges Ted's hand and whines softly to be let out.

— You know we've really got to talk about your finding an apartment.

— Not now. It's been a long day. I got a call from your brother, Chip. He wants to have a special meeting of the board. Reece is going to set it up.

His words have come out gruff and breathy with ill-contained emotion. He has washed his hands and is fussing with the towel, looking for an excuse to change the subject.

— How are you coming with the acknowledgements? I need to see your list. There are a few I need to write myself.

— When? Next week? Next month?

— Why not tonight?

— Not the list. The apartment.

— You said when things are settled. Nothing is settled yet.

She gets a bottle of pinot noir out of the refrigerator and pours herself a glass without offering him anything.

— How about the first of the year? Or wait! I've got it.

Valentine's Day. Her voice edges into nastiness.

— Well damn it! What do you want me to do? Move out now? Before the holidays? Don't you think that might be a bit awkward for everyone?

— You're stalling, she says, sipping her wine.

— I'm thinking like a Ward. If I ignore this, it will go away.

— It won't work. Not this time.

The rebuke has lost none of its power for the years that have elapsed. Surely she cannot be leaving him now for that one brief indiscretion committed so long ago. Her remark sears through him, alerts him, and rights him. Rational, he thinks. Stay rational.

— You haven't even seen a lawyer yet, have you? Do you know who you want? Reece can't do it, you know. We haven't discussed how this will hit the children and we haven't talked about a settlement. Do you know how much you'll need? Do you want alimony or cash? I'd have to sell some stock, and that's not simple.

— Oh all right. 'Til January then. But that's it.

His logic has thrown her off balance. She finishes the wine, walks into the mud room, and picks the Blazer keys off the board by the door, pulling her denim jacket out of the closet.

— I'm going to a meeting at the hunt club. They're trying to start some kind of new therapeutic riding program here. Oh, I ate already, but there's plenty of food in the fridge.

— You shouldn't drive when you've been drinking. One of these days you're going to get stopped.

— Not likely. This is Leesville, not Parkersburg.

He knows what she is doing. Stabilizing, compensating, pushing through the way she would after a bad jump when she must regain control before the next fence. He has seen her do it a hundred times and admired her for it. It is one of her strengths as a rider, her quick recovery, her coolness.

Stuck with no other company, he lets Beau in, watches as Virginia drives too fast down the drive and pours himself a stiff Scotch. It's almost eight, too late for network news, so he fumbles through a couple of television channels before finding a nature special on the eruption of Mt. St. Helens. The power of it shocks him, rumbling, shaking spitting orange red lava into gigantic black clouds. The camera pans across the desolation, miles and miles of skeletal trees exfoliated, flaming, crashing down on the seared smoking earth, a preview of hell. The comparison is so obvious; Virginia will hold Dolly's death inside her the way she held his infidelity and her disapproval of Volly until it blows like Mt. St. Helens, creating total emotional destruction. He hopes that time and the holidays will summon enough good memories to justify a reversal. The journal could be good therapy. He wants her with him for what lies ahead. He finds some frozen lasagna in the freezer, plops it into the oven and checks his watch. He thinks, now what, notices the red spiral notebook on Virginia's desk. He hesitates a moment then picks it up, feels a little guilty but more defiant. What he finds has nothing to do with a divorce but recounts a rambling story about her father and some chickens that she has never mentioned. How important can it be? He skims to the end.

I didn't understand what had happened that day but it didn't take long to figure out the way things worked. Dolly managed everything including Big Ben. Sam didn't tell me 'til later that he had seen it all along, that Dolly did the same thing with the boys. If we had talked about it, maybe we would have spent more time fighting Dolly instead of fighting with each other, but we were Wards. We went to church on Sunday, we were polite to our elders, and we did our best, because we were Wards and constantly reminded.

Dolly was hard on us but she made obedience and achievement worth our while. She picked out our clothes and our friends and the schools we attended and the sports we played and rewarded us with praise and lots of toys. We had the finest equipment available, went to the best camps. If we wanted to ski, she took us to Vail. When Warren showed an interest in tennis, she sent him to Florida in the middle of the winter to work with a nationally known coach. Nobody could say the deal wasn't a fair trade, but we didn't understand the quid pro quo. What we didn't understand was that the grades and awards and trophies accrued to Dolly as our mother as much as they did to us.

She kept trophy pictures on the piano to remind us. Chip with his swimming medals and Warren with his expensive rackets and Sam in his Scout uniform. I was there too, astride Charlie, my first hunter, a blue ribbon clenched between my teeth. I didn't even win Ted for keeps. She took him too.

He thinks of his own upbringing, how different it was from hers. Anyone knowing them would think she was the one who had everything, but he sees that she was denied what she needed most, attention and affection. She tried so hard. How sad for her to feel so used. He loves her more for what she has accomplished on her own and he wonders why Dolly, as intelligent and generous as she was, was blind to her daughter's need.

Ted helps himself to another glass of Scotch, loses his optimism in a chill of comprehension.

We never understand, do we? Not as children, not as adults. Parents have conflicts and traumas and needs of their own, but we demand that they make the right decisions for us, even in retrospect.

He replaces the notebook on her desk as she left it. Depressed and lonely, he eats his lasagna out of the aluminum tray and tosses it in the garbage bin. No one in charge. So much unfinished business. Obligations left dangling, like the sympathy notes Virginia is ignoring and the one that waits on his desk from Mary Helen.

This is going to be some god-awful holiday season.

12

Thanksgiving weekend, 1988

Two weeks pass with no jarring disturbances. Life at the farm feels almost normal. Sam and Billy join them for Thanksgiving dinner at the country club in spite of Virginia's misgivings. She thinks they are appearing at a social event far too soon after Dolly's death.

— It's not a social event, Ted tells her. — It's dinner and we have to eat up our monthly minimum.

When they enter the club, see the crowd, she reminds him. — Not a social event? Then what would you call this?

Surrounded by people they have known for years, people who welcome them expressing concern and caring, they allow themselves to take the comfort offered but speak sparingly to one another. Billy, staring at his plate, hardly speaks at all.

The following Sunday Ted is reading the *Times* when Virginia comes in trailing the fresh clean scent of a winter day. She is wearing jodhpurs and a marled turtleneck sweater. It echoes the golden shades of her hair. He misses touching her, wants to stroke that golden color the way he used to at night in bed when he cradled her in his arms.

— I found Dolly's diaries, she says.

— Good morning to you too. He smiles, amused at the way she jumps in to the middle of a conversation without warning or preamble. She pours a mug of coffee and sits down opposite him at the breakfast table.

— The diaries, plural? When? he asks.

— Yesterday. While I was in town. I should have asked Sam in the first place.

You look tired.

— Haven't been sleeping well.

He has neither shaved nor dressed. The freshness of her and the unexpected concern make him feel old and sour, but he senses an opening and so he tries to engage her.

— You saw Billy?

— We're doing the right thing, aren't we?

— We're doing what the doctor suggested. It's just 'til he finishes at the academy. Why? Did you notice any change?

— No. I think he's happy. Sam says he is. He seemed so … settled there.

He hears the note of regret in her voice, as if she has failed her son because the home she has made isn't the best place for him. She misses him. What Ted misses is the father-son relationship that might have been.

— He'll be a senior in high school next year. I guess at his age, any place is better than home.

— They've bought more fish tanks, bigger ones this time. Sam says they're going into business together raising tropical fish.

— I told you that a few weeks ago, he says. She sips her coffee.

— Oh? I guess I wasn't listening. She tries another tack to see if he's receptive or snarly. — Has the bank picked an administrator for the trust yet?

— Not as far as I know. When I talked to Reece Friday, he intimated that your brother Chip was staying on the case.

— I've meant to ask you, can Sam afford to keep Montvue? I asked him about paying some sort of room and board for Billy but he brushed me off.

— Don't worry about Sam. Dolly got Chip to set up a stock portfolio for him after the accident. She was right about one thing. Your brother may be a jerk but he's a very good stock broker. Sam tells me his account has been quite productive. Chip got him into some Silicon Valley stocks that look promising. Between that and his mill stock, Sam's fine.

— What about Ward Real Estate? Chip asked about it at the reading of the will, Virginia says. Greedy jerk! He'd love to get his hands on all that land you and Dolly were playing with.

— The real estate business has always been kept exclusively between Dolly and me. Dolly inherited some money from her mother. She told Reece to put what was left of it and the profits from her share into a non-profit foundation after her death. I'll still be running the business. The foundation is another matter. We'll have to find a director eventually and a few more board members. Until then Reece can handle it, or we can turn it over to one of the banks. Reece says Dolly was interested in funding scholarships for business women.

— Huh! Virginia says. — That's a surprise.

Having worked late into the night on his computer searching for answers to the business dilemma he faces, he will renew his search today for information about the possibility of selling the mills as a block. The prospects do not look good but he decides not to tell her for now.

— There's a lot Reece never told us. It must have been hard for him, he's so fond of you. Not being able to tell you about the codicil.

— Lawyer-client privilege. Ted shrugs. — It's a beautiful thing.

— You're not angry about it?

— I was but I've adjusted. Just grateful we've got an ethical lawyer. They don't all come that way, you know.

— Any coffee cake left?

— Toaster oven.

She helps herself and refills her mug.

— What did you find in Dolly's diaries?

— There was one for every year she lived at Montvue. So much. I didn't know where to start, so I didn't look into any of them. Maybe another time. But I picked up a pack of old letters. Decided to take a shot at those first.

Virginia rejoins Ted at the table where he has resumed reading the paper.

— Could you put the paper down?

— What is it?

— I wanted to tell you now, I think it would be good for me to get away for a week or two after Christmas. I don't know where yet or for how long, but I need a change of scenery. I've already lined up an extra girl to exercise the horses.

He is surprised, frowns, questioning silently, but he makes no comment.

— There's something else, she says. That phrase, "there's something else," is a device she uses. It means there's something more important.

— I've decided I'm not going to take the horses on the circuit this summer. I may not show them at all, even at the Leesville Annual. The physical effort … it's too much for me. My arthritis … She leaves the sentence hanging, fingers the copper bracelet on her arm.

Ted looks at her hands, the blue veins rising, the joints, obviously swollen. Her hands have aged. She flexes them, her characteristic gesture, fingers curled into palms, extending and closing, extending and closing. They don't match the rest of her. He wonders why she is thinking so far ahead to the summer when they have yet to get through the holidays with their diminished family and their broken marriage and no Dolly. He's not sure that her planning so far ahead is a good sign.

— You might want to see a rheumatologist. And have you thought any more about seeing Mason again? Maybe we could both …

— No. She cuts him off, picks up the sports page and pretends to read.

He knows better than to push her, so he follows her lead and raises the paper again, shielding himself, turning a page as if he were reading too.

A door had opened. For a moment, he thought the old Ginny was back. This is the first semblance of a decent conversation they have had in a month. Ted is reminded of their arrangement when he visits Montvue and observes Sam's fish tanks, the mollies and the tetras swimming around and around, crossing and recrossing in one another's wake, never touching. He has to try again.

— I'm surprised you didn't get into the diaries. I thought you were so anxious to find them.

— Sam told me they were in her room. He says it's time Annie and I cleared her things out of there before it turns into a shrine. There's some jewelry and the doll collection. What in the world will we do with that? I'm going down this afternoon and make a start.

He is encouraged by her use of the plural pronoun, but the door slams closed with her next sentence.

— I hear there are some new condos going up near the college. You should take a look at them the next time you're in town. You might enjoy being close to John Wesley.

Once again, she has shifted into another subject. He studies her, trying to gauge how else his wife has changed. He can't map it out exactly, but he senses a difference since Dolly's death, as if she's been given permission to be herself. The business with the horses for instance; it's not like her to plan ahead. Without a clue as to how to continue what has begun, he sits across from her, watching her read the Sunday paper in puzzled silence.

Their paths cross again early evening when Virginia comes up from the barn. Ted is leaving for the monthly dinner with the Big Five.

— I may be late, he says.

— If you go by Montvue, see if Annie wants any help with Christmas dinner. Do you think we should do it up here?

— No. It's too hard on Sam in this weather.

— Thanks for reminding me of what a thoughtful sister I am. She's making a bad joke but he takes her literally.

— I can't say anything right, can I? Will you be home tonight?

— Yes. But I'll probably turn in early.

Ted asks himself where else would she be normally except here at home, but he recalls their earlier conversation. Her recent behavior has been more social. Driving into Parkersburg, Ted begins to think for the first time that Virginia may be quite serious about divorcing him. She is obviously considering her alternatives. Perhaps he should consider his as well. Given the surprise codicil and the issues it has raised, he has conveniently compartmentalized, avoiding consideration of what his life might be like six months from now, a year, or two years even. Logically he would turn to family, but Virginia's family has become his family with all the attached quirks and foibles. He wonders how his relationship with Sam might change, what his children will feel, how and where he might live, spend his time. Nothing remotely pleasant occurs to him. He likes his life the way it is, or was.

13

Sunday, December 11, 1988

Dinner for Virginia is a ham sandwich and a glass of wine. She takes a second glass into the library, lights a fire, and tosses her red spiral notebook into the trash basket. The packet of Dolly's letters she drops on the coffee table. She watches the end of the evening news, wavering between eagerness and reluctance where the letters are concerned. She was reared not to read other people's mail, and yet, if Dolly hadn't intended her to find them, why hadn't she gotten rid of them? She checks the postmarks; the one on top is dated April 1959. Holding the packet of letters in her hand, she is struck once again with a sense of her mother's presence. The feel of Dolly's stationery, the musty smell of documents left untouched for years.

Without warning, a moan rises from her gut, flooding her chest and throat, roaring in her ears and bursting from her in the form of huge wracking sobs. Tears pour down her cheeks. She makes strangled gasping noises. She can barely breathe, sobs uncontrollably. She can't see. She can't stop. She gives into this sudden rush of emotion because she can't do otherwise. She feels horribly sad without understanding why. Is she grieving? For her mother? Her marriage? Her youth?

— Ted. She calls his name, hugs herself in an effort to regain control. There is no choice but to let the spell work itself out.

Slowly the worst of it passes. She thinks of Sam, decides to call him just as the phone rings.

— Not much on TV, he says. Thought I'd call and see how you're doing.

— Better now, she says, still breathing erratically, she blows her nose.

— Not so good, huh?

— I don't have any secrets from you, do I?

— It's the twin thing. When was the last time you cried … lessee … when you had to put that big old horse down.

— His name was Frankly Honest. Dumbest name! He was green as grass when I got him, but he was a real sweetheart, eager to please. There was something about him … he knew me from the start. He tried so hard to do what I asked.

— You talkin' about the horse or your husband?

— Too soon, Sam. I can't laugh yet. She is calming down, hiccupping but coherent. — I hate this time of year.

— I thought you came down here yesterday to get Dolly's diaries.

— I told you when I left. You were so absorbed in that stupid football game you didn't even hear me. There were so many of them I didn't know where to start. I ended up with a packet of old letters instead.

— I got Jesse to bring a couple of the diaries down when you were gone. You'll be disappointed. They read like old plantation journals. Dolly recorded everything from the cost of her antiques to notes on the Big Five meetings and the daily change in the price of cotton. We even get an occasional mention if we won something. I forgot we had chicken pox at the same time.

— It was in the middle of the summer and they sprinkled the sheets with ice water to keep us cool so we wouldn't get sweaty and scratch.

— And they kept the room dark.

— And Dolly told me we'd be scarred for life if we touched our faces. She said she'd get Annie to tie our hands down if we even tried.

— Annie put cotton gloves on us both. I felt like a sissy.

— That was when we got the rabbits.

— Bugs and Peter. Granddaddy swore they were both boys but he was so wrong.

She laughs, remembering Dolly's consternation when the first litter arrived. —.And their descendants have lived happily ever after in College Heights.

— Mostly in the backyard right here at Montvue.

— It's yours, Sam, You can say so. Call it 'my house.'

— This place will always be Dolly's, he says. — And Ginny?

— Yes?

— What's so scary about asking for help? Promise you'll think about it, okay?

— I don't need help. I've got you.

— I'm worried about all this stuff that's going on. So much up in the air. I know it's bothering you too. I'm telling you. I had good luck talking to Mason. Just give it a try. Or find somebody else if you don't like him. Please?

— Okay, she says. — I'll think about it. Hey, I love you.

— Likewise. 'Night baby sister.

Five minutes later Virginia is considering her reflection in the powder room mirror. It does not flatter. Her eyes are slits, her nose pulses, swollen and red, and her forehead feels impacted, stuffed as tight as Annie's Thanksgiving turkey.

— We are a family raised on clichés and adages, she says to her mirror image, wringing out a damp wash cloth and quoting from *The Ward Book of Proverbs.*

— Blood is thicker than water. Kiss it and make it well.

She has created a rinse-wring-pat sequence in the hope of ameliorating the pain in her nose and the stinging in her eyes.

— A stitch in time ... Marry in haste ...

The effort falls short for her face, but the rest of her feels much better thanks to Sam.

— Never put off 'til tomorrow ...

Virginia takes two aspirin and looks at her watch. A little after eight. Ted won't be back for another hour or so. Might as well get on with these letters. Probably just something else to throw away.

She puts a small log on the fire, goes to the kitchen for wine and returns to take up the letters Dolly has written to Sissie. She could throw them away unopened or ignore them or toss them in the fire, all options she considers, but she's a Ward. Wards finish what they start.

— Here we go, Beau, she says, reaching down to pat the dog. *Reality as Seen Through the Eyes of Dolly Ward.* Subtitle: *Down the Rabbit Hole.*

April 30, 1959

Dearest Sissie,

The steeplechase is over for another year and what a day it was! Chip's latest girlfriend stood him up and Virginia announced that she's getting married. Can you imagine?! Right in front of the whole family!

There I was with my oldest son moping around like a love-sick calf and my youngest son drinking too much beer and running off to one of those awful port-a-potties all the time and betting on the horses and my daughter issuing ultimatums. She just marched right up to me and said Ted and I are getting married!

Well I nearly had a heart attack. The truth is she's sooo physical, if you know what I mean. She's like Daddy was, so impetuous and careless for the feelings of others. She's one-tracked as a cow going to the barn when she sees something she wants and what she wants right now is this nice young friend of Sam's named Ted Brunson. Not the Charleston Brunsons, this boy is from Fort Hill. His parents are merchants and he has an uncle in real estate who has done very well. I checked them out. He's not one of our kind, but he's very sweet and bright enough according to Sam, and we can use him in the business if Virginia persists in this insanity.

Anyway boys can marry up a lot easier than girls. He's got at least another year to graduate from John Wesley and that counts summer school. Poor thing! Virginia's got him wound up so tight he's about to explode. You know how boys get at this age, caught up between honorable intentions and lust. He adores her and she's teasing him. Sissie, I tell you, it's downright disgraceful to see my daughter behaving like a common hussy. She was all over him right there in broad daylight. I called her over and told her so but she just laughed! I shudder to think what happens between them after dark. Chip says I should send her off to Europe right now for a couple of months but it wouldn't help. She's stubborn and vengeful. No telling what kind of trash she would pick up and drag home just to get even, some phony European count or something like that. Be glad you've got boys, Sissie. A daughter is a constant worry, and I am absolutely sure Virginia is capable of running off with him to Pageland where they wouldn't even need a license and getting married and she might as well tell the world she's pregnant and had to get married. I am trapped! If I get her on birth control pills, it's like giving in to her. The worst of it is Virginia isn't one bit subtle. She as much as told me she'd have him one way or another, threatening to drop out of school before graduation or contrive to get herself thrown out. It wouldn't take much. She's come close enough in the past. I may have to give in but I won't budge on the wedding. We will do the wedding properly at St. Luke's and have the reception outdoors at Montvue. I always imagined Virginia's wedding in the spring when the azaleas bloom, but she won't wait. We'll have to pray for a cool June and forget the azaleas. We could go to either of the clubs, but I think a home reception says so much about the family and I am counting on your being here to help us out. I just don't see how I can put a wedding together in two months, but it looks like I'll have to.

But back to the steeplechase: Chip was sulking because his current flame didn't show up. You know the family by the way. She's Henry Bruce's daughter from Greenwood. He was at Georgia

Tech when we were at Agnes Scott and I swear he was the handsomest man I've ever laid eyes on except for Ben Ward himself. I've known since Christmas that he was chasing her because he bought her a monogrammed silver cigarette case and charged it to me, three hundred dollars' worth. You can believe we had a few words about that little bill! On the other hand, a cigarette case is cheaper than an engagement ring, so I just hope it's really over. I didn't like her anyway. She's too glamorous looking. Women that showy are not trustworthy and my boys seem to go for that type.

By the way, Mother's peonies are in full bloom. I filled the wine cooler with them and used one of the crocheted tablecloths on the folding table over a pink cloth with the silver candlesticks. We won the prize for the most beautiful table setting!

Your Kissin' Cuz, Dolly

— Crap, Dolly. This is a bunch of crap, Virginia says aloud. Beau lifts his head at the sound of her voice. It's all wrong, she thinks. But the part about Chip and Mary Helen Bruce is juicy news. I should tell Ted that Chip got there first. She'd sleep with anybody that would buy her a drink, much less a sterling silver cigarette case. And about that silver cigarette case, that explains a lot. The rest of it? Dolly got that wrong too. If Ted were here … Virginia stares into the fire, remembering.

It was mid-April. A warm sunny day that smelled like hot charcoal briquettes and fresh cut sweet grass. Noisy, bright, like a fair. Six races spread out over a long hilly track. Tough for the horses but exciting. Picnickers dressed to the nines, a hat contest, the Wards out in numbers with guests and peripheral family members amassed as they were every April. John Reece was there paying court to Dolly. I had been drinking mimosas, sitting next to her. When the first race began and the men crowded down to the rail to get a better look, I just blurted it out.

"I'm going to marry Ted Brunson."

"Marry? You'd better stop drinking before you make a complete fool of yourself. And pull your skirt down, I can see halfway up your thigh."

"I mean it, Dolly. Right after I graduate."

"Mean it all you want, but if you persist with this foolishness, you'll embarrass yourself and that nice young man. You're too young, Virginia. You're going to graduate from St. Mary's in June and go to Europe exactly as we planned."

"No, Mother. I'm not. I'm going to marry Ted Brunson and I'm going to do it this summer. Your way or my way."

"That's enough Virginia." It was her mildly exasperated voice, the edge still distant.

"You know the rules at St. Mary's. They won't give me my certificate if I'm married. Or pregnant."

Dolly's head jerked around like a snapped rubber band. "Are you threatening me? A child so spoiled and lazy you've never even washed your own stockings? Marriage is for grown-ups. What kind of a wife do you think you'd make for that young man? And where do you intend to live? In one of those tacky little apartments near the college?"

"We love each other."

Dolly laughed. "You've got a crush on him! He's your brother's friend. He's being nice to you because of us."

Ted walked up with a Bloody Mary in his hand for Dolly. "Mrs. Ward?" he said.

Virginia thought how handsome he looked and how innocent. Full of expectation and good will and honesty and she stood up and said, "I told her."

For a minute — it was quick, just the tiniest moment — the three of us were caught in a magnetic field, enormous charges of emotion and will racing between Dolly and me. Dolly gave a little shiver, like when they say a rabbit ran over your grave, and the question was settled. I had won. But you'd never have known, watching Dolly. She smiled at Ted, relaxing into her gracious public self. She stood and, taking his arm, she said, "Let's get some lunch. Annie made her famous brownies for dessert. We think she puts a little bourbon in them but we've never been able to catch her at it. Sam says she uses Alice B. Toklas's recipe, whoever that is!"

Virginia stands, stretches, says to Beau, — Come on dog. Time to pee.

Beau rises and follows her to the back door. Outside the air is brisk and the sky is clear. She smiles thinking how Ted loves the night sky at the farm, crowded with visible stars, no light pollution. He taught her how to find the constellations. She sees Orion, tries to find Aquarius, shivers, goes back inside.

Big mistake remembering what happened so long ago. Probably not accurate. We are all the heroes of our own stories. Ted would remember better than I do. I didn't understand then. I didn't know about having a daughter. Dolly wasn't giving in to me. I didn't really win anything. She was giving in to me, the way mothers do in decisive moments, weighing immediate versus long term needs and assessing the odds. She was irked because I had pre-empted her, choosing a husband for myself, but she didn't smack me down because she saw what was happening. I watched her thinking. Ted solved two problems for her at once. He was smart enough to help run the mills, at least as smart as her own boys, and brave enough to take on her unruly daughter.

When Ted comes home an hour later, he finds her on the den sofa, her feet curled up under her. He recognizes Dolly's handwriting instantly on the sheets of stationary scattered on the coffee table and feels a twinge of sadness.

— What's all this about, he asks, bending down to pick up a page.

— Wait! she says. — Don't get them out of order. Do you remember that Christmas the year before the wedding?

— I wanted to give you an engagement ring but Sam said Dolly would have killed us both.

— I had bought a beautiful cashmere sweater for you, brown to match your eyes and a Braemer. They were the rage then, imported from Scotland. I bought it when I was home at Thanksgiving and stashed it on my closet shelf. When I got home for Christmas three weeks later, it was gone. I asked Annie and she didn't have a clue. Then at dinner that night, Dolly couldn't wait to nail me. 'Virginia,' she said, 'I've been meaning to ask you what in the world were you thinking about charging a fifty dollar sweater to me? Well of course I found it and returned it the minute I got the bill. You'll just have to find a less expensive gift for your friend, whoever he is.'

— She knew it was for you, Ted. We'd been dating all summer and I wasn't seeing anyone else. Dolly knew how I felt about you and so did Sam. He was so angry he slammed his napkin down on the table and left the room. I sat there and ate and let her simmer. I wasn't about to leave and give her the satisfaction even if I had to sit there all night with Chip and Warren snickering. Know what Sam told me later? Chip had shown him the sterling cigarette case he'd gotten for some girl he was trying to impress. Sam said it must have cost Dolly at least two or three hundred bucks.

— But you did give me a cashmere sweater. It was a V-neck, baby blue, and the first cashmere I ever had.

— I borrowed the money from Sam. He always had cash, probably blackmailing Chip over some trashy girl he was dating. He can be pretty sneaky when he needs to be.

— Are you coming down with something? Your eyes are red. You sound …

— No, no. I'm fine. Just need another glass of wine. How 'bout you?

— Sure, he says. He sits, waiting until she returns from the kitchen, wondering what she has read in this pile of old letters.

— Where did you get these?

— They were in Dolly's room. She wrote them to her cousin Sissie and someone must have returned them after Sissie died. Here, she says.—Start with this one. I was a year late making my debut because I took a fall in October and splintered a bone in my leg. I was still in a cast. She included my individual picture along with the regular family Christmas photo of all of us together. The dress was so big, the hoop, the crinolines. I look like a ship under full sail.

— Great description, he says chuckling.

— Okay, okay. I know how funny I looked.

— You looked gorgeous. And very young.

— This letter, she says. — Dolly sends the picture then she goes on at great length to describe each one of us. This part about Warren's girlfriend, just listen to this: 'Who'd have thought it,' she wrote. 'He's the one with a steady girlfriend. She's nobody he can marry of course. Her daddy works in the #2 Plant, but she's a sweet little thing.'

— Wonder what she thought of me at that point? I didn't have a pedigree either.

— Do you really want to know? Here's one about the '59 steeplechase.

She lets him discover the Chip and Mary Helen connection on his own, but watches his face for a reaction. His expression never changes until he finishes. Then he smiles at her.

— You are one tough cookie, he says. — Standing up to Dolly like that. But it worked, didn't it?

— Sure. For you. I had to get a job while you finished John Wesley. And that apartment! Lord! Not room enough to cuss a cat.

— Aw it wasn't that bad. At least Dolly sent Annie over once a month to clean up and to bring in some real food. Wish she'd taught you to cook before I got you.

— You told me you liked hamburgers.

— You didn't like the job teaching kids to ride?

— It didn't pay very well. She sits down again and sighs.

— A fifty-dollar sweater against a three-hundred-dollar cigarette case. Southern women are such fools for their sons. It's because so many young men died in the War Between the States. We're still not over it, never will be.

— Any more secrets revealed? he says.

— Just that one about Chip getting stood up. I thought you'd be interested.

— About Mary Helen? I was one in a long line, I suspect. You still don't trust me, do you?

She shrugs, sighs, as if to say, you don't understand.

— Strange, looking back through these letters. I had always felt I won you fair and square in a shoot-out with Dolly, but that's not what happened at all. She liked you and she was a little bit in love with you herself.

— C'mon Virginia. That's ridiculous.

— Not the way I was, of course. And maybe not right off the bat. But later. When she had to take over from Uncle Young? There you were, a young Lochinvar who rode out of the east instead of the west. She loved you because you helped her save the company. Face it, Ted, that was Dolly's main interest in life. The charities, the church, her children, we were all secondary to Ward Mills, Inc. If you hadn't proved out, I believe she would have married one of the Big Five to keep the company going and she would have made the poor guy sign a prenuptial agreement to that effect. Ward Mills, Inc., was like a sacred trust to her.

— You're being pretty hard on your mother.

Virginia is pacing, thinking out loud, not editing her thoughts.

— Am I? I don't think so. Look at the way she reacted to our marriage. It was a business deal. A long shot maybe, but you were the only game in town at that point and she had what you wanted, so she negotiated a trade. I was her bargaining chip. Your business brains, your influence on Sam, your obvious work ethic. She got all that and you got me. Short straw.

— I'd have found you sooner or later. If you'd married somebody else, I'd have had to break it up.

— Really? Don't try to charm your way out of this.

— If you believe anything I've said for the past thirty years, then believe what I just said.

— I glanced at the next couple of letters, she says, denying what might have been a tender moment between them. — The next one in line is Dolly's version of the accident.

— I'm not so sure Dolly intended for me to read these letters.

— My mother never left anything to chance, Virginia says. — She knew what she was doing, turning her room over to me.

14

Tuesday, December 20, 1988

Ted wakes to silence. Strange bed, hotel room. Atlanta.

Opening the blackout curtains, he sees the skyline swathed in a heavy drifting fog, not unusual this time of year, but inconvenient. No planes will leave until it lifts. His sinuses are throbbing. When the front pushes through, he is likely to have a migraine. He needs to beat it home.

The trip has not been a success. Too close to Christmas and the year end to expect any serious business deals. He should have known. He met with a potential buyer who offered such a ridiculous price for the three mills in and around Parkersburg that Ted almost laughed in his face. The word is out. Ted wonders who is responsible.

The fog makes him feel invisible. He considers calling Mary Helen, knows she lives in Dunwoody. Divorced, she has taken her maiden name back. Funny, he thinks. That we still use that phrase, maiden name, as if she could reclaim her virginity. He wonders what she looks like now. He could stop by just to say hello. No lust, just curiosity.

Dumb move, Ted.

The heat pump has blown on him all night; could be he's coming down with a cold. He orders breakfast, gulps down aspirin with his coffee, and checks the televised weather forecast. The news is not encouraging so he arranges to rent a car. His brain cleared by caffeine, he thinks he may be able to get back to the farm in four or five hours. If the fog is localized, if he's lucky getting out of town, if there are no pile-ups on I-85. A few extra miles to the Parkersburg airport and he can drop off the rental and pick up his own car.

He cheers up at the prospect of driving home. He dislikes flying and only did it to save a couple of hours. So much for that. Driving gives him a chance to regroup. He doesn't consider the time lost, only reallocated for analysis and evaluation. He appreciates the consistent silence. No phone calls, no interruptions. He welcomes this chance to think through Dolly's letters and her motives for leaving them where Virginia would find them so conveniently. He thinks of Virginia, of the conversation they had earlier. What she wanted, what she needed from Dolly was attention and affection. What she got was discipline and a clear understanding that her brothers came first. Poor Virginia. He cannot imagine why she wants to revisit the accident now, twenty years later. What can be gained by resurrecting a tragedy that scarred them all?

Traffic is not as bad as he expected. Within forty-five minutes he's past the worst of it and heads north toward home. The phrase tumbles into his subconscious. Book title: *North Toward Home.* Author: Willie Morris. He is not the first ambitious Southerner who has found his personal climb exciting but strenuous.

He pulls in at the Lavonia rest stop. Too much coffee. Getting out of the car, he observes a man with a small boy coming out of the rest room. The boy, who is tugging at his reluctant zipper, has a thick shock of dark hair like Billy's.

Passing the Anderson exit, he drives within sight of the motel where he once met Mary Helen, where Warren swears he saw them. He remembers the place and the year. July 1969, Woodstock, Nixon was "Vietnamizing" the war, Neil Armstrong walked on the moon. No matter. To the Wards 1969 was, first and forever, the Year of the Accident.

By 1969 after ten years of marriage he had begun to understand. The Wards and their counterparts among the Big Five maintained their own personal almanacs, unaffected by world and national events unless they raised the price of cotton or lowered tariffs. President Kennedy was shot, then Martin Luther King, then Bobby Kennedy. None of it seemed to touch them.

A minor addendum to the Ward family chronicle might possibly include the onslaught of his mother's dementia and the cancer that lead to his uncle's death two years later, the year his son was born. It might also include a small reference to the fact that in 1969, Ted nearly lost his own life, or at least his soul.

He thinks again of that weekend as he crosses the Lake Hartwell bridge, its flat precast abutments like the one that had saved him. It was the annual convention of the Textile Manufacturers Association in Hilton Head. He remembers drinking too much at a party Dolly threw that first night, recalls flirting with Mary Helen. As usual Virginia wasn't there, busy running a show for the pony club. About ten, feeling slightly ill, he retired. He was up during the night with nausea and vomiting, a flu bug most likely or a touch of food poisoning. Golf course hot dogs. He opted out of the Saturday morning foursome and slept in. Sam got an early tee time and finished nine holes by eleven in spite of a slow drizzle which increased to a full blown rain storm by the time they left. Fortified with a Coke and saltines, Ted had driven the first few hours until they escaped the rain. Sam insisted on stopping in Columbia for Hardees' sausage biscuits. Sam took the wheel and Ted, suffering from the effects of a bad night, dozed in the passenger seat beside him.

He was still sleeping when the car swerved off the road. Ted, buckled loosely into his seat belt, was tossed sideways and felt an enormous jolt as the front grill hit the abutment. His head slammed into the dashboard. His chest strained against the shoulder belt. Sam's new car had a low center of gravity and came equipped with shoulder harnesses. Otherwise he would have been killed or too seriously injured to rescue Sam. Looking back he thinks he must have been crazy. In one twenty-four-hour period he had set himself up for a fling with Mary Helen and lied to the family, to Sam, to the police, and in a strange way to himself.

Snow begins to fall as he nears Leesville. By the time he reaches the driveway at the farm, a fluffy confection covers the property like icing on a cake. The barn roof, pastures, all vanishing under fat white snowflakes, drifting without a sound in a light wind and dissolving under the wheels of his car as he shifts into low. Waiting for the electric garage door to open, he looks through the kitchen window, sees Virginia watching. For him, he hopes. But he suspects otherwise. She will be worrying about the horses and the snow.

— Good trip? She asks as he comes in.

— Not very, he says. He hangs his coat in the closet. He drops his bag at the foot of the stairs.

— There's a fire in the den. I'll get you a drink. And here, she says, handing him another of Dolly's letters. — You should read this before we talk.

— Virginia, I am exhausted and half sick with a cold and this ridiculous hunt of yours for something significant in these old letters is, well, it's futile. There's nothing there. None of this is significant. We've got real problems to attend to. This is a waste of time.

— No more after this one, I promise. I just found it. It's about the accident. I'm going up to take a shower. Please. Just read it.

— Is this never going to end? he says, taking the letter from her.

He gathers a handful of salted peanuts from a dish on the bar and takes his glass into the den. Warmed by the fire and the Scotch and the comfort of his favorite reading chair, he begins.

Dear Sissie,

You were so sweet to send the flowers to Sam. They lasted and lasted. I can't remember if I thanked you when we talked. Sam is coming back to us but so slowly. They tell us he has been in no pain but that's hard to believe. I think they dope him. They talk about therapy but I know in my heart he will never walk again.

When it happened the rest of us were in Leesville where Virginia and Ted bought that farm.

I had flown home from Hilton Head to see Volly's first pony club show, once around the ring on a lead but she loved it! And I was keeping an eye out for Sam's new car, a red convertible. They were due late that afternoon. The show was almost over and I turned to look one more time and that's when I saw the uniform. You know how things stick in your mind's eye? Well I can see that blue shirt as clear as day right now with two creases down the front where the laundry had folded it and those dark glasses like mirrors. Such a polite boy. "Mrs. Ward?" he said, "I'm afraid there's been an accident." Of course they all know us. The boys got enough tickets growing up, especially Sam.

I tell you, Sissie, I was as hollow inside as a brown paper grocery bag. I heard "hospital" and the next thing I knew we were in the car, following the police. Warren had picked me up at the airport. Thank goodness he was there to drive me. When we finally got to the hospital there was no place to park near the emergency room and I told him to just let me out. There I was in my culottes at the emergency room of Parkersburg General Hospital and ambulances roaring in and the girls at the desk couldn't find a single one of the doctors we know. There was something awful in the air. I couldn't get a good breath. I was having an awful premonition like the one I had the day Papa died. I just knew they were both dead and nobody would tell me the truth.

I looked down the hall to the treatment rooms and I saw Ted's back. Warren was right behind me and called Ted's name. When he turned around there was blood all over his shirt front and one side of his face was swollen the size of a pumpkin. I got it into my head that the blood was Sam's blood and for a minute I thought I was going to faint because my brain told me if Ted was alive, then it was Sam that was gone.

Ted looked awful. He said something about how he had done his best and if Sam had only had his seat belt on. Then his knees went out from under him. Warren and I half caught him and we sank down on one of those nasty brown Naugahyde benches. The bandages had stopped the bleeding, but he must have been in terrible pain.

Warren was running around hollering for a doctor and then he came over to us and said he's alive but we can't see him. They've got him in x-ray right now.

I tried to comfort Ted, I really did. I told him I knew he had done the best he could and that's all any of us can do and that's when he started sobbing. I never had seen a man cry like that before. A nurse finally came and collected Ted for some kind of test. That left me and Warren in that dingy waiting room sitting on a plastic bench with that television blaring those grey jerky pictures. Live from the moon it said across the bottom of the screen. There were the astronauts lumbering around like those giant balloons at the Macy's parade.

Virginia returns just as he finishes.

— I don't remember crying, he says.

— You had a concussion. We all cried when we found out how serious it was. Even Warren.

— Where were you?

— Thirty minutes behind Dolly and Warren. I had to close down the show and find somebody to see to the horses and Volly. I was frantic by the time I got there.

— Surely … I can't believe I never talked to you about how it happened. I never told you? I thought I did.

— You told me a little, she says. — And the others told me the rest. The police, the people from the second car that almost hit you when you were pulling Sam off the road. I got all the essentials. When you got better you avoided talking about it.

She leans forward and takes the letter from him, ties it carefully into the packet with the others. His face is drawn, his eyes staring into the distance. She has forced him to relive a terrible experience and she's sorry.

— The farther I got from the accident, the easier it got for me to deal with it. Like a picture in my brain getting smaller and smaller. Finally it all but disappeared. I don't see how resurrecting it now can be of any use.

— It's all right. Like you said, it was twenty years ago. It doesn't matter anymore.

But, she thinks, it does matter, doesn't it? Or you wouldn't be reacting like this now.

By morning, Ted's cold has developed into bronchitis. Trying to lie down makes it worse, so does talking. The intimacy which might have reconnected them in the wake of reading Dolly's letter has blown off like the freak snow storm of the day before. From the window in the breakfast area, they see that the snow is nearly all gone.

— More coffee? She says.

— No, he says. Before he can thank her, he is overcome by a series of hacking coughs.

— Have you heard anything from Reece about the bank trustee?

He thinks she's not really interested; just making conversation.

— Don't badger me, Virginia.

— I'm not badgering you. They sure are taking their own sweet time.

— It's less than a week 'til Christmas and they've got all their year-end reports to organize for existing clients. They won't have time for us until January.

—Well, I just asked. You don't have to sound so patronizing.

Ted's response is interrupted by a series of hacking non-productive coughs.

— Don't you think you should see a doctor?

— Great idea, he says sarcastically. — I should go sit in an office full of people who are sicker than I am and wait for an hour to be told to go home and go to bed?

— He could give you some antibiotics.

— And then I'd get sicker than I already am. You know what they do to my digestive system.

She thinks he is being deliberately secretive about his Atlanta trip. He sees no need to confess to a failure, to follow a dead end. She gives up.

— Go back to bed, she says. He camps out on the den sofa instead.

Ted welcomes periods of sleep whenever the cough allows. He dozes periodically, snoring. Because he sleeps so much during the day, he watches late night television, falls asleep leaving the set on overnight, which annoys her. She rises early to feed and water the horses, waking him not quite intentionally. She has stopped writing in the red spiral notebook. She retrieved it from the trash, but shelved it with the few cookbooks over her desk. Writing seems useless. She is hoarding old grudges.

The tension is draining what energy she has when she has finished her chores at the barn. She has decided that divorce drags on as tediously as marriage. The explanations or lack of same, the dishonesty, the barely veiled hostility. She wants it over and she wants him out, but she keeps hesitating. Before there has always been something to push against, to rebel about.

Now the choice and the consequence are hers alone and she questions her own judgment. Right now he's sick and pitiful. When he was well the protective caring aspects of his nature were easy to accept in spite of his recent abrasiveness, brought on as she knows by the alligator he is wrestling, her family's business. She has committed to the divorce, but finds that getting her way is more complicated than she had imagined. She hasn't pursued the obvious next step, which is seeing a lawyer. She doesn't know why she's wavering, needs to talk through her initial decision and rekindle her dissatisfaction. She has fantasized about what her life would be like without Ted.

And there is the other question about what actually happened the day of the accident. She needs closure. She needs to talk to Sam.

Dolly's letter tells only a part of the story. She's heard Ted's limited version, not much information there. His concussion was an excuse. She thinks Ted was too emotional to talk about it at first and too embarrassed later because he had broken down in front of Dolly at the hospital. She has never asked Sam directly because she can't bear to hurt him.

Tell me, Sam, she thinks, how did it feel? That's what they always ask on TV. How did it feel to get thrown out of the car, to spend those weeks in the hospital completely helpless? What was it like, Sam? Those months in rehab, those leg braces they tried that rubbed your flesh off in bloody hunks you couldn't even feel. What's it like, Sam, to live your life sitting down, never to stand up like a man? Tell me about this accident that changed the handsomest, funniest, most charming boy I have ever known into a pitiful cripple. And tell me, while you're at it, why it hasn't made you cynical and hateful or downright crazy.

She has never asked him because all the implications, all those unasked questions would echo behind her words. But she has read between the lines of Dolly's letter. There is more to the story. Like other family myths, this one has been sanitized and enhanced and totally embraced. There's nobody left to ask but Sam. He always tells her the truth, even when she doesn't want to hear it.

— I'm going into Parkersburg, she says. — I have to talk to Sam.

Forty-five minutes later, Virginia stands behind Sam's wheelchair rubbing his shoulders. Surrounded by green warmth and wavering filtered light in the sunroom at Montvue, the soft bubbling sound of the aquariums soothes her. The room is a grotto, a fitting place for the exchange of long-held secrets.

— Ted knows you're here? Sam says.

— I want your story about the accident. I read Dolly's version in a letter I found upstairs. She wrote Sissie all about it, but it doesn't ... I don't know, it doesn't ring true. It's all about Dolly.

— Not surprising.

Sam lights a cigarette and she notices his hand shaking, sees how slack his muscle tone has become. Paralysis is a misleading definition of Sam's condition; his disability is not static. It works constantly on his body, degenerating his joints and connective tissue, softening him, and turning his body to flab.

— Where to start, he says, sighing. — Lessee. You and Dolly expected us at the pony club show. I didn't care when we got there, but Ted didn't want to disappoint either of you. You know how he is once he makes up his mind. Mary Helen was there at the convention. You knew that.

— She was helping Dolly with the party.

— And helping herself to your husband in your absence, he says.

She crosses her arms, recognizes that she has assumed a defensive posture, and shifts her position.

— We ran into them Friday night at the dinner dance. Ted took her out on the floor a couple of times but I don't think they got it on that night. What's the matter? Sam says. Virginia has made a face and hissing sound, drawing in her breath.

— Makes me sick to think about it.

— Then don't. As to that weekend, I don't know when the affair started. Ted and I have never discussed it. They could have gotten together later that night. I wasn't paying attention. Ted said he turned in early. Said his stomach was upset. He was tucked in and snoring like a hog when I got in about one thirty. Maybe it started that weekend. What difference does it make? For my money it's not like Ted to move that fast. Anyway, it poured overnight and the golf course was a soggy mess. I missed three gimmes in a row on the front nine before the real rain started up again. Ted had the car loaded and was waiting for me. He wouldn't even let me change clothes. I told him he should have flown if he was in such a damn big hurry. We didn't talk much on the way home. He drove as far as Columbia and said he had to stop to get another Coke, his stomach was still bothering him, and I was hungry for a sausage biscuit. I had some Bloody Mary mix and vodka in the trunk, so I stirred up a little hair of the dog to see me home. Ted said he hadn't slept much for throwing up. I never heard him, but I was pretty drunk by the time I got back to the room. I remember he said he didn't like the new seat belts with the shoulder harness. It bothered him because of his upset stomach, so he loosened it. I never even hooked mine up. So, I let the Mustang roll between Columbia and Parkersburg. It was sweet, ya know? He was asleep and I had an excuse to run her without him bugging me about speed limits and cops. Ten thousand miles we must have driven together over the years and he never once failed to warn me about speeding except that one afternoon. We hit the turn off onto 175 ahead of schedule. You know where it happened, about ten miles from Parkersburg where the two-lane goes around that big curve over the river. Must have been the angle of the sun on the windshield. I looked away from the road for a minute and I felt the right front wheel bump off the asphalt. When I tried to pull her back, she jerked out of my hands. We were headed straight over the embankment. I grabbed the wheel and slammed on the brake but she started into a spin. I think I yelled for Ted to get out. I made a diving roll out of the car, like off a horse, you know. You go with the forward motion and fall soft. Or maybe I didn't jump. Maybe the door flew open and I was thrown out. I slammed my head on something, a log that had fallen off somebody's pickup. That's what they told me later. Most of me was still in the highway. I couldn't move.

He has stopped looking at her, focusing instead on a spot between them. His words come out in wheezes, slow, strung out. She hears the shock in his voice, his surprise and disbelief. As if he still can't comprehend. He is no longer talking to her. Only to himself.

— I heard sounds coming together. Tires screaming, the thud. Flat, final. No reverberations. I felt it. Or I thought I did. I tried to get up or roll out of the road but I couldn't lift my head. I didn't hurt anywhere .... just couldn't move. Can't see anything much ... just sky. Crows flying up there... screaming inside but nothing coming out. Nothing but car noises, tires, then the thud and everything stops. No sounds... just time passing and smelling burned rubber and wet grass. I hear steam hissing and I think oh Jesus it's going to blow up and I have a sweet taste in my mouth and know it's blood ... and I'm trying so damn hard to roll over to get away from that car that I know is going to blow ... and I can't ... I can't ... move.

His cigarette has burned out in the ash tray. When he stops talking she finds herself clutching the sofa pillow to her chest.

— Lying there ... tall grass around my head and shoulders ... saw this bug climbing a stalk, weighing it down over me. Like nothing had happened to disturb his day. Here's this enormous black beetle about to drop down my shirt front and I am thinking how can I stop him and then I remember the car is going to explode and it won't matter. My teeth started rattling and I was so goddamn scared and then I heard Ted coming for me, calling my name. Calling me in this croaky voice … I couldn't understand what he was saying. I could hear him but I couldn't understand the words except he was calling my name … Sam, Sam … then he was beside me, hanging over me. He looked awful. He had a big cut on the right side of his head and his eye was swollen shut, turning purple. I could see the blood pumping out of a cut running down the side of his face. He saw I was alive and he started saying the same thing over and over. He was pulling me out of the roadway and saying it over and over. 'I was driving,' he said. He kept saying it. 'I was driving … Sam it's really important … Remember I was driving.'

— I said who cares. Nobody's dead, for God's sake. He grabs me by the shirt front and lifts me off the ground and I try to knock him off but my arms won't work. He is right in my face whispering and his blood is splattering in my eyes and he said, 'Get this straight now you stupid son of a bitch. I was driving. There's another car. We hit another car.' He eased me back down on the ground off the asphalt and when he stood up I could see his pants were torn and his knees were bleeding like he'd come across the road on his hands and knees. Then I heard the others, the people from the other car. I heard more cars stopping and I just closed my eyes and prayed to go to sleep. I knew if I just went to sleep everything would be okay when I woke up. That I'd be able to feel my arms and legs again. But it didn't happen that way. So I just kept asking for them to give me something to make me go back to sleep again.

She reaches for his hand and holds it lightly. He thought she would interrupt, be full of questions, but all he gets is her "I love you" look. It almost chokes him.

— There was an open bottle of vodka in the back seat. The cops would have thrown the book at me. You know the rest of it.

— Please. Ted's not so good with the details.

— Sometime a week or two later when the doctors had figured out I would live, the police came to the hospital. Ted was right there. They told us the people in the other car were shaken up but not seriously hurt and that my insurance would cover everything, but Ted realized I'd lose my license as well as my insurance and the cops would nail me for reckless driving and DUI. If anyone was really hurt in the other car, it could have been much worse. We had sideswiped them when we went into the spin. Turns out it was just a fender bender. I never have figured out how Ted got to me so fast. Thank God it was a back road, took the cops a while to get there and by then Ted had everything under control. You know what's really funny? If the third car had come around the curve a few seconds sooner, the driver would have run over me lying halfway out there in the middle of his lane. He couldn't have helped it. They were the ones who went to the nearest farm and called the EMS. Like Dolly said, I'm one of the lucky ones.

The irony cuts through her.

— For a while I couldn't get any of it straight in my head and then it started coming back in small pieces but nothing connected. Like I'd wake up from a dream hearing my own screams or trying to scream and not being able to. Then I started getting the sounds. The way the tires screeched, and that thud when the car hit the abutment. Like some huge book closing.

For a moment there is no sound but the gurgling of the fish tanks. He focuses on her face, sees the pain there.

— Ginny? Are you okay? It really wasn't as bad as I make it sound. I never felt a thing.

She knows he is lying. She wipes a tear off her cheek, sniffing. Stretches her fingers and balls them into fists.

— I should have been at the hospital more.

— Your husband had a concussion; you had a three-year-old kid and a horse farm to run. Dolly did everything that needed doing and then some. There wasn't room for another Nightingale, believe me.

— I never even said I was sorry. Dolly told us we shouldn't talk to you about it.

— The time I spent in the hospital is mostly gone. Sedation I guess. I don't remember much. And I thought I'd get well. For the longest time, I really thought I'd get over the paralysis. Dolly had me convinced I'd be as good as new. At the rehab place, they gave me a brochure to read while I was waiting to check out. I memorized it. *With early therapeutic intervention, a little determination and courage, and familial support, paraplegics can learn to lead a relatively normal life.* After that I cried a lot. Didn't help much so I quit. Went to see Mason because I was feeling so damn sorry for myself. He put my feet on the right path, so to speak.

— Oh Sam.

He pats her hand. She bends forward, presses her forehead against his hand. Her hair falls into a part and he sees for the first time how much gray grows amid the blonde. He remembers how the top of her head looked when she climbed into the tree house, uninvited and determined. She sits up, looks at him.

— And?

— And the story has a moral, baby sister. I told the cops Ted was driving, just like he told me to. He told them about sun blinding him. The accident didn't cost him anything because he had a clean record and no liquor on his breath. I was out of points and my premium was so high the company had already threatened to cancel. Ted knew that. He covered for me and kept me out of trouble. If somebody in the other car had been seriously hurt I don't know what would have happened.

— If somebody in the other car had been hurt, you'd have told the truth, she says. — You'd tell me, wouldn't you? If you need anything?

— Sure babe, but you don't have to worry. The fish business is working out just fine. She understands. He is talking about Billy.

— I never said thank you for that either.

— You let him come. Hey! Enough of this. You want to fetch me a beer?

She gets a can from a college-sized refrigerator he keeps in the sunroom. She flips it open, starts to hand it to him and instead takes a swig the way she used to when they were kids swiping PBRs from the kitchen under Annie's nose. Finally, he smiles.

— Your turn, he says. You said there was something else?

— I've asked Ted for a divorce. I should have done it years ago, right after his little fling.

— You are way slow gettin' past that. Are you are still hanging it over his head?

— I can't help it.

— Just quit it! None of us is perfect.

— I know. And the truth is I almost left him then, before Billy was born, but Dolly talked me out of it. I didn't come to you because you were just beginning to respond to therapy and you're his best friend. I knew you'd take his side. I was mad with him for a long time when we found out you were … paralyzed … because he was responsible. I had to remind myself that he saved your life.

— And that's it?

— He was more married to Dolly than to me.

Sam reaches across the space between them and takes her hand. She is surprised at how cold it is.

— Ted has done a lot for our family, Ginny. He loves you. He always has.

— Then why did he cheat on me?

— You were obsessing over the horses. You weren't there for him.

— You've done more to raise Volly and Billy than he has.

— Because he thought that was the way you wanted it.

— I can't do it again Sam. I can't sit by the bedside and watch somebody I love die.

— But you can take a thousand-pound horse over a six-foot jump. You don't have to worry about me. I've got a living will. No extreme measures. Is Ted ill?

— No. I mean I don't think so.

— You don't know how to fight, Ginny. You only know how to fight back.

The room is quiet except for the gentle murmur of water running through the filters of the fish tanks. Virginia is looking down at Sam's hand. He turns his palm up and laces their fingers together. She looks up, sees the concern on his face.

— Have you talked to Reece?

— Haven't talked to anybody but you. Ted says he needs some time to straighten out the curve ball Dolly threw us with this trust business. And … there are so many details…

— Take your time. Be real sure. And talk to Reece. You're gonna need a lawyer. You know he can't handle it, right?

— Yes. But Ted says he can recommend someone who will.

— Better yet, talk to Mason.

— You're pushing.

— You need to be pushed.

— I don't know about Mason, she says. — When I went to see him at first it was about Billy, and then he started prying into things that were none of his business. That's why I quit. I've worked through most of it on my own.

— Doesn't sound that way to me. You're still licking your wounds. You don't have to tell him anything you don't want to. For what it's worth, I like the guy. Ginny, I do not want to see you grow old alone. Dolly's gone. You can make the marriage work.

— I'll give it some more thought, she says. She hugs him gently and she's gone.

Slowly, because his muscles have stiffened from sitting in the same position for so long, he wheels himself to his accustomed spot between the window and the television set, pulls the remote out of the side pocket of his chair and hits the power button. A NASCAR race flares onto the screen.

He has not told her what haunts him, the one thing he always thinks about when the accident is mentioned, whenever someone brings it up unintentionally or when he is overcome with discomfort and frustration and depression. The one thing he always remembers is Ted bending over him, lifting him off the ground by his shirt front, telling him what to say, and calling him a stupid son of a bitch.

Somehow during the next five days Virginia can't find the space, a slice of time large enough, to contain the conversation she wants to have with Ted about what she has leaned. The truth about the accident and Ted's role play continually in her brain in the scant time she finds herself alone or without chores. First thing in the morning when she wakes up; last thing at night when she's too tired to do anything but fall into bed, she mulls it over, considering the risk Ted had taken and the cost of living with his decision all these years.

For everyone else, the days are consumed with Christmas. Sam asks that Billy stay with him over the holidays, a request neither Ted nor Virginia can refuse. Christmas at Montvue without Dolly and the usual commotion will be hard for him otherwise; it will be bad enough as it is.

Friends are generous, perhaps because of Dolly's death. Packages arrive, placed in a growing mass at the base of the twelve-foot tree in the entry hall. Then three days before Christmas Eve, Volly comes in. Ted and Virginia pick her up at the airport and meet Sam and Billy at the club for dinner where the halls are literally decked.

— I forget from year to year what a great job they do, Virginia says.

Volly goes straight to the tree in the middle of the ballroom, loves it.

— The decorations are so different from last year. Just look at the size of those glass balls, big as grapefruit! I wonder where they came from. Never seen anything quite like that, not even in California.

It's a standing family joke that everything where Volly lives is bigger and flashier than it is on the East Coast.

— Look Ginny, Sam says, the Macauley girl brought her twins.

— And the Wrights have all six grandchildren. Handsome bunch.

Big Five families smile, acknowledging the Brunsons with interest and some curiosity. Ted notices, amused. He assumes there is speculation about his next move. Volly sees old friends across the room and goes over to speak while Sam wheels to the assigned table docking his chair with some help from Billy, who moves chairs out of the way. Virginia chats briefly with a couple who live near Montvue. They check in on Sam from time to time and she wants to thank them and make sure they keep it up.

The spirit of the season, Ted thinks, observing. It may be temporary but it compensates for the heaviness of the fall. The music, the cold air, the congeniality. So many people at the club they know, children; grandchildren. Everything festive, everyone happy. As if reading his mind, Sam echoes his thoughts.

— We may be fooling ourselves, but this is nice. Really nice.

They gather at the farm on Christmas Eve. Volly has done the gift shopping, says she planned her strategy on the plane.

— Everybody got at least one thing they like. Hurray! I'm a success.

Momma, the tree is beautiful. You're a success too.

Kind words from Volly! Virginia finally relaxes.

— This may actually work out, she says to Ted, who is pulling corks on some Bordeaux to go with the duck. By noon, the Montvue gang, as she calls them, arrives with dinner, most of which Annie has cooked ahead of time. Good wine and open fires warm them. There are the traditional holiday phone calls to and from Atlanta. They have dinner at one, so that Billy and Sam can get to Montvue before dark. Billy is the designated driver, his most cherished Christmas gift the arrival of his learner's permit in the mail. Volly decides to go into town with them, sensitive to the emptiness of Montvue, this first Christmas without Dolly.

— I'll come back day after tomorrow, she says. — I want to catch up with some old academy friends.

— Interesting, Ted says, how Volly keeps up her Parkersburg contacts.

Finally Ted and Virginia are alone at the farm. They clear the table, working smoothly together as they load the dish washer and straighten the kitchen. He has laid a small fire in the den, comes in with a glass of wine for each of them.

— Happy Christmas.

— Your cold is much better, she says.

— Yes. Nice party.

— Before ... she begins, — before Christmas actually, when I talked to Sam, he told me the truth about the accident. I understand the chance you took, what you did. You saved his life and covered for him and took a huge risk. I know you didn't do it for me, you did it for him, but he's my twin. You know better than anyone how close we are. I wanted you to know ... there aren't enough words ... I can't ... She stops.

— Thank you, she says.

Ted cannot remember the last time he has heard this gentleness in her voice.

15

Wednesday, December 28, 1988

Virginia is thinking about sex.

She doesn't mean to. She doesn't want to. She can't explain why. Could be the weather. Palm Beach is experiencing the warmest winter in years. She is staying at the home of a fellow St. Mary's alumna, Jo Anne Hunter, a seasoned veteran in the war between the sexes. On her third marriage, Jo Anne has offered complete privacy but has generously included Virginia in numerous invitations to cocktail parties, dinners, and charity luncheons available in high season. Mostly Virginia declines, but once she has dined with an older, wealthy gentleman from New York who lives next door. Since learning she is a Ward of Ward Mills, Inc., he has become aggressively charming. When she can escape his attentions, when he plays golf or tennis, she spends carefully chosen hours beside the pool, reading, nursing a slow tan, swimming when she gets too hot, and writing in the red spiral notebook, retrieved from the trash can the day after she tossed it. She feels compelled to keep it, as if seeing her thoughts written down makes them truer. But she is still thinking about sex.

Confident at fifty that she has progressed beyond the point where it matters, the opposite seems to be startlingly true. She is awakening orgasmic in the middle of the night.

She reaches down beside the chaise for the tanning lotion, spreads it on her arms and shoulders and across her chest and adjusts the wide-brimmed visor to a more comfortable position. The visor she found in the closet of the guest house. She is reading *Peachtree Road*. She knows all about girls raised in the South and the excuses they make.

Fanning herself, she thinks maybe this is some sort of delayed menopausal reaction. She skipped through "the change" without serious symptoms except for a few hot flashes. Her gynecologist has told her it is because she's in such good shape, for a woman her age. She hates that phrase, "a woman her age." The French have a nicer way of saying the same thing: a woman of a certain age, many of whom, or so she is told, take younger men as lovers. The problem is that she doesn't want a younger lover. Older women with younger lovers have a nervousness about them. Besides, those things never end well. What if all she wants is the tender, careful lover she has had since she was eighteen?

At the doctor's office for her annual check-up she had scanned the categories of the skillfully worded questionnaire: Which term best describes your sexual activity? Frequent, occasional, inactive, satisfactory. Circle One. Ted and I have hit all the categories, she thinks.

The sun is too much for her. The guest house mini fridge in her mini kitchen is stocked with eight-ounce Coca-Colas. She wants one, but it's not quite ten o'clock. Not on her diet and too soon to go inside. She worries that missing the rigors of daily horse training she will gain weight. She turns the chaise so she can see the ocean, waves flaunting pompadours of white foam, young people, all buff and healthy, strolling in the surf or running on the damp sand where the water has cooled it. She closes the book, which has lain open in her lap. Jo Anne joins her, stretching out on an adjacent chaise.

— Cup of coffee? she says.

Virginia shakes her head. — No, but thanks.

— You look like you've got something on your mind. Wanna talk?

— Sure you don't mind?

— Honey! Jo Anne smiles. — Like Miss Dionne Warwick says, that's what friends are for.

— Surprise! It's my marriage.

— Uh-oh.

— I'm afraid so. Until Mary Helen Bruce came along, everything was fine. That bitch. Okay I may have provoked it ignoring Ted, flirting with one of the show managers. It was so unimportant I never told him. A little groping behind the barn and that was it and besides it was the year of the accident. The important thing was that Sam was alive and we had reason to hope that physical therapy would fix the paralysis.

— Sounds like you were having a rough go.

— Actually I was optimistic. Ted had to have some plastic surgery, a couple of procedures on his face. They left him with a faint scar on his cheek — very sexy, but he hated it. Said it reminded him of the accident first thing every morning when he shaved. He spent a lot of time running up and down the road to Parkersburg, running the mill, and trying to keep Sam's spirits up. By then we had settled in at the farm and Volly was showing promise as a rider. At five, Volly was the size of the average seven-year-old and she was fearless.

— Your pride's showing.

— I wanted another child but Ted wasn't himself. I guess it was taking him longer to heal than I realized. He seemed unusually quiet and preoccupied. I was very busy managing my first three-day event, something I had committed to six months before. Lots of paper work and field prep. I worked late and got up early. Ted was at the office all the time because Uncle Young Ward had retired. I was having the covered arena built. We were on such separate tracks. I don't see how anyone could blame me for a little snuggle behind the barn. That's all it was.

— Nobody's blaming you but yourself.

— Actually our sex life was great. No complaints there. Then I got pregnant and he slept with another woman. Boom! And he did it more than once.

— Honey! Jo Anne says, faking outrage. — I would never

have pegged him for the type. She makes a "tch-tch" disapproving sound and frowns.

— Me either. He confessed and broke it off when Warren caught them. You remember Warren. Didn't you go out with him once? When you came to Parkersburg over spring break our first year. We went up to the lake house for a cookout?

— He's the short one, right? I was more interested in the taller one but he didn't know I was alive.

— Of course Ted said he was going to break it off anyway, but I didn't believe him. I think he expected to get away with it. Except for Warren, he might have. And my dear brother! He couldn't wait to tell me. Called me the next day. He said he and Chip had been suspicious ever since that convention in Hilton Head the weekend of the accident.

— When Sam was paralyzed?

— Yes.

Moving her legs off the chaise lounge, Virginia stands, stretches, pulls her bathing suit down in the back and up in the front.

— Why do I keep replaying his infidelity in my head?

— Because it still hurts. Go on. Tell me the rest.

— When I confronted him, he apologized, sort of. He said he was sorry I had to find out that way. Like there's a good way to find out something like that. His confession was so stoic, not mea culpa or please forgive me. Just 'it's over and it wasn't much to begin with.' He made it sound so simple, like something he picked up from my brothers and their buddies. And then he changed tactics and tried to explain and it made me sick to my stomach.

— Umph. Men! They're all alike, Jo Anne says, fingering the large diamond ring on her left hand.

— I kept imagining he was comparing the two of us. She's tall and thin and I'm not. She looks like a model, tons of curly red hair and white, white skin. I was pregnant and you know what that does to your hormones. I couldn't stand the thought of sleeping with him but I hated sleeping without him.

She strolled over to the pool, climbed two steps down the ladder and scooped a handful of water over her shoulders and arms.

— He made it so easy. Never pushed, never questioned. I convinced myself that I didn't need sex, that it was nothing more than a messy inconvenience, that marriage without it would be just fine. She hesitates for a moment.

— Thinking back now, I wondered if Dolly knew, before I told her, I mean. She was being unusually thoughtful and kind, probably because of the pregnancy, but maybe the peace between the two of us that spring meant more than it appeared to. Chip and Callie were talking about getting married, finally. She was planning a trip to Santa Fe for the wedding that summer. It didn't dawn on me 'til later that Warren might have told Dolly too.

— From what you've said about your brother, that makes sense. I thought he was a little creepy.

Virginia climbs out of the pool, shakes off the excess water, and sits on the foot of Jo Anne's chaise.

— It never occurred to me until now, but Dolly could have set up what happened next. Mary Helen's husband got an offer from a company outside of Atlanta, and six months later they were gone. Not that the problem was completely solved. Atlanta's only three and a half hours away. I was pregnant, emotional. I couldn't believe he'd give her up so easily. Ted was the only man except Sam I ever trusted and I couldn't bring myself to trust him again.

Then Ted's mother sold the store and moved to the Methodist Home the same year his uncle left Fort Hill and moved to Charlottesville. Too many abrupt changes for him to accept easily. Poor guy, he seemed so alone and so sad. I reached out to comfort him, put my arms around him, and sensation took over. That's it. That's how Billy was conceived. Afterwards I decided that maybe the affair was my fault, that I hadn't been as attentive to Ted as I should have been. So I lost ten pounds fast, got my hair streaked for the first time. I thought I looked pretty good for a thirty-one-year-old woman with a five-year-old and a new baby. Even Dolly noticed. She said I had it all. A smart girl-child, a horse farm in the country, a husband who loved me, and now, a son. I guess I did, but I couldn't believe her.

Virginia stands, moves to the companion chaise, sinks down onto it and into her own thoughts. They lie quietly for a few minutes, two old friends, middle-aged women, wondering where to go from here. Virginia picks up her story where she left off.

— If I'm honest with myself, I'm bored. Ted works all the time. We haven't taken a decent trip in ages. The children are almost grown. What do we have left?

— You don't think this has anything to do with your mother's death?

— Absolutely not. You have been such a dear listening to all this. Thanks, girlfriend! I'm gonna take a dip in your lovely pool, and then I'm gonna start packing. She swims four laps easily and climbs out of the sparkling blue water.

— There! I'm better. It's time for me to go home and face up to my decision. What I need is a new outlook. A new version of me, some sort of makeover. Think I might have a little work done. Nothing major, just a tuck here and there.

— You've never lived alone, have you?

— No, but I can imagine what it would be like.

— You're not going to like it.

— Can't be any worse than what I've got now. You know what they say. All the disadvantages and none of the advantages.

But what if Sam is right, she thinks. What if all I need is to talk to Mason? What if leaving Ted is nothing more than a reaction to Dolly's death? What if I'm wrong?

Virginia drops her bags at the foot of the stairs and heads directly to the telephone.

— Hey. I'm home.

— Baby sister! How was Florida?

— I stopped by on my way from the airport, but I missed you.

— I went to get a haircut. Billy's out running with Rhett, the kid I hired. I'll get him to call you when he gets back.

— What kid?

— Long story. Want it now?

— No, she says, no time. I'll be down first thing in the morning. How are things going?

— Neat and sweet, sugar pie. Are you feelin' better?

— I guess. Right now I've got a million things to do. I'll see you tomorrow. About ten? Billy will be there, right? I've missed you both.

She is miffed at having to make an appointment to see her own son, hates the delay, but looks around and squares her shoulders. The pile of mail on the kitchen counter is intimidating, the maids have not cleaned the floor around Beau's food mat and the oven is dirty.

Home sweet home.

A cold January wind gusting from the northwest covers the sound of Ted's car approaching, but she hears the automatic garage door grinding open. She has just hung up her coat when he comes into the kitchen, a handful of dry leaves skittering in behind him. Ted bends down and picks them up.

— Hi, she says, as casual as if she has been on a thirty-minute grocery run rather than lolling in Florida for two weeks.

— You look great, he says. His sad eyes tell her all she needs to know.

— What's this about some kid Sam has hired?

— Name's Rhett. He's taking courses at the university extension, training to be a physical therapist. Jesse's showing his age.

Sam needs more help sometimes, getting out to the car, that sort of thing. How was your flight?

— Fine. I went by Montvue on the way home. They're not cleaning those fish tanks often enough. Dolly'd have a fit! The house smells musty, like boys' socks. I'm going to tell Sam to crack down.

— Let Sam handle it and the boy too. He walks behind the counter and drops the leaves into the trash compactor.

— Any news on selling the mills? She says, ignoring his rebuff. — I met a man in Palm Beach who might be interested.

— Reece says the bank has proposed setting up a meeting. We'll know more after we talk to them. In the meanwhile I'm going back to Atlanta tomorrow to meet some people Reece has scared up.

— Are you planning to see Chip and Warren?

— Not if I can help it.

She puts her red notebook in the desk drawer.

— I got a lot of writing done while I was gone. What were you like?

— What do you mean, what was I like? he says, wondering what this question has to do with anything. Walking toward the bar, he asks if she wants a drink.

— Please, she says, — just some wine. When you were a child. What were you like?

— You know all that. I was just a normal kid. I didn't come into my own 'til I got to John Wesley and met Sam. And you.

— I stopped at the Green Mart on the way. Brought you some shrimp. Won't take a minute to whip up some salad and some grits.

— Thanks. I'm getting tired of Mrs. Stouffers.

After dinner, he scrapes the dishes and puts them in the dishwasher.

— I'm going up, he says. — Gotta leave early to make that seven-thirty flight to Atlanta.

— 'Night, she says. She is watching *Wheel of Fortune* to see what Vanna is wearing.

An hour later he is in bed reading the new Michener book, *Alaska*. He likes travel books, has wished they might have taken more trips together but there was always some reason she couldn't make plans — Dolly, the horses, the children. He hears her letting Beau in, decides he's too tired to be polite, and quickly turns off the bedside lamp.

She pushes his door open gently.

— Ted, are you asleep?

— Not quite. He keeps his eyes closed, but hears her coming into the room. She sits on the bench at the foot of the bed.

— So what happens next? What if this deal tomorrow doesn't work any better than the last one?

— There are other possibilities. He hopes she will accept that answer and go away.

— You're still hell bent on selling?

— It's best.

He opens his eyes, pulls the pillow behind his head. No escape.

— Something will open up. All we've lost is the element of surprise. There's been plenty of speculation since Dolly died. A buyer will surface eventually. The company's in good shape. He wishes things were as simple as he makes them sound. He wants to put a deal together before the banker shows up for two reasons. A proposal to buy would validate the soundness of the operation and it would play to diversification.

— I'm afraid of Chip and Warren.

She is standing at the foot of the bed, untying the bow of her blouse. She kicks off her shoes.

— They'll try to run you off before you make your move.

— I don't think so. He doesn't tell her that they can't run

the company without him or that he has a contract. Or that his management has been a major asset. Or that he doesn't understand why, if she is so eager to divorce him, she's undressing in front of him.

— You don't know them like I do. You'd better care. We need some sort of strategy or we're going to lose.

— Let's wait and see how this thing works tomorrow. A thought is drifting in the back of his mind as elusive as lint.

She paces back and forth at the foot of the bed, a pattern for her when she is thinking. He cannot help but notice the way her skirt clings to her hips as she moves.

— We'll have to find a way around them.

She's saying "we." He wants to keep her talking to see if she will keep saying it.

— Has Sam told you his suspicion about the codicil?

— Oh yes. Just like Chip to pull a fast one. Or maybe the baby theory is wrong and he just told Dolly the truth. That you planned to sell the company as soon as possible.

— Dolly knew I wouldn't do that if I thought there was any other way.

— But she was on heavy pain medication by then. Makes you wonder what really happened, doesn't it?

She picks up her purse from where she has dropped it on the bench. A pack of cigarettes and a lighter fall out.

— I thought you'd stopped.

— After we get through this I promise.

There it is again. We.

— I'm sorry. I know you hate my smoking. She puts the cigarettes back into her purse. When she bends forward to collect her shoes, her hair falls forward and he notices how the sun has bleached it. That and the tan. She is a woman of summer.

— I'll go now. She picks up her shoes, stops in the doorway. When she turns the chandelier in the hall highlights her body in profile.

— Could you start the zipper in my blouse? My fingers hurt. From carrying the bag. She balls up her fists and stretches out her fingers with obvious discomfort, comes to sit on the edge of the bed with her back to him. He obliges.

— One more thing.

As she turns to face him, her blouse falls off one shoulder. He shifts *Alaska* to cover his instinctive reaction.

— I thought about Dolly's letters a lot while I was in Florida.

She stands. Pulls one arm out of her blouse and holds it in front of her chest.

— Oh never mind, she says. — You'll laugh at me.

— Have I ever?

— I think Dolly read those letters over before she died and edited them. Threw away some of them and kept others. The sequence is peculiar and there are fragments that don't make any sense.

— You believe she meant for you to find them? Some kind of message in a bottle?

— I don't know, but I'm not done with them yet. Or she's not done with me.

Is that it? he thinks. No "thanks for listening"? Is that all I get out of this? A curt goodnight and a divorce?

16

Monday, February 6, 1989

Virginia is stuck in a motel room in Athens, Georgia. Sandlapper, her youngest horse, has developed a tumor that the local veterinarian is reluctant to treat. He spotted it on one of his regular visits to the farm to check the horses, give them shots or medication if needed. He's new, young; Virginia likes him because he treats the horses as individuals, remembers their names, chats them up before his examination as if they were human.

— I'm sorry Mrs. Brunson. We can excise the tumor here and send it off for analysis, but we don't do a lot of surgery and I'd rather Sandy sees someone with more experience. I've got a friend on the faculty at the university vet school in Athens. You and Sandy would both be better off there. I'll call him and get back to you.

She calls Ted at his office. —I can't waste any time getting Sandy to Athens. I should be home by the end of the week. And have you see the weather reports? You should come home as soon as you can. There's a storm on the way and the weather man says it's going to be a doozy.

She loads up and leaves after lunch, missing his arrival but beating the predicted snow storm by two hours.

Ted is stuck at the farm. Not that he minds. He enjoys the solitude. The freezer is full and so far the electricity has not gone out. With Virginia away, the two horses in the barn are a problem but the handyman has called. He can get the truck halfway up the road, as far as the barn.

— No sir, Mr. Brunson, he says. — I don't muck them stalls.

— Well you'll have to for the next couple of days, Ted says.

— Virginia's girl called. She's got a tree down across her road and she can't get out.

— Extra work means extra pay, Mr. Brunson.

— I understand. Could you pick up a newspaper and a couple of chicken salad sandwiches for me on your way? And don't forget to check the pressure gauge on the water pump while you're here.

The Christmas tree is shedding, browning and forlorn where it stands in the center of the hall, surrounded by sectioned cardboard boxes. They have always disassembled the tree together, but Virginia has ignored it for a month and now she has left, saying only that Ted and the handyman can do it. Ted has managed to accomplish a small part of the job, taking the ceramic cardinals off the tree, his sole responsibility every year because of his red/green color blindness. Virginia has never trusted him with the more complex tasks of sorting and re-boxing the glass balls before.

It's a bad sign, this business of not sharing. Cooperation is a part of all good marriages. Just as he must depend on Virginia to select his neckties, she needs his help with back zippers. He hopes there will be no reason to wear a tie before she returns. More than that, he hopes she will miss him, will reconsider.

Ted suffers from a kind of memory-laden lethargy. He shuffles through Dolly's letters once again, hoping to find a key to Virginia's behavior. He wonders why no one told him about Chip and Mary Helen. It would be so much like Chip or Warren to use the information as one-upmanship, an "I had her first" crack, just to embarrass him. He finds it amusing that the woman who became his mistress had spurned Dolly Ward's adored oldest son. Or perhaps he spurned her and the affair with Ted was nothing more than soap opera revenge. The fact that Virginia has thrown the short-lived fling in his teeth a dozen times means that Sam knows about it. Whatever Virginia knows, Sam knows eventually. Perhaps he will ask Sam the next time he's at Montvue. Just for fun. Oh by the way, Sam … any of the Ward boys ever sleep with Mary Helen Bruce before I got around to it?

Dismissing the idea with a chuckle, he looks around. The house is a mess, dusty, in need of a good vacuuming. The maids can't come to clean. Taking advantage of his isolation, Ted has not shaved for three days. He considers it an accomplishment simply to walk down to the barn every morning to get his paper and pick up the basic groceries the handyman delivers. He is, as Volly would say, someplace else in his head. Slogging back up the hill with Beau wallowing through the drifts beside him, he thinks of the snow storm that kept them in for almost a week one winter when the children were small.

Volly saw it coming and called them away from the Super Bowl to watch. The farm lay in the middle of a localized phenomenon: snow was approaching from the southwest and the northwest simultaneously, swirling through the gap and over the ridges obscuring houses, trees, lights, the mountains themselves until it muffled the farm in a gray twilight silence.

Standing at the glass wall of the kitchen, his arm around his wife, his children beside him, watching outsized flakes, yellow in the flood lights as they drifted soundlessly, Ted had never been more content.

Alone at the farm, he feels that same sense of suspension and safety, as if time has no meaning. He has gained a brief reprieve, a chance to refuel. Virginia calls to ask about the situation. Satisfied that the two horses are being cared for, she elects to wait another day before coming home. Getting the trailer up the hill in snow could be treacherous. As far as he knows, she has not made a move about the divorce. She's all talk and no game.

He doesn't know how to interpret her hesitation, explaining it to himself as part of the getting through the holidays.

— It's never easy, that first Christmas after someone dies, Reece said, calling to check on him. — You want everything to be the same way or totally different and either way is impossible.

Before the storm hit, Ted drove past the condominium complex near the college. Buying a unit there does not seem nearly as irrevocable as what will happen when he tells her he's done it. If he buys a condominium, another step will be taken in a narrowing path that leads to divorce. He doesn't want to be the one to take that step.

Another day, another dollar, he says to himself. But there will be no trip to Parkersburg to the office today. The secondary road to the interstate refreezes at night. He'd need chains to get out, and then he'd need to remove them for the highway. Too much trouble.

With effort he puts on his boots and whistles for Beau, goes out, down to the barn to get his paper. Chilled from his walk and from cleaning Beau's feet when they return, he kicks off his boots in the mud room and pads into the den in his socks. He stretches out on the sofa and tosses the afghan over his legs. A relic from Virginia's brief handicraft period, it consists of an interlocked series of multicolored squares in an openwork pattern. Virginia had made it the first winter they were married. It comforts him, heightens the feeling of her presence in the house. He stretches out on the sofa where they have laughed, cuddled children, made love. Whatever happens he knows he will never escape the need that he has for her. She is his center, his motivation. The physical bond between them remains as undeniable as the snow on the driveway, for him at least. But he wants her to have what she wants, even if that means he must move out.

He falls asleep, waking an hour later, cramped and uncomfortable, to the sound of Reece's voice on the answering machine.

— Ted? Good Morning. Sorry to drag you down from the farm but there's something we need to discuss at your earliest convenience. Please call me when you get this message.

Under the stimulus of bright sunshine, the snow has begun to melt. Icicles drip off the gutters and the sound of moving water is everywhere. Ted makes coffee, feeds the dog, and returns Reece's call as soon as he can focus.

— Shall I meet you at the club for lunch? I can't get into town much before noon. This Christmas tree's a damn fire hazard and Virginia's arranged to have it hauled out this morning, only I haven't gotten the decorations off yet.

— The tree can wait. I've heard from the bank about the children's trust and you and Sam and I need to look at the details before we meet with their appointee. Sam's available after eleven. I've also done some research on the possibility of selling the mills. Why don't you meet us at Montvue? That would save him from coming out in the cold.

Showering and shaving, Ted thinks how glad he is the holidays are over. He was equally glad to see Virginia go. In a nasty argument the day before she left for Palm Beach, she had told him that he was responsible for telling Volly about the divorce and she wanted it done before Volly's imminent return to California. He refused, reminding her that the decision was hers and so were the consequences. He has exhausted his strategies for deception trying to preserve the image of their marriage over the holidays for the children's sake, but in her absence, he has come to terms with her reality. He will see that realtor she has mentioned when he goes into Parkersburg to talk with Reece and Sam.

He is tempted to let the tree go as is, balls, lights, and all, but he sees that doing so would cause another fight for which he has no inclination. Dressed and ready to go, he drops the balls randomly into boxes, pulls the strings of lights off, and leaves them in a tangled heap on the floor.

An hour later as he is dropping his coat on the bench in the front hall at Montvue he calls out to his son, whom he sees watching cartoons in the sunroom. Billy comes to meet him, as usual unresponsive to Ted's hug. He has gained some weight, but his body feels fragile and boney.

— How's the fish business? Ted says.

— Sam says they're not breeding because they aren't used to being here yet. It's hard to keep up with how many of them are in there but you have to, so you know when to add new ones. And there's a formula for the water. It has to be warm but not too warm and the pH balance has to be … Billy looks away, distracted by an explosive sound from the television set.

— I … I haven't quite got it all yet, he says.

— Sounds like you're catching on fast, Ted says, grateful for the obvious enthusiasm, he pats his son on the back.

— I forgot, Billy says. — I was supposed to tell you that Mr. Reece and Sam are in the library.

— It's okay. I was headed that way anyhow.

The room he enters is antithetical to Montvue, strongly angular and masculine in this feminine house. Floor-to-ceiling bookcases line opposing walls. Sparsely furnished, the library is dominated by the portrait of Ben Ward over the mantle and by Dolly's working desk, inherited from Ben's father, the governor. It sits in front of long double windows overlooking the deck and garden.

Since Dolly's death Jesse has rearranged the furnishings to allow space and clearance for the wheelchair that both confines Sam and gives him mobility. He has rolled himself behind the desk into the sunlight. A pair of leather captain's chairs face the desk; two identical love seats flank the fireplace where Reece stands, warming his hands before the fire, shifting his weight from one foot to another as he does when there is a problem to be resolved. Sam smiles at Ted as he comes in.

— Late as usual.

— Couldn't find Virginia's handyman. If he hadn't had the radio turned up so loud, I'd be hunting him still. God-awful stuff he listens to. Racists and evangelicals.

Reece shakes his hand and passes him a file folder from a pile on the desk.

— This is interesting. We've been assigned a young woman as co-trustee. Her name is Gretchen Bennett.

— Sounds like a good Southern name, says Sam. — Where's she from?

— She's originally from New York.

— City or state? Not that one isn't as bad as the other.

— She was born and raised in the city, Reece says. — But her father is from eastern North Carolina.

— So we won't know anybody she's kin to? Sam says.

— Possible but not likely. She's young, but a little older than Volly. Graduated from Duke summa cum laude and has an MBA from the Darden School at the University of Virginia. She's been with the bank two years now. They tell me she's quick and charming.

— You courtin' her, Reece? Sam says.

— I'm just relaying what I've been told, says Reece with a smile. — She was long-listed for the U.S. dressage team. She and Volly may have crossed paths at some regional horse show, or perhaps Virginia knows her name. The bank has prepared an extensive document for our approval, which she is eager to present to us.

— Which you have read already and don't much care for, judging by the tone of your voice, Ted says helping himself to coffee from the carafe Jesse has put out for them. He sits down again across the desk from Sam.

— Does that 'us' include me?

Reece clears his voice in a characteristic manner.

— For as long as you are president of Ward Mills, Inc., and the parent of two of the beneficiaries, and my boss, yes.

— Your Miss Bennett won't object?

— No, Reece says. — If Sam will assure me he won't harass her. She sounds like a very reasonable young woman. Incidentally, she prefers Ms. to Miss.

— I've looked over the paper work and this trust is very precise and fairly typical. That's a good thing. Setting up a trust like this one is nothing new to the bank. When I spoke with her, she mentioned that the presentation she'd like to give us has to do with diversifying the holdings.

— And the will allows for that?

— Perhaps you thought the codicil altered Dolly's earlier intent? It didn't. The will states that the trust is to be managed so it will grow. For the next ten years, the trustees control Dolly's stock. Who knows? The bank may agree with you. Perhaps the trustees will feel that holding a large amount of a single stock in one company is detrimental to the interests of the beneficiaries, well ... you see why the will was worded as it was.

— And you worded it that way? Ted says. — With Dolly's consent?

— The will remains as Dolly wanted it originally. My client was a very sick woman when she created the codicil. She was only interested in making the one change, leaving her personal stock to the trust rather than to you, Ted. My guess is she viewed the trust as a way to buy time. To keep the operation intact until prospects for the industry improved. She left the original language in the body of the document alone. It's a question of ultimate worth, Reece says. Now and in ten years time. We can only guess, but based on the way textile manufacturing stocks have fallen, it is reasonable to assume we've lost twenty-five percent of the company's value since 1975. Reece clears his throat again as if reluctant to continue.

— Hard as I tried to explain, that possibility was beyond Dolly's comprehension. I don't mean to imply any criticism. We all tend to overvalue our own possessions. The fact of the matter is that big banks have been known to let a small trust, anything under five million, languish. Over the years even a sizeable trust can lose value to the point that all it does is pay the management fees. I suggested that we needed a firewall against that possibility, so Dolly agreed to give the majority rule on trust matters to Sam and myself.

Sam and Ted exchange glances, acknowledging that neither one of them has read the will *in toto*, understanding that Reece has deliberately left options open.

— There is one other small point, Reece says. — The bank may suggest that my being your corporate attorney, a trustee, and a stockholder represents a conflict of interest. I may have to retire.

— Terrific, Sam says. — Just what we need right now.

— The trust is not a bad thing, you know. It may simply stretch out the resolution of our problem. That can only work to the advantage of the beneficiaries, provided the trustees act responsibly rebuilding capital. If you held all of Dolly's stock, Ted, the offering price might not be presented fairly and you'd still have to fight off the boys in Atlanta. With the bank involvement, we have a way of securing an invaluable outside assessment of what the company is actually worth and we open a door to all the bank's connections.

— Ward Mills, Inc., is worth what somebody is willing to pay for it, Ted says. — But I suppose we can't decide the issue until we talk with Ms. Bennett.

Reece has been standing before the fireplace but moves forward to take the chair opposite Ted, but addresses his remark to Sam.

— The bottom line is that the trustees have ten years to make this situation work out the way Dolly intended. You two realize better than most there may be no market, even if we decide to sell, but in the foreseeable future, that could change.

— Any more good news? Ted says.

— I'm afraid so, Reece says. — A matter that has come to my attention confidentially. Warren has let it be known that he is quite unhappy with Dolly's will as it excludes him from his mother's estate. I suspect that Chip isn't happy either and is fueling his brother's apprehension.

— They're not crazy enough to try and break the will, are they? Sam says.

— Stranger things have happened. Warren and Chip are mentioned in Dolly's will directly in relation to the ownership of Montvue and as previously gifted recipients of financial help. That could be a saving grace. Once they have time to think about it, I believe they will realize that the trust opens up other possibilities for both of them as well. If Chip and Callie were to have more children or if either couple adopts, the balance of the stock in the trust could shift in their direction. And that's just one of a dozen scenarios for how this situation might play out.

— Reece, Sam says. — When you drew up the codicil, Dolly didn't mention why she wanted the change made?

— She did not. Your mother's mind was quite clear, if that is the unasked part of your question. She knew what she wanted. It was not up to me to challenge her motives or to dissuade her, nor is it my place to explain to either you. Ted, I have made the inquiries you requested regarding a sale of the company. I suggest we discuss that later. Our conversation with Ms. Bennett should take priority.

— How available is she? Sam asks. — Would she come here or do we have to go to her?

— She'll come here, Reece says. — Are we agreed then? Shall I call her for an appointment?

— Here's the phone, Sam says, turning the instrument towards Reece. — Like they say in that new Nike ad: Just do it. How about a drink to celebrate?

— Thanks, Ted, says, — but I've got to go across town and buy a condo.

17

Tuesday, February 7, 1989

Virginia fills the time in Athens with visits to Sandy and chilling walks around the campus. A few students have returned from semester break early, but for the most part the campus, a monument to Southern architectural style of the last century, sleeps under half a foot of snow that has caught the town and the university unprepared. Daytime television bores her and the paperback novel she picks up at a nearby drugstore isn't much better. Accustomed to more activity and more people, she waits for the snow to melt and for Sandy to heal. The doctors have excised the growth as a prophylactic measure and to her relief, it's nothing but a benign fatty tumor. Its location on his neck concerns the vets. There are stitches that need to mend at least partially before the horse can be safely loaded into the van and manage the long ride on the interstate without reopening the incision.

— Can't be too careful, they tell her.

Virginia packed in a hurry and inadequately, thinking she'd be gone three days at the most. When she runs out of clean clothes, she locates the nearest launderette and gathers up her things, turning her jeans and shirts wrong side out and emptying pockets. Tucked into a zippered section of a plaid flannel jacket she rarely wears, she finds an old, crumpled envelope, folded in half.

Hotel stationary? What's this? When was the last time I wore this jacket? Ah! The day I went to Montvue in search of Dolly's diaries.

Turning the envelope over, she recognizes Dolly's hand writing.

Must have discounted this because of the stationary. Postmarked Santa Fe, NM. June 10, 1971, the week of Chip and Callie's wedding. Virginia sits on the unmade bed and begins to read.

Dearest Sissie,

I never thought I'd live long enough to see this day, a child of mine getting married in a hotel bar and on a Sunday no less!!! Callie and Chip say the view is wonderful, but it's going to be like the rest of this place, hot and windy. Six stories up on an open air terrace and I've already got a nosebleed from the dry air and palpitations, as Mother used to say. My heart is pounding when I move around at all. They say the air is so thin because of the altitude that normal people coming from somewhere else can't get enough oxygen. I'm just glad the rest of the family isn't here to see this charade.

I don't like Santa Fe. The trees are runty and they give off a sweet smell and although the town is nice — there's a pretty little square in the middle — the city is surrounded by flat sandy desert where nothing can survive but lizards and prairie dogs so they say. They make a great to-do over hand-woven rugs and weavings of various sizes and the jewelry, mostly silver with turquoise which they put on big heavy belts and necklaces that look like horse collars. The food is certainly different. They serve chili peppers and beans for breakfast and not a sign of grits or one single biscuit.

The sun blazes down and then it either rains or gets cold at night and the opera is outside, can you believe it? Callie says the Santa Fe Opera is world famous, but it's hard to see why, way out here in the middle of nowhere. The building, if you can call it a building, is like a big arena with no roof and the strangest thing, there's no back to the stage. You look straight through at a mountain range. Callie got tickets for two operas and they last three hours each so we'll be midnight getting back to the hotel. She says they can't start until eight because they have to wait until the sun sets, what with that wide open theater. She has a small part in one of the operas, a maid or some kind of servant, but she says the leads are going to be famous someday so we should pay attention.

Virginia skips over the next page, something about two of the singers.

The main reason I'm writing is to tell you about another family mess. Ted showed up at my room yesterday morning and told me Virginia says she's going to divorce him. I asked him why and he hemmed and hawed and finally said he was in trouble because Virginia found out he was having an affair. He said he didn't even try to deny it, because he was about to break it off anyway.

Sissie, I tell you, I was in shock! But when I looked him in the eye I knew it was true. He can't lie to me. Those big brown eyes of his were so sad. He had that same look about him for weeks after the accident, like a lost puppy. You know how a stray will cower around your legs, knowing you might kick it any minute but it's so desperate it takes the chance. That's the way he looked, hopeful and fearful at the same time. I asked him if the woman was somebody at the office but he said no, it was that awful Bruce woman Chip used to date. She lured him into it, I'll bet. I don't know whether I was more mad or disgusted.

How could any man in his right mind be fool enough to let a little amour destroy what he'd spent twelve years building? He must have forgotten, it's not just his marriage, it's his career!! I've got an investment in him. We all do. If he'd just kept his mouth shut, or told Virginia it wasn't so, but, no. He just had to tell her the truth. He said he didn't think she'd make such a big deal out of it, but I understand and I can't blame her for being furious.

Of course he wants me to intercede, so now I've got to convince Virginia not to pursue the divorce because if she does Ted will surely leave the company high and dry. After all the time and energy I have spent bringing him along, I don't have enough energy to start over. Another year or so and he can run the mills with a little help from Reece and eventually from Sam (as soon as he's back on his feet).

There is more, but Virginia has read enough. Sitting in the semi-darkness of her motel room, she folds the pages and slips them into the envelope.

Dolly knew all along and Ted's the one who told her. How to deal with that? Why didn't she tell me the truth? At least Ted was honest. I guess he didn't tell her I thought I was pregnant. That's like him.

Reading Dolly's letter invokes memories and emotions she prefers to ignore but cannot escape. Remembering Santa Fe hurts in part because she found the place so achingly beautiful. The harshness of the landscape, the mystery of the surrounding desert, the Jemez and Sangre de Christo ranges, purple in the sunset, all touched her painfully. Having discovered Ted's affair she wrapped the beauty into her pain, unable to feel anything but anger and disappointment.

"I'm sorry you had to find out this way."

Did he think there was an easier way to find out something so demeaning and humiliating? It was like getting a tooth filled without Novocain. Straining for an apologetic nuance, she forces herself to review what he said and the way he had said it. There was no repentance, no regret. He never offered one of a dozen excuses might have allowed her to forgive him, and so she didn't try.

The trip to Santa Fe had been one long nightmare. Looking toward the mountains she saw the contours of a woman's long slender body, like Mary Helen's. Watching young lovers kissing in the evening shadows of the square, she saw Ted kissing Mary Helen and felt a physical wrench in her gut. At the wedding she thought to herself, how sad. One marriage beginning as another disintegrates.

"I'm sorry you had to find out this way." The words circled in her brain the way an old phonograph needle circles near the center of a record when the song is over. If she hadn't told him about the conversation with Warren, how she had quashed him, maybe she could have found a way to warn Ted off, making a joke about middle aged men and their silly meaningless affairs. She might have said something about how wives are the last to know and that suited her fine, just fine.

Their life together was so good. Past tense. Had been so good. He kept telling her how happy he was with the farm, how much he adored her, how proud he was to have a beautiful daughter like Volly, how he loved his job at the mills. She didn't understand then. She still doesn't understand how he could do it to her, to them.

Seventeen years later, in a motel room in Athens, Virginia puts the pieces together, finally understanding how her own culpability, her misplaced guilt and her over-active imagination had led her to make the most damaging mistake of her life right there in Santa Fe. She had decided to talk to her mother.

"Dolly," she said. "I need to see you. Can you spare me a few minutes?"

"I was just lying down for a little rest, but come on," Dolly said.

Walking down the hall, taking the elevator to the third floor, Virginia tried to focus on what she wanted to say. Dolly had unlocked the door. Virginia knocked and entered, found her mother stretched out on the bed with a damp cloth over her eyes.

"You shouldn't have left the door open," Virginia said.

"I knew you were on the way and I had to lie down," Dolly said. "I've got the most excruciating headache."

"I understand. I've got one too. A big one," Virginia said. "I need your help."

"Well that's a surprise," Dolly said.

"Here's another one for you. Ted's been having an affair."

Dolly sits bolt upright, dropping the cloth to the floor.

"Oh no," she said. "Not Ted."

"Yes Ted," Virginia said. "He admitted it. He says it's over, but I don't believe him."

"Virginia, you poor thing!" Dolly said. "This is not good for any of us. Why did he do it? Have you been fooling around with some of those horse people? Did he catch you carrying on with another man?"

"Dolly! Of course not. Not that I haven't been considering it."

"That's not going to help. I'll talk to him and get this all straightened out."

"What would you say?"

"I don't know. I'll have to think about it."

"Can you keep him busier? At work, I mean. Find some more for him to do? He's spending too much time playing golf and hanging out with that crowd at the country club. And going to all those stupid Big Five meetings. Can't you send somebody else?"

"Are you very upset?" Dolly said." You're not going to do anything rash, are you?"

"I thought about divorcing him, but there's Volly to consider," Virginia said. "And I love him. We've built a life together and I don't want to throw it away. But I can't tolerate cheating."

"I know, I know," Dolly said. "My poor baby." Dolly reached for Virginia's hand. "We can fix this. Don't even think of a divorce. That's not going to do you any good. Let me sleep on it. I'm sure we can come up with a solution."

On the plane flying home, Virginia asked Ted to change seats so she could sit with Dolly.

"But we were going to discuss some business," he said.

"I have some business with her myself," Virginia said.

By the time the plane landed in Atlanta, Dolly had persuaded Virginia to wait a while. A divorce, she said, would destroy not only the Brunson family but it would threaten the Ward family as well. Dolly explained that Ted had become very important to the business.

"We need him at the company right now," she said. "Later, who knows? If I give him more to do, you'll have to live with him, make whatever peace you can between the two of you. This 'thing' has to stop of course. People live together all the time after these things happen, provided it never happens again. Be very clear with him about that. Distract yourself, buy some more horses. I can help more with Volly. I don't see enough of her as it is. Take a trip. Go to Paris. You two don't get away enough. I'll keep an eye on my granddaughter. She can stay with me."

The truth was Virginia didn't know what she wanted. At the time, Dolly's solution seemed logical, even more so after she confirmed her pregnancy.

18

Friday, February 10, 1989

Reece has moved forward, scheduling an appointment with his new fellow trustee, Gretchen Bennett. Ted meets them at Montvue. They are standing in the front hall, opposite Dolly's portrait. Ted has arrived just as the hall clock strikes ten. When the reverberations subside, Reece introduces them.

— Ms. Bennett, Ted says, shaking her hand. — I've been looking forward to meeting you.

He sizes her up quickly. Tall, about Volly's height. Not pretty in the ordinary sense, but open faced and attractive with even features and a sprinkling of freckles.

— I'm glad you were able to be here today, Gretchen says to Ted.

— I appreciate the inclusion. Proper, he thinks. Business-like.

She brushes a wave of shiny dark hair away from her face, hooking it behind her ear.

— Your son has been showing me the fish, she says. — He seems to know so much about them.

— He does indeed.

— When he learned I work at the bank he asked if I'd like to see his ledger. It's fairly complex and quite detailed. Your brother-in-law says Billy manages that end of the business himself.

— He's always had a knack for math, Ted says. — His socks may not match, but he can reel off the first hundred numbers of Pi for you in a minute.

Reece stands to one side listening. Gretchen turns to face him. — I appreciate your patience, too, Mr. Reece. It took our textile people a while to assemble the information we need.

— Actually we had not expected this project to have a speedy resolution. Sam's in the library. Shall we join him?

One sofa has been pushed back against the bookcase and two chairs have been drawn up at a right angle. Sam has rolled in near the fireplace.

— Don't even think about making a move on this pretty young thing, he says. — I saw her first.

—Sam, Reece cautions, — Ms. Bennett might not appreciate your particular kind of compliment.

— Pay no attention to him, Ted says to Gretchen. — Wards always expect to be at the front of the line.

She takes no apparent offence and sits on the sofa opening a large attaché case that she has placed at her feet.

— If you're ready, I have to give you the background spiel first, she says, pulling weighty professional looking notebooks out of the case. — I understand that the three of you know all this, but you asked for the bank's point of view. It's part of my job to explain the situation as we see it so you'll know we've done our homework. We may have developed a somewhat different view from yours.

She hands each of them a notebook, slick cover, full color, pages of graphs, charts, and statistics.

— For future reference, she says, — or you can follow along. The charts back up the analysis. She takes a deep breath and begins speaking without notes while Sam, Reece, and Ted give the packets a quick look.

— Ten years ago, the industry was prospering. Overall textile manufacturers had close to a twenty-percent sales increase in 1977. Management viewed the infiltration of labor unions as a constant threat and did everything in their power to subvert organization except to attend to the obvious, pay scales and working conditions. Workers were not faring well by any measure. Pollution and noise levels inside the mills were terrible and pay was low, roughly four dollars an hour. Gretchen pauses for a moment.

— If I'm stepping on toes here or if you have any evidence to the contrary with what I'm saying, please let me know, okay?

— Go ahead, Reece says. — So far your assessment is quite accurate.

— Thank you, Gretchen says. — Going forward then …

She flips open the report and continues, again without notes.

— In 1981 the Supreme Court upheld the government's requirement for cotton dust standards. The necessary adaptation of the mill buildings and the addition of newer, quieter machinery proved costly in several ways. Owner investment in new machinery and automation resulted in cleaner operations but also in significant layoffs. That's the point at which you consolidated your operations, closing the outlying plants in Union, Gaffney, and Pacolet and building your #3 plant here in Parkersburg.

— Imports nearly tripled during the early eighties and, as you know, the Congress has not been responsive to your plight. Your Big Five, as you call them, have fought creatively with their advertising campaign but more and more business keeps leaving the continental United States. To make matters worse, you overestimated the ability of your lobbyists to get the tariff bill through Congress. As if the industry weren't already hit hard enough, mergers and corporate raiders have trimmed the ranks of independently-owned manufacturing units by half.

— Finally, she says smiling, — we get to the point. This is where we find your industry in 1989, depleted and endangered. Smaller family-owned operations like yours still have options, but they are shrinking fast.

— Our responsibility as one of the trustees is to work with the company to establish viable strategies for the beneficiaries in compliance with Mrs. Ward's will. We can use the bank's resources to help you implement those strategies. It would help if we knew what long-term plans your board has in mind. What is it they anticipate? What do they expect?

— Sam has the answer, Reece says.

— The three of us represent the family and the company, Sam says. — My two older brothers are minority stock holders because my sister and I vote our stock with management. That would be Ted here, Mr. Brunson, whom my mother named as president of the company shortly before her death. That's a clear indication of who she trusted. I don't know exactly how much stock Reece has but I'm reasonably sure he is with us. As to my older brothers, they may be greedy and mean, but they aren't stupid. Well, one of them isn't anyway.

Gretchen lowers her head trying to conceal an amused smile.

— We find it curious that your brothers haven't approached you about a possible buyout.

Reece looks from Ted to Sam, turns to Gretchen.

— It was virtually impossible to convince Mrs. Ward of the impending crisis in the industry, he says. — Traditionally we had done things a certain way. Dolly expected those rules would always apply. I suspect Chip and Warren shared her refusal to face reality. Then once the family was apprised of her diagnosis, any sort of disruption would have been out of the question. With Chip and Warren, one never knows quite what to expect, but if I were to hazard a guess I would say they do not want the mills for themselves, they just don't want anyone else to have them. They understand the picture could change if Virginia should decide to vote her stock with theirs. Still, with the trust holding Dolly's stock, I think we can maintain control, but we haven't gotten a clear count since the sixties, although we believe we have approximately two hundred shares outstanding. We plan to announce a stock holders meeting shortly.

— About Virginia's stock? Sam says. — Not to worry. She would never vote with Chip and Warren. She can't stand either one of 'em.

— As we see it, there are four reasonable choices, among them creating a holding company, a long complicated process. Your family dynamic in this case does not seem to lend itself to that option, but it would be possible to bring in outside management and allow the family to act as overseers.

— Equally unattractive from our standpoint, option two would be to sell off the entire company now to the highest bidder with no guarantees as to keeping the business open. You could pay out the employees as far as the money goes, and board up the mills. Sam has told me that he and Virginia have discussed the ramifications this would have on the people who work for you, some of whom are second or third generation Ward employees.

Gretchen turns again to Ted.

— Your wife and brother-in-law feel that although this plan would leave the family relatively unscathed because of other investments you hold, it is a betrayal of those people who have made Ward Mills the company it is today.

— Virginia feels very strongly on that point, Ted says. — However, I don't believe your analysis about selling is accurate. Quite the contrary, I see it as a viable alternative.

— I understand, Gretchen says. — But our figures argue to the contrary. We can go over them in depth with our textile experts later if you'd like.

— Thank you. I'd appreciate that.

— A third option would be to put you in touch with a mergers and acquisitions firm who can come in and strip down your operation and probably make a little money. In any event, we as trustees have ten years. We can be pretty aggressive, for a conservative old-fashioned bank.

Sam begins to cough.

— Can we take a break? he says. — I need to get my inhaler.

— May I get it for you? Ted says.

Sam shakes his head. Wheezing, he wheels out of the room.

— If you'll excuse me, Reece says. — I'm going to the kitchen for something to drink. May I bring you anything, Ms. Bennett? A Coke or tea?

— A glass of water, please, she says. — And please, call me Gretchen. She stands, walks behind the desk to the window.

— This place, she says. — It's so beautiful.

— Yes it is. Reece tells me you grew up in the city? Ted says.

— I was very lucky. My father worked for one of the big three accounting firms. His Southern charm worked so well with his first major account, they let him stay until he'd been through all the firms they serviced in the metropolitan area. It was quite a list. They had that four-year rule then, if you remember.

— Probably not a bad idea even now, Ted says. — Four years with any single client is long enough. I understand you ride. Volly, my daughter, does too. Or she did before she got bitten by the art bug. She's in California getting a masters in art history.

Gretchen flips her hair behind her ear in an unconscious gesture.

— I look forward to meeting her. We seem to have a lot in common. I love contemporary art too. I used to spend every Sunday I could at MOMA when I couldn't get out to Connecticut to my horse.

— We'll see what we can arrange this summer. She'll be home in June when she finishes her class work. I think she plans to write her thesis here.

Reece comes in followed by Annie with a tray containing an ice bucket and four glasses, which she puts on the desk. Reece pours a glass for Gretchen and one for himself. Sam returns, visibly more comfortable. Ted leans against the desk, perching on the front edge. Reece stands before the fireplace. Gretchen takes a seat and begins again.

— There is a fourth alternative, she says, one which we favor. Your industry, or parts of it, will survive but the organizations and products will look entirely different. The big companies will go international — some have already begun — the smart smaller ones will specialize. If Ward Mills, Inc., can find a comfortable niche, then it can not only survive but prosper. This is obviously in the best interests of the trust beneficiaries. We have some specialists at the bank who can make suggestions. For instance, we worked with a small manufacturing company in Alabama that produces exclusive jeans for selected designers and retailers and we helped another find a market for rubber-backed automotive floor rugs. But if the trustees and the stock holders, both in and outside the family, agree, we're still only halfway there. The decisive factor will be leadership. Who will be in charge?

Gretchen turns to Ted who stands, moving away from the desk, as if separating himself from the possibility.

— It's obvious that you are the logical choice, but I understand your reluctance to continue as president because you have expressed a decisive interest in selling. My guess is that you have not even considered going forward because of the risk factor and because you know your two brothers-in-law will object to whatever you do. You're playing it safe because of the trust. With you out of the picture, you think they may be more, how should I say this, malleable? The three men chuckle.

— That's unlikely under any circumstance, Sam says.

— How unfortunate, Gretchen says. — Their cooperation would make things much easier. Oh well … she sighs, shrugs.

— Granted this approach isn't foolproof, but it has advantages for you and your children in the long run. And I'm convinced it's doable, that is if Mr. Reece and Sam and I can talk you into giving it a shot.

— You've discussed this with them? Ted says.

— Only superficially. My colleagues and I would have been remiss in suggesting our plan if it were unrealistic.

Ted walks to the chair opposite Gretchen and sits down.

— I'll admit I'm surprised, he says looking at Reece and Sam, acknowledging their involvement. — And I'm flattered. But the situation with Chip and Warren. He frowns. — They would expect some part of the action, some role. That's not unreasonable.

— After reviewing their business experiences, Gretchen says, I don't see how the bank could honestly support any managerial role for either of them. They've been away from the business too long. They are both heavily involved in their own careers. For either of them to assume additional responsibility just isn't practical. They'd be a thorn in your side, but no solution to your present situation is without drawbacks.

— I need to think about this for a few days. To discuss it with my wife. And I'd like to talk further with your people about alternatives I may have overlooked.

— Of course, she says, getting out her day planner. — I can set that up for you right now if you'd like. I'll also need an accurate count on shares, so I'm glad to hear about the proposed stock holders meeting and suggest you get on it ASAP. Gretchen stands, gathers her materials, and shakes hands with Sam and Reece.

— I know you want to work on him, she says. — I'll be on my way.

After Gretchen leaves, Sam suggests a martini on the deck before lunch. Sounds good to Ted. The day is warm and sunny; an unexpected thaw has brought temperatures into the low seventies just three days after the blizzard.

— This can't last long, Sam says, wheeling himself out. — Holler for Jesse, will you? He's all set up and waiting. Tell him Mr. Reece will accept his favorite aperitif, the French vermouth.

— Always the considerate host, Reece says, bowing courteously. — What do you think of our Ms. Bennett?

— She's not one of Sam's beauty queen types, Ted says, — but she has a confidence about her that gives her credibility and she's obviously done an excellent job putting this report together.

— I like her, Sam says. — She knows her stuff. And I like the way she talks. Slow for a Yankee. Like she's put the brakes on for us poor Southern slobs who can't listen as fast as we ought to.

— I don't see that as patronizing, Reece says. — It's more practiced civility. She attended Southern schools for seven years.

— Duke's not Southern, not anymore. Good thing we like her, Sam says. — We're stuck with her.

— If you have reservations, I could ask the bank to …

— No, no. I can see her working well with Volly at some point. If she's still around in ten years.

— The time will pass much more quickly than you expect, says Reece.

— About Virginia, Ted says. — Are you sure?

— Once Reece explains it to her, Sam says. — It's a business decision, best for her and the children. Whether she divorces you or not. And besides, even if she voted with them they'd still have the trust to contend with. And you, brother? You will give Ms. Bennett's suggestion serious consideration?

Ted shakes his head and chuckles.

— Damn it, Sam. How did I get myself into this briar patch? I thought I was marrying one Ward and here I've ended up with all the rest of you crazies for two generations, going on three.

— Don't give me that crap, Sam says. — You've loved every minute of it. Shuffling that real estate around, fighting off Chip and Warren. It keeps you young. You're nowhere near ready to quit and I for one believe you are most unlikely to bail on us now. Swear to God, I never knew why my sister took to you like she did, but she must have seen some brains behind those big brown eyes.

— Boys, boys, Reece says. — Stop playing. Think it out. Just be sure you include Virginia. And it might not be a bad idea to update Volly too. She will be the first grandchild to inherit her shares of the trust outright. It makes sense to keep her in the loop, even if the resolution is ten years away. Or I can talk with her as well as with Virginia, if you'd prefer. He stands, on his way.

— Haven't seen enough of you at the office lately, Ted. His tone implies a mild reprimand. — Things can get sloppy when the boss isn't around. We may need to make a few personnel adjustments. Nothing major, but we skipped our usual year-end reviews. Time to take a look at pay scales and promotions.

Leaving his Vermouth glass on the table beside Sam, he walks into the house, through the sunroom. Pausing in the front hall, he turns, looks up at Dolly's portrait. The hint of a smile crosses his lips.

19

Monday, March 13, 1989

Mason's office doesn't have a waiting room. He shares a small building downtown with an architect and a lawyer. The modest foyer holds two straight chairs, a small table with a day-old newspaper, and a plastic plant that needs dusting. Virginia presses the buzzer beside his name to announce her arrival. Opening the door of his office, he offers his hand to her.

— It's good to see you, he says, smiling, underlining "good" by inflection.

Virginia remembers the room, bland as a sandbox. Dr. Mason himself is just the opposite. He radiates good will, one of Virginia's initial objections when she met him.

"Shrinks are supposed to be neutral," she told Ted. "Mason is too enthusiastic."

"You're holding it against him because he's pleasant?" Ted said.

Ten years ago she did, but not anymore. She's here to talk about Billy. She doesn't want to make up her mind yet about being a client herself, not just yet. This visit is more like an interview or a test drive. For reasons she doesn't fully understand, Virginia is cautious where Mason is concerned.

— So much has happened since I was here last, she says, noticing that in this place the opposite is true. Nothing has changed. The walls are still a nondescript light green, randomly covered with diplomas and citations. Shutters at the single window modulate the cheery spring sunlight, but Virginia imagines how sterile the room must look in winter, devoid as it is of decorative devices or personal references.

— Yes, Mason says. — Time has a way of re-ordering our priorities.

Squeezing his chubbiness past a large over-crowded bookcase, he sits down behind his desk, bare except for a single file folder. — How can I help?

Virginia wonders why bald men think wearing beards compensates and why a psychologist of Mason's reputation would see clients wearing a plaid open-necked shirt and no tie, displaying a sprout of chest hair. He seems calmer than before, a shallow wash of gray at his temples, a gathering of wrinkles around his eyes.

— I don't quite know where to begin, she says. Her voice sounds unfamiliar to her, muted and hesitant.

— You're here to update Billy's situation?

Virginia nods, forces a small smile, which he returns before opening the file folder.

— Billy was originally diagnosed as developmentally delayed. I saw him originally when he was six. He's … what … eighteen now? Virginia nods.

—He's had special schooling?

— Some extra tutoring in a few courses, that's all. He graduates from the academy this year, or … maybe the year after.

— Good! Good for him. Now, tell me about him.

— He's a whiz at some things, like math for example. He can solve equations in his head that Ted says he can't figure out with paper and pencil. But then he's slow with others, like jokes and ordinary conversation. We have to keep reminding him to look people in the eye when he's talking to them. He's tried to pass the test a couple of times, but he still doesn't have a driver's license. He gets so nervous …

— That's not unusual for any teenager. In the meanwhile, he's had no remediation for his condition? No medication?

— My mother … we didn't think it was necessary. Billy leads a sheltered life. He seems comfortable with what we have provided for him. I don't think anyone would describe him as handicapped. Virginia takes a quick breath, experiences the familiar defensive discomfort.

— It makes you uncomfortable to talk about it?

— No, no. That won't help Billy. He's quite a swimmer now, on the school team. But out of the water, he's awkward physically. He fell and broke an arm last fall. He's still recuperating, but he's much better. And he seems stronger lately and a little more self-aware. He's working out and running. He and my brother Sam are in business together breeding and selling tropical fish.

— So, you've noticed some changes?

— I thought it was wishful thinking.

— Perhaps not. I've recently read about some interesting research done by a psychiatrist in Germany. It hasn't made the *Diagnostic and Statistical Manual* yet, but I think it will soon. Forgive me, I should explain. The *DSM* is our professional guide book. It documents a series of symptoms that, when grouped together, form an identifiable syndrome. This new one is called Asperger's Syndrome. You know your son better than anyone else. Let me review the symptoms with you and we'll see if any of them might apply to Billy.

Mason picks a magazine from the shelf behind his desk, opening it to a page marked with a scrap of paper. — 'Asperger's is characterized by abnormalities of communication and interaction; by a lack of social and emotional reciprocity; by restricted and repetitive interests and behavior.' Does that sound like Billy?

— In general, I guess. Is that it?

Mason refers again to the article in his hand, glancing up to catch Virginia's reaction to each symptom as he mentions it. — 'Some children have a heightened sensitivity to sound or light or both. Some have highly developed musical or mathematical skills.' You mentioned that Billy is good with math. Basically Asperger's is a high-functioning form of autism.

— I saw *Rainman*, she says. — Billy isn't like that.

— That's a movie, Mrs. Brunson. Hollywood is known to distort facts for dramatic effect. Real-life situations are more variable, each patient different. The new theory allows for a more exact range of behavior and symptoms, but nothing is all black or white, especially in my field. Unless we update Billy's capacities, we can't be sure of anything, but your sense of his development is encouraging. Asperger's children tend to improve as they mature and as they are made aware of their own particular circumstances.

— But there's no cure?

— It's more a matter of degree, Mason says. — Therapy helps. With awareness on the part of the patient, some of the behavioral patterns can be changed. We can do the additional testing if you'd like, but I'd want to review this information with your husband first.

— Yes, of course, Virginia says. — And my brother Sam should be a part of any conversation we have about Billy. Our son lives with him. It's more convenient for us and for him if he sleeps in Parkersburg. Early swim practice, late swim practice, homework, you know how it is.

— And when did you lose your mother? Mason asks, his voice softer.

— Five months ago. In October.

— A heavy loss for your family and the community. If I remember correctly your family, you and your brothers, are very close?

— Not so much. Except for Sam and me.

— Asperger's can be very difficult to live with. If that is Billy's problem, it has been hard for you and your husband and your daughter. She's an adult now, isn't she?

— Raising children, even so called normal ones, isn't easy.

— We could talk more about that later if you like, Mason says. — I don't mean to cut the session short, but I can use the time to set up the testing.

— Yes, she says without hesitation. — Please do.

— Has Billy been treated by medical doctors exclusively? Has he seen a psychiatrist or a psychiatric social worker to your knowledge?

— No, I don't think so. I can ask his school counselor.

— You'd know. The school would have needed your permission. I must warn you that there is some controversy about this diagnosis. You won't find much information about it in standard sources, but I still have my notes on Billy's original testing when he was younger. It can't hurt to take another look. If he's willing.

— If Sam says it's okay it will be fine with Billy.

— Good! My assistant will call you and your husband to set up a convenient time.

— If she could call Sam first. As you know he's a paraplegic and his schedule is complicated.

— Of course, Mason says. — Very thoughtful. We'll make it as soon as possible. He stands, but hesitates.

— If I might, you seem to be a woman who is trying very hard, Mrs. Brunson. I sense a lot of anxiety. I can prescribe something if you'd like.

— No, she says. —Not just yet, thank you. But I would like to see you again. Sam's been badgering me. He knows me very well and he thinks talking with you would be good for me.

— And what do you think?

— There are things I need to face, to work out. Talking to an impartial person might help.

— By all means then. Just call my assistant and tell her when you're free.

Virginia gets to her feet, reaches across the desk to shake Mason's hand. He holds her there for a moment, looking at her closely.

— Losing one's mother can be a traumatic experience. Don't underestimate the effects for you as well as for the rest of your family. How do the kids say it? He smiles. — Can you cut yourself a little slack?

Virginia drives straight to Montvue to tell Sam what Mason has said. To her disappointment once again, Billy and Rhett are out running. She invites herself to lunch in the hope of seeing them when they return. She and Sam are in the dining room enjoying Annie's homemade vegetable soup when the phone rings and Jesse comes in.

— It's Mr. Brunson, he says, speaking to Sam.

— Have you talked to Ted about this?

— Haven't had the chance.

— If he asks, are you here?

— Sure.

Sam rolls across the hall to the library. She can hear his voice but cannot distinguish words. She looks at him expectantly as he wheels himself back into the dining room.

— Ted says Volly's coming home for spring break. He wants me to take her down to the beach with Billy and Rhett. He says it will be good for her to see how the three of us operate. That's typical. He's planning ahead.

— For what?

— The inevitable. Billy's likely to outlive all of us and somebody's going to have to be in charge.

— Don't be so gloomy, she says. — I'm not invited to the beach?

— He said he thought you were probably too busy. He's not going to stay, just coming down for the weekend. He told me he hasn't moved yet. What's the hang-up with his condo?

— The bathroom tiles. He asked me to help him select colors. Don't look at me like that. He had to ask somebody, and then we got into trims and moldings. The tiles are imports. They should be in next week.

— So whose condo is it anyway?

— I promised to help with the basics to get him off the dime. He'd stay at the farm forever if I didn't. It's not a big deal. After thirty years I know what he likes better than he does.

— You don't have to apologize for helping your husband. Maybe Volly can take over the decorating for you when she gets here.

— Fine with me, she says, ignoring the humor. — I just want him out of the house. He looks so needy. Makes me feel guilty.

— Have you two talked about Ms. Bennett's suggestions for Ward Mills, Inc.?

— A little. He gave me a notebook to read. Too fat.

— Do it, baby sister. Make the time. We need her on our side and we need to tell her you are too. She's the one controlling Dolly's stock and she's got a big old bank behind her protecting that trust. We need you both on our side. You understand?

— You mean my stock. Why am I the problem? What do we need stock for anyway?

— You could ask Reece, but I see the stock as a way to keep us interested, pay us for being cooperative, and pay the boys not working for Ward Mills, Inc. In a closely held company like ours, its how the income is paid out and how the value is transferred from one generation to the next. I haven't been full time since the accident. Ted lets me keep an office but I'm just taking up space over there and we both know it. Ted's secretary is setting up a stock holders meeting to locate some missing certificates. You realize, don't you, you could change the whole equation by voting with the boys?

— Hmmm, Virginia smiles. — So Ted's talked to you about the divorce? He thinks I'm mad enough to join forces with those two? I guess that's why he's being so nice about moving out.

— Like I told him, Sam says, — I don't think you could ever get that mad. Sam rolls closer and takes Virginia's hand in his.

— Sweetheart, he says. — This game you're playing with Ted. Stop it. It's childish.

As if on cue, Billy and Rhett thunder into the front hall.

— Perfect timing, Virginia says. — Hello there!

Looking around the room, talking immediately, Billy is in constant motion.

— We did seven miles around the Heights, he says. We try to do that much every time. It's good for your heart rate. I'm checking my pulse. It's good.

— I'll take a nice sweaty kiss, Virginia says, and then you two could both use a shower.

— Sorry about that, Rhett says. — Nice to see you again, Mrs. Brunson. He trots upstairs behind Billy.

— He seems presentable enough. Is he living here too?

— Not yet.

Virginia pushes her chair away from the table.

— I've got to go. Mason's assistant should contact you shortly. I told her to call you first. And I promise I'll talk to Ted tonight about the trust and your new girlfriend.

— Don't I wish.

Virginia gathers her jacket and purse from the front hall bench, comes back into the dining room.

— He knew I was coming into town today. He didn't even ask if I was here?

Ted beats her home. She has bought steaks to grill, potatoes to bake. She plans to make a salad. It has been a while since they sat down together over a meal.

With daylight savings time approaching, Virginia is spending every possible minute with her horses. She anticipates working them twice a day once the weather warms up. She usually leaves meals for Ted in the refrigerator, but she has promised Sam. Over several glasses of wine, Ted takes her through the information from Gretchen Bennett, trying not to influence her decision, trusting her to see what's best.

— Did Sam tell you where he and Reece come down on this? Reece said he'd talk to you but I thought I could explain it a little more simply.

— It's pretty obvious they want you to stick around. Sam

said we need to resolve it but we're stuck until the stock holders meeting.

— What do you want out of this?

— What's best for the children. And I want you to be satisfied too. You've put your best years into this company.

— Thanks. I guess I'm not quite over the hill yet.

— Of course you're not.

— I told Sam and Reece I'd have an answer the first of the week.

— And you're agreeing to see Mason? About retesting Billy?

— Good idea, he says, — but I do think Sam should be in on any decision.

— Without question.

When he goes out to retrieve the steaks, the sun has fallen beyond the mountains and the sky is streaked with orange, turning to red, to blue, to purple.

— Look at that sunset. It reminds me of the burning of Atlanta in *Gone with the Wind.*

— Like you actually see the colors?

— Well, he says, — I can see them changing. When did we see that movie? Did you read the book? I never did. Must have been in the fifties. Strange what you remember. There were grown men sitting in that theater actually crying.

— You know what they say, the South will rise again. What's going on with Volly? I was with Sam when you called.

He shakes his head.

— You catch me off guard when you jump like that. He takes a sip of wine and reorients. — All she said on the phone was that we have a few things to talk about. All talk and no action; the Brunson coat of arms.

— You sound irked.

— She's got some big decisions ahead of her and I'm not sure Parkersburg is the best place to make them. And you might be a little irked yourself if you were getting kicked out of your house.

Ted holds out his hands in a supplicating gesture. — Hasn't this been pleasant? Can't we go on the way we are?

— Don't start. It's settled. You'll be moved by the time she gets home.

— Possibly. But what if I'm not? You can't expect Volly to stay here.

— She'll stay right here in her own room. When's her break?

— Next week. She hasn't made any reservations yet. She called to see if it was okay for her to come.

— And I suppose I'm to blame for that too? she says.

— It's nobody's fault, but if we're going at it tooth and nail the whole time she's here … He shrugs, leaving the thought dangling.

— Ted, please. Whatever it is we can't deal with it 'til she gets here.

A week later, Ted goes to the airport to pick up his daughter. Her plane is late. Due at four, it is rescheduled to land a little after five, the peak of rush hour. For a regional airport the crowd is unusual, especially around the gate where Volly's plane is expected. Some of the boarding passengers have looked at him as if he were familiar. Perhaps they have seen his picture in the local papers or perhaps they like his tie, a gift from Volly. He knows he looks substantial, like someone who might be important, a senator perhaps. He doesn't think often about the way he looks but people have noticed him more in recent years. Volly says it's his hair, sprinkled with gray, thick as ever. He still misses his crew cut, but agreed to Virginia's suggestion that this longer style is more appropriate for a man in his position. Volly says he has grown more handsome as he has aged.

Someone bumps him from behind and he turns to scowl, as two young men push past him. The shorter one nudges the taller one, tilting his head in the direction of the deplaning area.

Ted follows the look and sees a statuesque young woman in a white suit stepping through the arched doorway of the plane. She wears a straw fedora, its brim falling forward over dark glasses. She has great legs.

For a second, he is one with the two younger men beside him admiring her. She lifts her chin, knowing she is observed and comfortable with the admiration. Without conscious thought, Ted pulls his shoulders back and straightens the jacket of his suit.

When she reaches the foot of the steps, she lifts her hat off and shakes her hair out, catching the waves in place by pushing the dark glasses onto the top of her head. The hair, its buoyancy and color, tugs at something inside him, evaporating in a surge of recognition. She sees him, smiles, waves, hurries past the two young men, not noticing as they turn to watch her.

She grabs his arms, hugs him, and kisses him on the cheek.

— Dad! I am so glad to see you.

— You look wonderful, he says. — I had forgotten how much you look like your mother.

— We're not fighting, Virginia says. — The marriage just isn't working anymore.

Volly sits opposite her mother at the breakfast table. She has taken the news of the divorce without comment. She has talked with Sam who has warned her of the friction between her parents.

— He thinks we should try to fix it, but I don't. I expected you to take his side.

— It's none of my business, but you've been together a long time. Isn't this sort of a radical step for people your age? Volly sees she has amused and perhaps offended her mother.

— Sorry, she says. — I guess it doesn't matter now.

— You mean it will when I'm older? Virginia says. — I'll be fine. I've never had a chance to live alone. I think I may like it.

— Sam and the boys should be here by now, Volly says. — It's been a long time since I've spent any time with Billy. I'm looking forward to this trip, and to the beach. She has decided to ride with them rather than taking a separate car. She lifts a wedge of Sara Lee almond-filled coffee cake out of the aluminum tray and puts it on her plate.

— Looks like you'll have nice weather, Virginia says. — I understand your father is coming down for the weekend?

— Don't worry. I'm not about to get in the middle of this. Think I've got time for another cup of coffee. She helps herself and sits down. Of course she is concerned, but mostly for Ted. But she's been away for the last six years and has deliberately separated from her mother emotionally. She is used to a dictatorial, impulsive parent and reacts like a daughter would who has suffered emotional abuse. The calmer she remains, the less likely she is to set Virginia off. Volly is as cautious around Virginia as one would be around a yappy little dog.

Virginia tries to find common ground, anything to reestablish their relationship.

— Speaking of time, Virginia says, — could you take some time while you're home to go through some of your old clothes? I'm getting a load together for Goodwill. Virginia laughs.

— What's so funny about Goodwill?

— I sound like your grandmother.

Virginia is trying to find some way to connect, some common interest.

— She made us switch out our seasonal clothes twice a year. First, we had to try on everything and see what would carry over. Then she and Annie hauled one bunch up to the attic and hauled the next season's bunch down. The first time your father came to visit, to actually stay at Montvue, Dolly was up in the attic and just happened to look out the window when he was leaving. She saw me kiss him goodbye. I got a good lecture after he left.

— Why?

— We were standing in front of the house, out in the circular drive beside his car. It was an old green Chevy Bel Air his uncle had given him when he graduated from high school. Dolly thought it looked so tacky, she made him park it around by the kitchen, but she let him drive around front to load his clothes and golf clubs.

— You were in your own driveway?

— But clearly visible from the street. And I was the one who initiated the kissing. Dolly didn't approve of public affection.

— Doesn't it bother you? To talk about it?

— About Dolly? No. Not really.

— No. I mean about when you were young and you and Dad were courting. I guess it was so long ago.

— Ouch! I thought … Look. I know you're here to talk to your father, but I'm still your mother, you know, and I care very much about what you do with your life. I'm seeing Dr. Mason. He's helping me get past some things I've ... The important thing is that I love you and I hope you'll give me another chance.

Volly looks at her mother, trying to decide how to handle this new approach afraid to take her mother's attitude seriously and afraid not to.

— Thanks, but … What can I say? Dad is my go-to parent. Maybe if we had talked more or sooner, who knows? But we didn't. Ah! Here they are. What you're saying … I'll think about it, okay?

Virginia decides to interpret the remark as a typical noncommittal California-style answer, goes out, and waves to the boys, vaguely remembering another of Dolly's aphorisms, something about the sins of the fathers.

20

Monday, April 3, 1989

— When you were little, Ted says, — your hair was so curly. You looked like the angel in Grunewald's *Annunciation.* They are walking on the beach where the retreating tide has left the sand packed and cool. A warm breeze from the south, blows Volly's long blonde hair out behind her.

— Been reading Janson's *History of Art*? she says.

— No, Ted says, but I've been reading Robert Hughes in *Time* magazine. Interesting writer. A couple of times I went to New York so I could see what he was writing about.

— And this all started when?

— About the time you switched your major. No need having children unless they're smarter than you are so you can learn from them.

— You might learn more than you want to know.

He lets the remark pass, resolved not ask too many questions. She has initiated this visit and she will tell him what she needs to, when she needs to. Like her mother, so much like her mother.

They pass a young couple going in the opposite direction. Holding hands, bumping hips from time to time, they smile over the small intimacy, the sensation of touching. Their connection is evident. Ted wants that for himself again and eventually for his daughter; this sharing of self with another person.

— I figured I'd get this master's degree and find myself a nice curatorial job in a museum somewhere and I'd be launched. She bends down to pick up a hinged coquina.

Ted, who is being very careful not to push her, doesn't respond.

— Art's not about art anymore. It's about money. I could probably get myself hired at an auction house by dropping the Ward name, but that would only be the beginning. They'd expect me to bring in clients from down here, family and friends with money to spend. I'd be an art pimp.

— A rude awakening, as your grandmother would say.

They walk on another ten paces in silence. The tide inches in, the water edging forward, fringed with the smallest hem of foam, almost soundless.

— The water's so gentle here, Volly says. — So different from the Pacific.

Ted hears a wistfulness in her voice, wonders what emotional tides have driven her home.

Ted and Volly splash gently through shallow tidal pools to the sound of gulls and the faint whistle of the wind stirring the sand.

— So what do you want to do now? he says. — Teach? Open your own gallery? Make art?

— Probably one of the above. Teaching might be fun, but you don't just walk into a college-level job and that's what I'd want. Maybe I'm just worn down right now by the phoniness.

— I know you're disappointed.

— Mostly in myself, she says. — I've been so naïve. I didn't realize how political the art world is. The pros have their own language, artspeak, and it's nothing but pseudo-intellectual bullshit.

— Whoa! he says, not ready to hear her use this language. He's a little embarrassed at his reaction.

— I'm ready to go back, he says, covering. — The wind … I'm getting sand in my eyes. As they turn, Volly combs her hair back with her fingers and ties her scarf on at the nape of her neck.

— I've been doing some research on West Coast collectors for the thesis. By the time the museums out there were big enough and rich enough, most of the best stuff was locked up in East Coast vaults. Some of the collectors specialized in obscurities, you know, like ancient Mayan pottery, which they could go dig up for themselves, or oriental kimonos straight from the Japanese black market. There's a taint to a lot of it, beside the fact that some people got into the art market either as an investment or so they could hobnob with the upper crust. There are a lot of hustlers, and it's not just the California types. Some of the collectors know little or nothing about art. They make a killing in some nefarious deal or even if it's legit they need to reinvest so the government won't get it. So they hire somebody from a museum to shop for them and make a modest donation with the promise of more and *Voila!* as Dolly would say, instant social status.

— Doesn't sound very healthy. Maybe you're well out of it.

— I hate to see what I love being used.

They walk on until they reach the steps in front of the beach house.

— Billy seems better, she says.

— Yes. Sam says the fish business is coming along nicely. Your brother will be undergoing some tests next week. We're hopeful that Dr. Mason's new diagnosis is on the money. Your mother filled you in?

She nods.

— And she told you about the divorce?

— Yes. I'm sorry.

— Me too.

— She wanted to talk more yesterday. She told me she's seeing Dr. Mason? Is that because of the divorce?

— I don't know. I think she's trying to recover from Dolly's death. They had some unresolved problems.

— I can understand why.

— Don't let it happen between the two of you.

— I don't think you should expect me to fix this.

— I don't. But maybe with time ... Promise me you won't give up on her.

— Okay. The word comes out heavy with breath, like a sigh. Volly looks out to sea, touches her cheek. She flashes back nearly seven years to the Leesville Horse Show, remembering Virginia's awful hateful reprimand. Pulling her off Ginger, slapping her in front of her friends, snatching the reins and leading her horse away, never to be seen again. "If you can't ride her right you can't ride her at all," Virginia said.

Volly puts her hand to her cheek, feeling the sting of that slap, the humiliation. She thought the worse of it was losing her Ginger, the horse bought just for her, never ridden by anyone else. But the worst part is now, realizing that her father never knew the real reason she stopped riding and showing.

They turn away from the water and wade through dry warm sand between the dunes. A narrow boardwalk leads to a shower where they rinse off their bare feet and collect their shoes.

— So, I guess I've failed to find a real career but I'm going to finish what I started, the thesis, I mean, and I've learned so much I can't begrudge the time spent.

Ted chuckles, gives her shoulders a hug.

— You're all Ward, sweetheart. Wards bow to no man. He looks up while she rinses the sand off her feet, sees Sam and the boys lounging on the deck like a family of lizards. He wants one more moment of her time and attention.

— Where do you go from here? he says.

— I'll keep you posted.

— Have you thought about coming home?

— I don't see many options for me in Parkersburg, do you? And the farm, well that's out of the question. You know what? I should have gotten an MBA instead of this useless art history degree. Then I could take over Ward Mills, Inc., like Dolly did when Uncle Young retired.

— Wouldn't put it past you even without the MBA. For a woman as beautiful and smart as you are anything is possible. He is a fool for his daughter and he knows it. He puts his arm around her shoulder again and kisses her temple.

Sam has sent Billy and Rhett shopping earlier. A cooler full of beer lies within reach and a plate of boiled shrimp with cocktail sauce rests on the table under a net cover.

— Good Lord, Sam, you are turning these boys into a couple of sun dogs, Volly says. — And this is your idea of dinner? Hasn't Annie taught you lazy things how to cook yet?

— Hush that fresh talk. Those two will never starve. They both know how to open a can of Vienna sausage.

— No way! Rhett says, speaking directly to Volly. — Why cook if we can eat green? Isn't that what you do in California? Yogurt and nuts and berries? By the time you come home this summer, we'll be rolling in fresh tomatoes and lettuce and beans and okra. Jesse's helping us make a garden.

Ted notices Rhett flirting with Volly, or trying to. I could tell him a thing or two about Ward women, he thinks.

— These two have turned into health food nuts, Sam explains. — No meat. Lotsa whole wheat and vegetables.

— Better put in an extra row or two for the rabbits, Ted says, looking at Sam.

— Family joke? Volly says.

— Got a bag full of 'em. Now git, Sam says, shooing the boys off the deck. — Have another run on the beach before the sun sets. Then you can go down to the pavilion and chase girls. Volly, stay here and talk to me. I've got a tale to tell on your momma since she's not here to defend herself. It's about her lemonade wagon.

Volly pulls one of the folding chairs near Sam while Ted goes inside to shower and find some real food. Time for wine and cheese and crackers.

— I think it was June or July. Sometime in the summer anyway 'cause the chinaberry trees were messing up the new sidewalk in front of Montvue. We hadn't been there long. When Granddaddy died Dolly rented the house on West Avenue and finally moved Miss Ida into a nursing home. Ginny and I must have been ten. That would have made Warren twelve or thirteen. Old enough to know better than to mess with your momma. But he's always been a little, how can I put it, a little thick when it comes to understanding women.

— That summer your momma made herself a traveling lemonade stand. She put an orange crate on the Radio Flyer wagon and somehow maneuvered one of Dolly's umbrellas to shade an ice bucket and pitcher. I thought it was ingenious. Ginny swiped the old jelly glasses from the kitchen and asked Annie for some lemonade to sell in the neighborhood. Annie was glad to help. She'd do anything to get Ginny out from under her feet. Every morning about ten-thirty or eleven when it was beginning to get hot, Ginny'd go down the street peddling her wares. The glasses knocked together and made music like the sound of the ice cream truck, so people knew she was coming. Most of the kids and all of the ladies out pruning their hedges or collecting their roses were willing to pay a nickel or two for a nice ice-cold glass of lemonade from such a polite little girl.

— Business was going pretty well until the day Warren decided to cut himself in. He jumped out from behind Dolly's japonicas and acted real sweet, telling Ginny he'd help her get the cart out across the street into College Avenue where she'd have more customers. He asked her how much she made in a day and she told him two dollars, which was both a lie and a mistake.

— 'Well I think I'll buy you out,' he said and threw a couple of old washers on the ground in front of her. She was too far from home to holler for Annie and Warren knew it. He grabbed the steering handle on the wagon but she wouldn't let go, so he pushed her in the chest and she fell backwards into a privet hedge and got all scratched up. Your momma didn't waste any time getting back to Montvue. She was one mad little girl.

Annie tried to clean her up, but she wouldn't have it. She wanted to stay all bloody and mussed 'til Dolly came home. And that was her second mistake.

— Before Dolly could get out of the car, Ginny was out front crying and yelling. Dolly told her to stop right that minute and asked what was wrong. Your momma told her, but good. 'That bastard Warren stole my lemonade cart,' she said, 'and I want it back right now!'

— Dolly was stunned. 'Where did you hear that word?' she said. 'Don't you dare ever use that word again. Out here in the front yard having a temper tantrum! Serves you right, young lady. A Ward going door to door like the Fuller Brush man.' Well, that set your momma off something fierce. She stomped her foot and yelled right in Dolly's face. "It's mine! It's mine! I made it!"

— Dolly told her she was about to get a whipping and that was the final straw. Ginny ran up the front porch steps and stood on the top one and screamed as loud as she could. All that accomplished was to get her sent upstairs to her room for the rest of the day. The next morning the boys and I were eating breakfast in the kitchen when we heard this ungodly noise. Of course we ran outside to see what was going on. It was your momma taking an ax to her lemonade stand. Warren started hollering, 'Stop! Stop!' He tried to take the ax away from her, but she choked up on the grip, swinging it around with both hands like she meant business. She told him if he came one step closer she'd chop his head off and I don't doubt she would have. He backed off and she hacked the lemonade stand to smithereens.

— Warren's face got all red like he was going to cry but instead he got real quiet and said he'd get her for it. She said, 'Nah, you won't. You don't have the guts to fight fair or the brain to fight crooked.' Chip grabbed the ax away from her. 'That's enough he said. 'You need to clean up this mess before Mother sees it.'

— The point is these are the genes you've got, Miss Virginia Dorothea. You're a Ward and Wards hold grudges and get even. Your momma's doing it now with your daddy. She's punishing him for something that happened twenty years ago. Dolly kept her reined in then, but she flipped when Dolly died, just had to express her independence. It's a losing battle, honey. I hope she'll see it in time. In the meanwhile, it's best if we stay out of the way.

— Amen, Volly says.

Virginia is out riding or at a meeting or doing whatever she must to stay clear of the farm this morning. Volly is gathering some of her old clothes for Goodwill and Ted is packing. His condominium is ready. He is moving out, and in, today. He'll miss Beau and their morning outings, although this spring their runs have become shorter and less rigorous.

He knows he can't take everything, has no room for all the accumulated material in his office. Virginia says he can send someone from Ward Mills later for the rest. He's leaving some of his things scattered around on purpose so she won't forget him, he hopes. To his dismay, his clothes and a few boxes of books and files have filled his car and the farm truck. Volly has offered to drive one vehicle and to help unload. Afterwards they go together to stock the refrigerator, pick up the few things Virginia has not thought of — candles, for instance, in case of a power outage. The transfer is accomplished so quickly they are both surprised to find themselves finished by early afternoon.

— We didn't need Rhett and Billy after all, Volly says, looking around his living room. She is unpacking a box of books, arranging them on one of two built-in bookcases.

— Dad! You brought the dancin' man! I'd forgotten all about him. And here's Dolly's birthday picture. Boy, do I look cocky!

— You were, he says.

She places the dancin' man on a low shelf and takes the picture across the room to an end table.

— I like this place. It's quiet. It suits you. Nice prints. You want to keep them out of direct sunlight. Want some help hanging them?

— From an expert? Ted says. — You betcha.

He locates the box he has packed with simple household tools, a small hammer, a couple of screw drivers, wire, and picture hangers. When they are done, they stand back together admiring.

— The artist teaches across the street at John Wesley, Ted says. — They say he's the best abstractionist in the South.

— He can hold his own anywhere, she says. — Good wall color for art. This shade, merlot, it's masculine. A corner room like this with so much light can take it. I like the new carpet smell, Volly says, sniffing. — Clean. You don't have to live with anybody else's footprints.

He understands. She is trying to make it easier for him.

— Who's your decorator?

— Your mother. I like the green chairs. They look good against those big trees across the street. By the way, have you noticed your mother is having trouble with her arthritis? All the years of working horses have caught up with her, and not being able to go at it full tilt is depressing her. Go easy on her while you're here.

— Sure Dad, she says, shaking her head, smiling, touched at his generosity of spirit. — You're a good man, Charlie Brown. Are we done here?

— Looks like it. Thanks.

— You need some time to just hang out. I'm going to Montvue and help the boys open the pool. Rhett says he thinks water therapy would be helpful for Sam. Of course we'll have to tell him we're doing it for Billy. Like he won't catch on. She gives him a hug and a kiss and starts out the door, then returns.

— I meant to tell you at the beach. When I graduated, when Dolly sent me that check, she wrote me a note, more like a letter. That generation, those women, they took the time to actually write down their thoughts. We're missing something important not doing the same thing.

— Do you keep a diary?

— Nothing interesting to put in it.

— I'll bet, Ted says.

— Anyway, in her letter Dolly told me she was proud of me for graduating from Duke and she said she hoped I'd find a nice young man to marry. Isn't that just like Dolly? She said that I shouldn't worry about my future, because I had spunk.

— High praise from Dolly, Ted says. — And you do have spunk. You'll figure out what you want to do.

— Gotta run, she says, kissing his cheek again and charging out, still full of energy, making him feel old.

He turns on the new television set, but discovers the cable has yet to be connected and the reception is limited to one local channel. He stretches out on the sofa, finds it agreeable, but he isn't tired despite the efforts of the morning, so he decides to go for a walk. The campus of John Wesley College beckons across the street.

He likes the leanness of the new fine arts building, the large expanse of glass on the front, and the new science building named for a classmate who has conquered Wall Street. The college has grown but maintains a suburban pastoral atmosphere. Large trees planted decades ago have matured, creating a shady arboretum on the old campus. He is comforted that it is so little changed and he grows nostalgic, remembering his college career, meeting Sam and Virginia, his first visit to Montvue, his wonderment at the Ward's lifestyle. Just as Dolly had written Sissie, he was not one of their kind, but he learned fast. The more he learned the more he realized he brought them what they needed, raw energy, determination, and a gut instinct that he trusted above everything. He still does.

Walking across the campus he feels a surge of gratitude for this place where he gained so much. He thought at the time that he could integrate easily into the Parkersburg crowd, and he did, but he wearied of their continuous entertainments, the tennis tournaments, the hunting trips, the stale jokes left over from a shared childhood. He shrugged off their initial disdain and made a place for himself on the basis of accomplishment. As an outsider, he developed his own perspective on their lives. Their kingdom was small but close knit. Absorbed by the increasing complexity of the games they played among themselves, they failed to see that the moat they had built around their castle was too shallow. What could possibly go wrong? Their underwear was ironed. They didn't even pump their own gas.

After they bought the farm, Virginia told him she had always been a reluctant participant in Parkersburg's vigorous social scene. The discovery that Virginia didn't like the lifestyle any more than he did made him love her more.

"It took me a while but I got the message," she said. "When we were growing up, the girls were using me. They wanted to hang out at Montvue because of Chip and Warren. They were considered very good catches."

Ted saw, even if she didn't, that her place in the group was hers to throw away because she was born to it. When she left, the group barely noticed.

He, on the other hand, had simply been bored, tired of the same conversations, the house parties, the benefits that kept them circulating among themselves like the fish in Sam's tanks.

"That's one of the reasons I loved you in the first place," she told him. "You weren't one of them. You weren't like my brothers."

Ted meanders back to Old Main, looks down the long green expanse of the quad, notes the expansion, new buildings bought and paid for by the Big Five and named accordingly, their legacy on the campus more visible than in the surrounding community. The Big Five and the rest of the Parkersburg crowd hasn't changed, but he sees them in a different light, feels almost sorry for their lack of comprehension, their missed opportunities, the good they might have done.

Ted is not without regret himself. He should have stayed more connected in Parkersburg, fought for the underdogs, for the people who worked in the mills, the politically manipulated and the children, most of all for the children. He thinks he is not so much different now from the young man he was when he arrived here thirty years ago. He still trusts his instincts, sees himself as more comfortable, surer of himself, more the person he was destined to become, but he hasn't lived up to the ideals instilled during a rigorously virtuous Baptist upbringing. In hindsight, he blames his lack of civic involvement on the geographic ambiguity created by living in one Carolina and working in another. Traveling across the state line every day, living at the farm has allowed him to avoid commitment to any number of causes and charities.

"You know, I have this one-hour commute every day," he would say. He has made generous donations on both sides of the line, salving his conscience.

Ted sees the family differently too. The Wards, like their peers born with money and friends, saw themselves as handsomer and smarter and more deserving. Dolly and Sam both had that presence that charmed and commanded. But it wasn't enough and they knew it, which is why he was welcomed so quickly. Later, when the bright aura of the textile industry began to fade, he and Reece, the outsiders, seemed to be the only ones who saw the sun sinking behind the clouds.

He looks up, sees the sky darkening ominously. Best to get inside before the predicted showers begin. On the way to the condo, he passes the old Ward home used now for faculty offices and meetings. He thinks of Virginia and her chickens, of how she lost her father when she was so young, of her reluctance to trust men, himself included. He sighs, trying to look ahead, always hopeful.

He has agreed to Gretchen Bennett's plan for reorganizing the company and will stay, working under an annual contract. He is talking with her associates about alternatives, he has not given up the idea of selling out altogether despite discouragement from all quarters. The stock holders meeting is scheduled, letters have gone out. Within a few months, the lost certificates will be declared null and void, the loose threads tied up. Personal loose ends will not be so easily mended. He knows he will never stop wanting to be with Virginia. He cherishes the unlikely possibility that his continued connection with the company might create an atmosphere for reconciliation.

Only this morning as he was passing her room with a box full of his toiletries, he stopped, looked in, saw the unmade bed, their bed. He put the box on a chair and lay down. burying his face in the sheets, inhaling memories.

Returning to his new pad, as Volly calls it, he checks the refrigerator for dinner, decides to have a drink first and watch the news. The oil spill in Alaska has spread. There's a piece on a telescope that is going to be blasted into space. Ted turns the set off. He feels restless, missing his wife and his dog and his hearth. He eats the first thing he sees among the prepared meals Volly has selected for him, garlicky chicken and pasta, and wanders into the bedroom with a new book by a young writer he's never heard of, a Mississippi lawyer named John Grisham. He intends to read himself to sleep. With no one to notice, he sheds his shirt and pants, tosses them in to the dirty clothes basket in his closet and decides to go to bed in his underwear.

He brushes his teeth, admiring the handsome tiles that bought him an extra week at the farm, and re-circles the condo to double check the locks. Volly's right. The living room looks good. Generously proportioned, high-ceilinged, more than he had anticipated, yet he feels confined and isolated. He returns to the bedroom, pulls down the quilted coverlet, sees that Virginia has selected white linens for his new double bed. Climbing in, he welcomes the clean impersonal new-sheet feel and smell, and settles in between the layers of smooth Egyptian cotton, milled, woven, bleached, sewn, and marketed by Ward Mills, Inc.

21

Thursday, June 8, 1989

Virginia yells across the ring.

— Tighten up the lead! She's frisky this morning. Don't let her hurt herself.

The filly doesn't like the inexperienced trainee. She's leading the horse through a series of exercises, circling round and round.

— It's called 'longing,' with a soft 'g,' Virginia explains, training the girl and the horse at the same time. — Don't bully her. She's got a soft mouth, but she's accepting the bit nicely. Be gentle. Talk to her. Horses are like kids. No two are alike. What works with one won't necessarily work with another.

She is thinking of her own two children. Wishing she had learned this elemental fact sooner.

— Here. Give me the lead. I'll show you.

She steadies the horse, takes the long line and the whip. Around and around. Slowly, carefully with lots of encouragement, the way you train a child, not by force but by force of habit, the way horses learn.

People too. She is training herself to live without Ted, but the house echoes with his presence in a way she had not expected. She catches her reflection in the night-darkened window, watching the road for the headlights of his car, repeating the nightly vigil, anticipating his arrival. The garden spot off the terrace where he cultivates a few tomatoes plants every spring lies fallow. His pillow still beside hers on their bed … got to get rid of that pillow.

Weekends are oppressively neat. No papers to wade through, no books to trip over, no croissants for Saturday breakfast. Ted always brought fresh croissants home on Friday night. Don't need those extra calories anyway. Bad habit, those croissants.

Habit, she thinks, sending the little filly into a trot. Need new habits. Don't like change. Mason says men are threatened by intimacy, women by separation. Get over it. Gently she slows the horse.

— Good girl, she says pulling her in and patting her neck. — Your turn, Virginia says, handing the horse over. — Give her another try at the trot. That's it! Good. Much better.

She hears Mason at their last session when she tells him she is better too. "Good, good," he said. "It's a matter of habit. You'll adjust to the solitude."

That part hasn't been so easy. She has the dog for company at night and the horses during the day. That hasn't changed, never will. The horses have to be stabled, feed, shod, groomed, and exercised. Every day. They are totally dependent. Appointments have to be made and kept with the farrier, the vet, the equine dentist. And the dog, Beau, has to be let in and out, brushed, combed, fed. The work she doesn't do herself has to be supervised. There's the handy man and the stable help and the maintenance on the house. Little things like changing fuses, she's had to learn. The power goes out during an electric storm. The generator fails to come on. Virginia panics, calls Ted, who sends the maintenance man from the company.

Worse still, she hates to admit she can't do it all by herself any more, hates it when she gets lonely, hates to acknowledge that living without Ted has made the long days at the barn seem endless.

— That's enough for today. You can take her in. Second stall on the right. Watch out for Sandy. He's gotten spoiled from all the attention and he's jealous. Be sure she has fresh water; she's put in a hard day's work. I have to go into Parkersburg. We'll try again tomorrow.

At four o'clock Virginia finds Montvue wide open, the front door screen unlocked, the air conditioning turned off, the way Sam likes it. She locates him by sound, hears beach music, and follows it out to the deck.

— Hey. It's me. Want a beer?

— Sure. Help yourself.

In spite of the heat, she comes to Parkersburg two or three times a week. She has appointments with Mason, with Sam and Billy, and not so often with Ted. Today she brings Dolly's letters for Sam. Mason has told her it's time to stop obsessing about them. She grabs two Dos Equis from the sunroom fridge and joins Sam on the deck.

— Where're the boys?

— At the gym.

— Volly still at the beach?

— Yup. The boys and I are going down for the Fourth.

— She's staying the rest of the month? By herself?

— Far as I know. Says she's working on her thesis. Something about American art in private California collections?

— It's good of you, letting her use the place.

— She said she has some sorting out to do and she wanted to be alone. She asked about the status of the foundation Dolly set up.

Virginia puts the cold bottle against her forehead

— I'm tired of summer already. It's so darn hot downtown. I'm all sweaty behind my knees.

— Good lunch with Reece? Sam asks.

— He brought me up to speed on the will. The estate should be through probate by fall. This beer, Dos Equis? Reminds me of Santa Fe. I brought the letters for you to read. If you want to. Dolly went on and on about the weather and the wedding at the hotel rooftop bar and she's hilarious on Callie and the opera. You were still in rehab, weren't you?

— When did they get married? 1970?

— June of '71. The summer I found out about Ted's affair.

She pulls a chair into the shade, props her feet on the lower deck railing, concerned that Sam seems to be losing all sense of family or personal history.

— How?

— How what?

— Earth to Ginny.

— Oh. Warren told me. I think they had someone following Ted. Or else it was a good guess. Ted didn't deny it. Why haven't we talked about this before?

— My best friend's married to my sister and he's having an affair? Wouldn't touch it. Totally a no-win situation.

— And you never asked.

— We weren't so close there for a while. You were busy with the kids and I was wallowing in my own emotions. I knew something was wrong between you two, but I figured it was one of those spells married people have. And as I recall it was a vintage year. Chip married, Dolly moved Miss Ida out, Billy was born. Wasn't that the year we gave the Ward house to the college?

— That wasn't until 1985. My idea. She takes a long swig of beer.

— And a good one. I was spending a lot of time at PT.

—Volly was starting kindergarten at the academy. We shouldn't have these spaces between us. It doesn't feel right.

— Look, kiddo, it took me five or six years to get used to this ... this contraption, and then I had to clear out my head. Sorry if I was less than attentive.

— I wasn't blaming you.

— Okay. What did I miss?

— Dolly did a number on me in Santa Fe. I didn't know about it until I found an old letter of hers that I had misplaced. She knew about Ted's affair because he admitted it to her and asked her to talk me out of divorcing him. She thought I'd bolt and she figured if I left Ted, he'd leave Ward Mills, Inc., and that scared her. She wanted to be the mediator and she was very persuasive. She said I should just get over it. The old Dolly in her prime, managing everybody's life. Made me wonder if Big Ben cheated.

— I doubt it.

— Why? Everybody in this crowd has affairs and brags about it.

— True. But how would you know?

— Common knowledge and hair dresser scuttlebutt.

Virginia takes another sip of beer. — Phew! This is hot. I'm going for another. How about it? Are you ready?

— Always, sugar, always.

She comes back out and hands Sam a cold beer.

— Before I knew it, Volly was in junior high school. She blossomed early. I was having a hard time with her and boys already and was grateful for any help I could get. Once Billy was at the academy too, it seemed perfectly natural for them to sleep here during the week.

— Dolly's story was that she was sheltering your poor abandoned children from your temper and your drinking. She wanted another chance, another family to raise. I guess she'd figured out by then she hadn't done such a hot job with us. Three of us had refused to live in Parkersburg. Would have been four if I'd had the choice.

— You do now.

— Too late. I like it here now that I've got it all to myself.

— The arrangement suited Billy. Ted didn't like it, but he didn't cross me. Billy got to hang out with you. He loved that. Volly was at the farm riding every weekend or off on the show circuit and Billy went along with us. I told myself I was sacrificing for them.

— Then why do you still feel so guilty about it? It's over and done. Volly moved down permanently when she was sixteen because she wanted to, not because you sent her.

— She was in a huff because I took her horse away when she made a mess of her ride at the Leesville Show. Her timing was awful, strides were off. I told her if she couldn't ride him right she wouldn't ride him at all. She was furious.

— And so were you, but not about that horse show. Something was going on between Volly and your friend the vet, right?

— How did you know about that?

— She told me you slapped her for sassing you. She said you over-reacted to a little innocent flirting. But you made her so mad taking her horse away, she came running to Dolly, telling her how you got loaded and abused your children and could she please, please come live with Gramma?

— Volly wasn't just flirting, or so I was told. He was twice her age and married. I'll never forgive myself for that slap, the only time I laid a hand on either one of them, but I — we — needed to get her out of that environment and Montvue was the most logical alternative. I never told Ted about the vet. He's so crazy about her I think he might have killed the man.

— She put on some show for Dolly. Said you were ruining her life.

— And Dolly believed her? She was a child. You didn't buy it, did you?

— Of course not. But it wasn't my business. I was glad to see her come. Figured her being here would take some of the heat off me. Once Ted was running the mills I became Dolly's new project. She upped her charity work and brought it all home 'to be nearby just in case.' She never missed a chance to parade her little volunteers out to the pool house 'to see poor Sam and cheer him up.'

Ginny is fanning with a straw hat Sam is supposed to be wearing.

— How can you stand this heat?

He doesn't hear, has retreated into memory.

— Women, women everywhere. Soft and sexy and good-smelling. That swooshy sound their nylons make when they walked — it was a damn mating call. Dolly had the idea that the accident had turned me into some kind of eunuch, but that part of me was far from paralyzed. His laugh is a dry wheeze. His voice, once so smooth and deeply resonant, comes from high in his chest.

— Think about it. Eye level for me is boobs. They'd bend over the chair to talk to me and I'd go crazy trying not to look down their dresses. Then I stopped trying not to and they stopped bending over.

— I'm sorry. I hadn't thought about that.

— Ted did.

— Stop it, Sam. I know what a nice guy he is.

— If you'd talk to him the way you talk to me …

— You sound like Mason. Maybe I should just pay you.

— Talking to me is like talking to yourself, sugar. Didn't Mason tell you that?

— Do you think Dolly did it on purpose, the women visitors and all that belated mothering?

— Dolly thought she could fix everything. The way she manipulated you, not telling you Ted had asked for her help … perfect case in point. When she saw I wasn't buying, she moved on to the next generation.

— The timing was perfect. Volly was mad at me about the horse. And the vet. I think she still is. And I guess I wasn't paying any attention. Volly and Dolly, two of a kind. I'll bet they got along famously.

— Yeah, Sam says. — Like oil and water. Dolly made rules, Volly ignored them.

Dolly hauled her car away and Volly didn't bat an eye. Just took up with an older, faster crowd at the academy and stayed out as late as she pleased.

— Dolly never said a word to us.

— And admit she was wrong? Of course not. It's a good thing Volly went to Duke when she did.

Sam leans across the distance between them and pats Virginia's arm.

— Why am I always the last one to know anything? she said.

— Honest Ginny, it wasn't all bad. You did me a favor. We started talking about the fish business that summer and that kept me sane. But now ... It just isn't enough for Billy. He still needs you.

— Don't make me feel any worse than I already do, she says. — I don't have very good mothering skills. Didn't have much of a role model.

— Water over the dam, under the bridge, whatever. We managed. I just want you to see the situation for what it was. Dolly was caught in her own web. She didn't want to let you down but she couldn't handle Volly any more than she could acknowledge Billy's problem. Ward men had to be tall and handsome and smart and really good at something. It was like he repulsed her because he wasn't perfect. I guess I fell into the same category.

Virginia looks away, hoping to hide the film of tears brimming over her eyelids.

—She was way too tough on him. He ran away once. Told Dolly he was going to the farm for the weekend. I knew he was up to something because he left me a note. It said, 'Don't forget to separate the pregnant mollies out or they'll eat their babies.'

— Where did he go?

— He was camping out on the back of the property. Jesse saw him out there and told me. He was home in time for breakfast.

— I'll be spending more time here, if that's okay with you. I talked with Mason about helping with Billy's therapy. He likes the idea. For both of us. He's found us a specialist.

— Good. That's good.

After a long silence, Virginia is the first to speak.

— Have you read any of Dolly's letters?

— Sugar, you're hunting for a message that isn't there. Making way too big a deal of nothing.

— Maybe. Mason says I'm trying to reconstruct a relationship with Dolly that I never had, but I think she left the letters for me as a way to apologize, to say she was sorry for being so hard on me. That last letter, the one from Santa Fe. She didn't need to keep that one. By saving it and leaving it where I would find it, she was admitting her mistakes.

— Pretty far-fetched, don't you think? She couldn't just say she was sorry? All those hours you spent with her at the hospital?

— I guess not. You know how hard it is for the Wards to admit they're wrong about anything.

— Are you done with the letters now? You need to let go. Come on up here with the rest of us and live in the present.

— Easy for you to say.

— Your call. If you want to be stubborn …

— Your saying I've got some fences to mend, right? Do you see much of Ted?

— Couple times a week. Oh Jeez, I forgot to tell you. Yesterday he said if I saw you I should ask you to call him.

She calls the office, arranges to meet Ted at his condo later. In Dolly's room to wash off the city grit and freshen her makeup, she notices that the silver dresser set needs polishing. She can't remember why they left it out when she and Annie cleared the room and stored Dolly's personal effects in the attic. The blinds, left open, allow the sun to fade the draperies. She wonders if Sam is using a professional cleaning service. Closing them she thinks, what a shame. That's all. No self-recrimination, no haunting presence, only a touch of sadness.

Maybe Volly … someday … if she'd want to live here? Virginia thinks. No, I guess not.

She has bought some dish towels for Ted, which she takes in.

— I went to see Reece today. She hands him the towels.

— Thanks, he says. — What did you two talk about?

— Pretty much everything. You told me to go see him, if I had any questions about the business or the stock or the trust, so I went. He's a very smart man but not much of a marriage counselor.

Ted decides to take one thing at a time.

— What did he say about the mills?

— Mostly what you've said all along, that the industry is in trouble and that it will take enormous effort for an operation like ours to survive. He also said that the company was in good shape because of you and what you've done for the past thirty years. He told me I'd be a fool to vote my stock with my older brothers who are most likely scoundrels as well as wastrels. Don't you love that word, wastrels? He said I'm a spoiled little bitch who has never known how well off I was.

— He didn't say anything of the kind.

— He said the wastrels part. He told me we'd have gone under in the '67 slump except for you getting us into the synthetics market early, and he said you did the same thing again when we went into housewares and that Chip and Warren fought you all the way both times. He pointed out, very courteously of course, that I haven't been the ideal corporate wife. He said I handed that part of my life over to Dolly just like I handed over the children, so I could stay up at the farm and play like I was Elizabeth Taylor in *National Velvet*.

— He didn't say that either.

— No, but it's true, isn't it? The reason you've treated me like a child all these years is because that's the way I've been acting. I've never done much to help you except get you out of this quagmire of a town and now I've pushed you right back into it. Reece says you love the farm as much as I do, but for different reasons.

— Sounds like you had quite a day. He wants to know if she consulted Reece for the name of a divorce lawyer, but doesn't want to ask.

— May I offer you a glass of wine or a drink? I don't have a big stash here but I can scare up a little Scotch.

— No thank you. I need to get on the road. I do want to talk about the children with you. Maybe this weekend. Could you come up for dinner Saturday?

— Sure.

He's a little disappointed that she's evading again.

She stands, looks out the window.

— Nice view.

— That's where it all started. Dear Old John Wesley.

— Seems like another life.

— More like yesterday to me. Would you like to walk over there? The campus is nice this time of day.

— Another time, maybe. Before I leave, how are things going at the office?

— Not bad. We've got some conversations going with Gretchen's bank people about zeroing in on a new market. It's small right now but has some growth potential. There's been some conversation about converting one of the mills to apartments. I'll keep you informed, if you'd like.

— I'd like. Better late than never, huh?

— Have either you or Sam been in touch with the Atlanta contingent? I don't call them unless they call me.

— Sam didn't tell you? Chip's asking questions about the foundation and he wants to meet your friend Gretchen Bennett when they come up here for the stock holders meeting. Sam thinks it might be a good move to put Chip on the foundation board, but I don't. He's enough trouble on the company board.

— Did Sam tell you Volly's curious about the foundation? What do you think about that?

— We'll see. It's probably another false start.

22

Wednesday, November 8, 1990

Take a good look, buddy. The elite of Parkersburg have once again come together to validate themselves. Good turnout, boys and girls.

Sam smiles, waves his goodbyes as Rhett pushes his chair into the sunroom.

— We're all related by marriage or we've got something on one another. It's how this crowd works. Don't be surprised if they act a little pissy today. They expected us to incorporate under the community foundation, but we did our own thing. They don't like mavericks.

Rhett pivots the chair, positioning Sam in his customary spot halfway between the French doors and the television set.

— Looks like the family showed up in force too, Sam says. This gets Rhett's attention.

— How many of these people are kin to you?

— 'Bout half of 'em. The tall guy's my oldest brother, Chip, over there with the lady with all that blonde hair piled up on her head. That's his wife Callie the opera singer and that good looking girl is their daughter Mimi. A little young for you, but she turned out nice, didn't she? In the living room you'll find my other brother, Warren, with his third wife. Damn! I've forgotten her name. Juanita was the first, or second. Grab Volly next time she sails by. She'll remember. Looks like about half a dozen Atlanta cousins showed up. Wonderful thing, Rhett. A big family like this one.

In the front hall Dolly's favorite silver wine cooler crowns the round center table, accommodating an arrangement of fall leaves and flora towering nearly to the ball of the chandelier.

Meaningless conversations rise like soap bubbles, transparent, weightless phrases combining in the library with the ring of ice cubes in cut crystal glasses and in the dining room with the tinkle of silver spoons on porcelain tea cups. An occasional riff of laughter floats through the late afternoon sunlight.

They stand apart, facing in different directions, moving from group to group. The cousins, the children, and grandchildren of Dolly Ward, gathered at Montvue for the announcement of the Ward Family Foundation, established as a non-profit entity dedicated to education. Specifics like mission statements and goals and the actual amount of money involved have been left deliberately vague. Virginia makes the announcement just after the antique hall clock strikes four. She is applauded politely.

Ted hears the clock in the upstairs guest room where he lies in the dark, the venetian blinds tightly closed. Demerol has dulled the pain of his migraine but the noise of the crowd below and the brilliance of the November afternoon have forced his withdrawal. His headaches have returned, keyed by abrupt changes in the weather, so he believes. Virginia says they are psychosomatic, caused by abrupt emotional upsets. His mother died a month ago, within a few days of the first anniversary of Dolly's death.

— Ted, Virginia says. — Are you awake? She has come in so quietly he has not heard. He smiles with his eyes closed.

— Yes, Virginia, I'm awake.

— You've slept over an hour. Can I get you a damp cloth?

— No, thank you.

— You'd be so proud of Volly and Billy. They're making a point of speaking to everyone. When I came up Billy was talking with your banker friend, Gretchen Bennett.

— And where are your older brothers? Sulking in the sunroom?

— Outside smoking, she says. — The party's going well. It should be over in another thirty minutes or so.

Ted doesn't respond, nor does he open his eyes.

— I suppose I should go back down, she says. But she doesn't. Instead she kicks off her shoes and stretches out on the other twin bed. She's smiling.

— Can't help but think about the first time you stayed over, she says. — I coveted this room from the first day we moved out here. I wanted it for my room because you can see the lake out the window and the pasture. But Dolly said the color was too grown up for a five-year-old.

She continues, speaking softly, as much to herself as to him.

— For the longest time I thought Dolly didn't love me. I still think she loved the boys the most. Then you came along and it didn't matter anymore.

Murmurs of conversation reach them from below. The guests are beginning to leave.

— I should be down there saying goodbye. Don't go away. I'll be right back.

Virginia gets up, wiggles her feet into her shoes, and goes out, closing the door softly behind her. Ted drops into a drugged sleep, awaking an hour later. The party noise has disappeared. The house is silent. He sits up slowly, carefully, testing for the pressure above his eyes. As he swings his legs gingerly off the bed, putting his feet on the floor, feeling for his shoes, Virginia reappears.

— Sorry to desert you today, he says.

— You couldn't help it. Feeling any better?

— A little light-headed, he says. I need something to eat. Any leftovers?

— Plenty. Shall I get you a plate?

— No thanks. I'll just splash some water on my face and be right down.

Virginia turns to leave but hesitates.

— I was thinking, she says. This could be the last time we're all here together. I don't mean to care about this house, but I do. I think it's part of my DNA.

— You don't want to live here, do you?

— Lord no. I just want Montvue to be here. Chip has suggested that we carve out an acre or two for Sam and sell off the rest, like it's his decision.

— Don't worry. The terms of the will are clear. It's Sam's for the rest of his life.

— Then it's Volly's?

— That bothers you, doesn't it?

— A little.

— Cross that bridge when we get there. But I wouldn't concern myself if I were you. I wouldn't be surprised if our daughter turns out to be a big city girl. She's looking for something and I don't think she's going to find it here.

— I'm afraid that bridge is closer than you suspect. I don't like to think about it, but I'm sensitive to Sam and I don't think he's feeling well. And there's something else. I know that selling one of the oldest mills was a part of your plan. Reece told me you thought you had that offer? From the Georgia company? It's possible that Chip blocked the sale. I know how hard you worked on the deal and for them to pull out at the last minute like that, there had to be a reason. What if you had sold and then found out about the trust?

— Never would have gotten past the board with so much stock.

She exhales in a tremulous sigh, an uncharacteristic sound for Virginia. In the darkened room, his wife only a few feet away, Ted hears resignation, but she hasn't left, hasn't finished. Without warning she makes one of the mental leaps that astound him.

— Mason said I was blocking and suggested hypnotherapy. You know how I feel about that kind of thing. Giving up control completely, but I did it because I wasn't getting anywhere with the journaling. He said it might relax my defenses enough to get the whole story out and it did. I wrote it all out in my red notebook. I'd rather you never had to know, but you may need to. In case Chip's using you like he used me.

— What did he do?

— Maybe it isn't even important ...

— If it's been this hard for you to deal with ... if I could have helped . . .

— No, I don't think you could have. Not until now.

He opens his eyes, sees her push her hair up in the back, fluffing it out with her fingers the way she does first thing every morning.

— All that's happened lately. Finding out about Billy, knowing we can actually do something, that his life is going to be fuller and better, and watching Volly begin to take responsibility like she has, it's like happily-ever-after but I know it's all illusion because they've got those Ward genes that screw things up. It doesn't do any good to get tired of your family. When you're ready I'll drive you over to your place. You're still full of medication. The boys can bring your car back tomorrow. The notebook's in my car.

Thirty minutes later, Ted unlocks his front door. He decides to sleep off the remains of the migraine overnight and deal with the red notebook in the morning when he feels better. He sleeps hard and long. Around eight, he pulls himself together, dresses, walks to the campus coffee shop for breakfast, and buys an extra latte to go. Once back at the condo, he takes up the notebook where he has dropped it the preceding evening.

Before air conditioning, we had a huge attic fan in the hall ceiling upstairs at Montvue. It roared like an airplane and made a draft that sucked the bathroom curtains in and made them billow out like little girls' skirts. On summer nights Dolly sent Jesse up to turn it on at nine before he left. By ten the downstairs was cool but it took longer for our rooms upstairs because the dormer windows were small.

It was the last summer Sam and Warren were camp counselors. Chip was home from college, working in one of the mills and sleeping out at the pool house. He smoked and Dolly wouldn't have him in the house.

June was awful, blazing hot days, no rain. When I couldn't get to sleep for the heat in my sheets I'd go down to the pool for a late night dip. We weren't supposed to swim alone or after dark but I did it anyway. The attic fan covered the sound of my footsteps on the stairs.

The first time there was no moon but the water captured light from somewhere, the reflection from town or the stars, I don't know which. I remember there was a breeze, light and warm and pushing the surface of the water into accordion pleats.

I dropped my nightgown on the grass at the shallow end and walked into the shiny blackness half expecting it to coat me with color, it was so dark under the surface, like car paint. The light broke up and spread all over my body as the water wrapped around me. It felt wonderful. I swam a lap of the crawl and backstroked from the deep end half way to the shallow end, where I could touch the bottom.

I had seen part of Swan Lake *on* The Ed Sullivan Show *and I raised my arms over my head with the backs of my hands together and fluttered my fingers together the way I had seen the ballet dancers do it. I balanced on my toes and stretched my head back, feeling graceful and cool.*

As my eyes grew accustomed to the dark, I could see the whole yard, the lawn, Dolly's rose garden, the big oak trees on the side of the house and Montvue itself. I lay on the steps in the shallow water and looked up at the stars. The wake I had created lapped against the sides of the pool and rocked me back and forth, so gently. It was peaceful, my hair floating out around my head, no sound but the crickets and a dog barking somewhere off in the distance.

I don't know if I smelled the sulfur of the match first or saw the cigarette glowing red in the dark. Fast as I could, I slid off the steps until I was up to my neck in water.

How long have you been spying on me?

Look at you, all grown up.

I couldn't see his face, only hear that voice, cool as the water around me.

I pushed off into the deeper water. He said something else, but the sound of the water in my ears covered it and he was there in the water swimming beside me. I could have climbed out at the deep end and run back to the house but I didn't. Instead I did a racing turn, thinking I could beat him to the shallow end and get my nightgown and then run, but he surfaced on my right, side-stroking and smiling at me. It was a sad half smile and he was looking at me in a different way.

My toes scraped the bottom and as I stood, he did the same. I was going to ask him to get me a towel, but he stopped in front of me and just stood there and waited. The water churned around us waist high and we stood there facing each other. I know I should have asked him to get the towel, but he was standing so close that I could see the water dripping off his hair. I reached out and touched a drop where it ran down his cheek. He put his hands on my shoulders, a light touch, and slid them down to my elbows. He didn't pin me, but he could have easily.

Some man will teach you, he said. It should be someone who cares for you.

Teach me what, I said. But inside I knew.

He cupped my breasts in his hands and it was the first time his eyes had left my face. I remember thinking he was going to try to kiss me or rub his body against me. It was like being in one of those dreams when you know you should move but you're so scared you can't and you have to just stand there and wait for whatever happens.

He never tried to hold me. He just touched me until I arched back against the coping with my arms stretched out and he slid his hand between my legs. I must have made a sound because he pulled away from me but I caught his hand. My knees gave way and I was floating in the water with his other hand under me and the pressure of his erection against my leg and noises in my head so loud I couldn't hear the crickets and the dog anymore.

Ted throws the notebook across the room and grabs the phone. She answers immediately, as if she has been waiting for his call.

— Ginny.

— You didn't call last night I thought … Did it make you sick? Are you disgusted with me? Her voice is nasal, tearful.

— No, no. No. I was just so tired I went straight to bed. You know how the Demerol affects me. Look. I hate to ask, but …

— But what?

— You wrote, 'The first time' … how long…?

Her voice is high pitched and strained.

— It wasn't incest if that's what you're thinking. He never forced me. He never even kissed me. It was only his hands. It was a game, like he was my teacher, like when he taught me to play tennis. If it hadn't been Chip it would have been one of the Atlanta cousins. I was the youngest, a girl, curious. When they came to Dacus, to the lake every summer, they were always making jokes about who had the biggest weenies. He was the oldest and he always won.

— I knew you never liked him. You've avoided him consistently. But this …

— That's the way we all learn about sex, isn't it? From our families? The Wards keep all the old traditions. We hide our crazies in the attic like we did with Miss Ida. We suspect our parents of having affairs but we're too polite to mention it and we diddle our cousins and the dear old aunties say isn't it wonderful how well they get along, how much they love each other.

Ted dares not interrupt, but he hears her anger, her self-disgust.

— And then when we have played all the games and the guilt begins to pile up, we're empty as sin and so we get saved or we get drunk. I considered the first possibility but find the second infinitely less hypocritical. She sniffs again. He can hear her pulling tissue from the box.

It was incest, he wants to yell into the phone. It was rape. The son of a bitch! It wasn't your fault!

If Virginia can only get halfway there right now, he is willing to stay around until she can swallow the bite she has bitten off. She will need him then.

— I'll kill him if you'd like.

— No. I hate I had to tell you, but he'll use it if he can.

— But now you've told me. So he can't.

— I wish you were here.

— I can be there in thirty minutes, he says standing, looking for his car keys and then remembering: the boys haven't brought the car back. It's still at Montvue.

— Damn! he says. — The car …

— It's okay, she says. — I'll be fine.

He thinks how small the iniquity for so long and great a pain.

— Writing about it … has it helped?

— Mason says it has.

— What do you say?

— I've never done anything harder in my life. Tell me it makes a difference.

— The difference is that you're free of it. Didn't Mason tell you that?

— I guess I needed you to tell me.

EPILOGUE

Thursday, May 11, 1991

Reece sits on the deck at Montvue, enjoying the scenery. Dolly's fabulous azaleas have come into full bloom, late but gorgeous. He's waiting for Sam, who moves slower this spring in the wake a long siege with bronchitis in December that kept him in the hospital for two weeks. It's after eleven when Sam wheels out from his quarters. Reece, who has been too busy to notice, realizes that just as Ginny has predicted, Sam is ageing. His stomach protrudes from lack of muscle tone and his hair, receding in the manner of all Ward men, is nearly colorless.

— Weatherman says we'll get more days like this, Sam says. — Summer's here again and a bit early. Well counselor, how are ya? Haven't seen you since the foundation announcement. Whatcha' been doin' with yourself?

— Trying to keep you and your family out of trouble, Reece says. — I've got an associate researching the procedures book for the foundation and I've been working with Virginia and Ted on their wills so I won't have to go through this circus again. If you haven't taken care of that yet, you can get yourself down to the office or I can send some samples out for you to look at. I'm too old to work through another internecine free-for-all with the Ward family.

— Crotchety, aren't we. No residual Easter spirit, huh?

— Actually I had a lovely holiday. I spent a long weekend with my sister and her family in Charleston, looking at condominiums. I'm going to retire at the end of the year and move there. Speaking of trips, I thought you were going to stay in Florida until April.

— Nothing would have suited me better, Sam says, but Rhett had to get back for classes. Gonna miss that boy when he graduates. Didn't know you had a sister.

— I expect Billy will miss him too.

— They'll stay tight. They're closer than I ever was with either of my brothers. Billy's signed up for a business course at John Wesley next semester and Mason found a therapist to help him with the Asperger's. Right now he's at the farm giving Volly a hand with the horses while Ted and Ginny are lounging on an island somewhere in the Caribbean. He's a first class rider, ya know. Seems to have an easy connection with all animals. Wants us to get a dog. Sam laughs his wheezy laugh. He shakes his head as if the idea is incredible.

— What about the fish business?

— He can handle both. At least temporarily. Ted and Ginny should be home by the first. Billy's talking about taking a course in programming. He's crazy about computers. Understands them a heck of a lot better than I do.

— Virginia sent me a card. Blue water, palm trees. Ted told me they were going but I didn't get any details. Are they reconciled?

— As far as I know, this isn't an experimental reconciliation. Ginny says it's just a trip. Whatever that means. Best thing about the current arrangement is that it's kept Volly around. Sam gives out one of his soundless laughs, throwing his head back. — She doesn't trust them to work it out on their own.

— I understand that Gretchen's been moved to the Greenville office and that she's moved her horse to the farm. She told me she thought Volly might be going back to school. Gretchen's hopeful she'll take over the foundation.

— Yeah, I know. I like Gretchen but she's meddling. There's nothing here for Volly.

—Giving away money can be a very satisfactory career.

— Speaking of giving things away, why didn't you tell Ted and Virginia about the stock Granddaddy gave Miss Ida?

— No need digging up all the bodies, Reece says. — We couldn't trace the certificates. We know your grandfather transferred the stock, and we paid the dividends as long as Miss Ida lived, but the certificates never surfaced. Miss Ida was past consulting by the time I started looking. Strictly speaking, those shares should have been part of your grandfather's estate and would have been added to the split between Young and Dolly, so knowing wouldn't have made any difference except for the embarrassment. If Dolly knew, she never said a word. You know how she felt about your grandfather's housekeeper.

— You mean mistress, Sam says.

— Gretchen tried to track them down too but she didn't have any more success than I did. By the way, the bank is doing a good job for us. We're well on the way to pulling Ward Mills, Inc., back in the black.

— Doubt it will ever make what it once did.

— Nobody will, Reece says. — What's bothering you? You aren't your usual cheerful self.

— Empty-nest syndrome. It's like those kids were part mine, ya know? They seem to be flying off in all directions.

— That's what they're supposed to do. You encouraged Volly's fling with Rhett, didn't you, to keep her here? The local grape vine picked up on it. You forget what a small world this is.

— They had something going there for a while, but it didn't pan out. She got bored and broke his heart. Too bad, too. He's a good kid. Honest, hard-working. The Ward blood line could stand another infusion of hearty peasant stock, as Dolly used to say.

— Now that we're all caught up on the family gossip, there's something you need to think about. Things will get more complicated when the foundation starts accepting grant applications next month. The secretary can work out of the pool house a little longer, but we're going to need more space soon and a professional executive director.

— Will the position be full time or could maybe a retired corporate lawyer handle it?

— I've served my time with the Wards. But I'll think about it.

— I don't mind having the office here. The coming and going, it's good. Gives me something to watch over besides the fish.

— And what about you, Sam? What do you need?

— So long as they keep renting lap dancers, I'm all set.

Reece laughs, shaking his head.

— When Annie and Jesse retire, what then? Have you ever thought they might want to leave Montvue?

— They won't. Dolly built that cottage just for them. They're part of the family.

— Times are changing, Sam. Don't make the same mistake Dolly did. You can't afford to live in the past.

— I am not like my mother, and if you ever say that again, I'll get Ted to fire you.

— Interesting family, Reece says.

— Virginia says we are classic Southern. Frankly, I don't see how we're that different from anybody else. For sure we came close to that riches to rags in three generations thing, but I'm betting families in Michigan have the same ups and downs. Actually we are quite exemplary. Look at us: no scandals, no murders, no alcoholics or druggies, no lurid divorces, not even any affairs to speak of. We never make the papers. We're discrete. We know what we need and how to get it. We look after ourselves. If you just cheat a little you never get caught.

— You're survivors, all of you. Reece stands, stretches his arms behind him, rolls his head from side to side. This is all very pleasant, but I've got to get back to work.

— Nice to see you, counselor. Come by any time.

— Take care Sam.

Reece walks inside through the sunroom. Conscious of the soothing sound of bubbling fish tanks, he watches for a moment as the mollies and the tetras circle in their safe transparent domain. And as always he pauses in the hall, looks to his right to the portrait of Dolly over the living room mantle. He hears the grandfather clock, the pulse of the household, checks his pocket watch against the quarter-hour chime, and moves on, out the front door of Montvue and down the steps.

ACKNOWLEDGMENTS

✦ For historical information, my thanks to *Textile Town*, edited by Betsy Wakefield Teter and published by the Hub City Writers Project (paperback 2002). The clear concise history of the textile industry in Spartanburg, South Carolina, provided the historical framework for my story.

✦ Also my appreciation to the *Book of Common Prayer* of the Protestant Episcopal Church.

✦ For their professional advice, expertise, and enthusiasm, thanks to Bertie Phayer, Carroll Brady, Jon Buchan, and Dwight Patterson.

✦ For ideas and encouragement and for their willingness to critique drafts: Jon, Bertie, Susan Beardslee, Virginia Lisella, and especially Rita Landrum, who was my first reader and who has never lost faith in me or in *The Dancin' Man*.

✦ For being the best mentor and friend a writer could have, I thank Betsy Cox who read and reread, advised and supported.

✦ For an amazing editor, Nora Gaskin Esthimer at Lystra Books and Literary Services who invested her time and expertise in *The Dancin' Man* far beyond any reasonable expectation. For Kelly Lojk, my gifted copy editor and book designer, and for a knock-out publicist, Cindy Campbell.

✦ And to my husband, Olin Sansbury, I offer public gratitude for his wisdom, his patience, and his willingness to listen and to advise. *The Dancin' Man* is a crazy dream that came true because of him.

Looking forward,
Mary Ann Claud
DECEMBER 13, 2013

CPSIA information can be obtained at www.ICGtesting.com
Printed in the USA
LVOW07s0058281114

415967LV00005B/321/P